MILEY TURNED TO ELIZABETH. "Did you hear what he said later?"

"What?"

"Well, I said something to Charlie, *Are you enjoying your visit?* or something like that, and he said that he really liked the scenery, but when he said it D'Arcy laughed the way he does, under his breath, like it was a joke. When I looked at him, he said, *It's just okay.*"

"What an asshole," Elizabeth said, and then she added, "Sorry, Mom."

Miley turned to Mom and said, "He meant that the girls were ugly."

"What a brat," Mom said and then smiled. "You're lucky he didn't take a shine to one of you. That'd been even worse, I think." They all laughed at this.

"Oh, he's all right," Jenna said. "Tiff told me that with just them he can be a doll."

"Right," Elizabeth said. "And school shooters love their moms."

Praise for Author

Tamara Linse

"Readers will be drawn in to the collection's world and will find themselves wanting to read more of Linse's intimate tales." —*Publishers Weekly* (starred review)

"Linse's wide array of believable characters, and her ability to return to the same set of themes without becoming repetitive or predicative, makes her a notable literary force. ... a notable debut from a very promising writer." —IndieReader

"Linse's gift for fiction lies in her seemingly offhand but richly engaging observations. ... Linse makes each journey relatable and emotionally textured while occasionally injecting her signature literary observations." —IndieReader

"By far, the author's greatest talent is her beautiful eye for detail. She has the remarkable ability to paint a picture with just a few choice words." —Books Direct

The Wyoming Chronicles

Moreau (adventure)
Pride (romance)
Solomon (adventure, forthcoming)
Eyre (romance, forthcoming)

Other Non-YA Fiction

How to Be a Man (stories)
Deep Down Things (novel)
Earth's Imagined Corners (historical novel)

Mechalum Space (as TT Linse)

The Language of Corpses (science fiction)

Pride

Wyoming Chronicles

Tamara Linse (signature)

Tamara Linse

willow

Print
ISBN-13: 978-0-9909533-8-8
Print (Amazon)
ISBN-13: 978-0-9909533-6-4

Epub
ISBN-13: 978-0-9909533-9-5
Kindle
ISBN-13: 978-0-9909533-7-1

Edition 1.0

For Elizabeth and Eli,
who love to read

"There are few people whom I really love, and still fewer of whom I think well. The more I see of the world, the more am I dissatisfied with it; and every day confirms my belief of the inconsistency of all human characters, and of the little dependence that can be placed on the appearance of merit or sense."

— Jane Austen, *Pride and Prejudice*

Pride

Chapter 1

Everybody knows that when an unattached rich guy comes to town, he needs a girlfriend. Obviously.

And Jackson, Wyoming, attracts its fair share of rich cute guys during the summer. Really, all you need to know about Jackson is that it's a hole—literally, there are obscenely beautiful mountains all around, but also all the local kids spend their time dreaming of getting up and out. You wouldn't know it by the toor-eests, though. Picture-taking, cowboy-hat-wearing, plastic-tomahawk-purchasing tourists overswarming the place for the months of June, July, and August. They're on their way to the Park—that's Yellowstone Park—to *experience nature*, or they own those houses you need a map just find a bathroom, the ones where the local kids pick up extra cash by working as waiters for big parties.

Jackson is a small town—it claims a population of about 10,000. That doesn't count, though, all the people coming and going all summer long. It's a madhouse. You think parking's bad in a city. People leave their brains at home. The town is hemmed in on all sides by mountains or national forest, with no room to expand, so you have to be a millionaire to buy a house.

The Snake River winds down through the valley, and land above and below the town is all privately owned. The town itself is on a grid centered around Town Square, with lots of touristy shops and amusements on every street. Town Square is the height of western kitsch, with its antler arches at each corner and staged gunfights every afternoon. Snow King Mountain and the ski slopes are to the south, and the National Elk Refuge is out in the valley to the north. Teton Village is a burb to the west up against the mountain—if you call seven miles away a burb. You think you need money for Jackson— the Village is even worse. Then way to the north is Yellowstone National Park and way to the west over Teton Pass is Idaho.

Elizabeth Banner, soon-to-be junior at Jackson Hole High School, toted the grain bucket as her sister Jenna, soon-to-be senior, scooped grain into the horses' feed bins. They were in the barn, with its smell of warmed wood, dusty oats, and fresh horse manure. The two sorrel mares, the red and white paint mare, and the blue roan gelding contentedly munched.

Both sisters had brown hair, but Elizabeth kept hers short and impish, while Jenna's was long and well groomed. Jenna's style was classic movie star—solid colors with tailored narrow waists and even doing chores she looked ready for a visit from Grandma—while Elizabeth liked jeans—jeans for school, jeans for church, jeans for work. Their mother tried to wheedle her into skirts, but since Wyoming dressy included jeans, Mom rarely got her way.

"Oh, he was just everything a guy should be," Jenna said as she patted the blue roan's neck, "smart, funny, and so nice!

And it's like, I don't know, he fits right in, even though he's got more money than God. Not stuck up at all."

"And don't forget good-looking," Elizabeth said. "I'm sure he's prettier than a speckled pup."

Jenna ignored her sarcasm and continued, "I didn't expect him to come over and talk to me."

Elizabeth shook her head. "What's his name?" She wanted to file it away so she could check him out. She didn't want some rich asshole dating her sister.

"Charlie something," Jenna said. "One of those snooty last names. Starts with a B." Then she added, to no one in particular, "I didn't expect him to actually notice me."

"You didn't? Really?" Elizabeth said. "Well, of course he did. That's the difference between you and me. When people notice you, you're surprised, but I never am. Why shouldn't he notice you? You're five-times more beautiful than any other girl in town. It's not a credit to him or anything. Sure, you think he's nice, but take a little credit yourself."

"*Eee-lizabeth*," Jenna said, wrinkling her forehead.

"Well, it's true. You like people too much. You never think about their motives. You've never said a bad word about anyone. Admit it."

"I always say what I think," Jenna said after a pause.

"That's just it. You're so smart, yet you totally misread people. I don't get it. People fake being nice all the time, but you—no—you don't fake it. You always believe in the best in people." She shook her head again. "Well, what was his last name? We can't check him out online unless you know more about him."

"Oh, right," Jenna said. She looked out through the wide barn door toward the snaggly-toothed white-capped mountains. "*Buh, bih,* something. It was like a town. *Bim, bit, bil. Bil*! It was like Billings."

"That might be enough. Do you know where he's from?"

"No."

Elizabeth bit her lip. If this guy was a creep, she wanted to know.

They finished up and left the gate open so the horses could go out to pasture once they were done. It was still cool, so the bright sun felt good on the shoulders. Mount Moran to the west was craggy blue-gray with the white snow scattered across its face like lace, and the cottonwoods and quakies along the creek rustled in the breeze. They were just coming up the two-track behind the barn when their younger sister Livie came tear-assing down the road in a purple tank top, short frilly skirt, and cowboy boots. Running in boots gave her an awkward duck-like stride. She stopped in front of them and stood there panting.

"Is there a fire?" Elizabeth said.

"Nah. I just felt like it," Livie said and turned to run back toward the house in her usual high animal spirits.

"Well, was there something you were supposed to tell us?" Jenna said loudly.

"Oh, yeah, supper's reeeee-ady," Livie shouted over her shoulder as she took off back toward the house, her out-of-control blonde hair flying out behind her.

"There's no way she's just ten months younger than me," Elizabeth said. Jenna snorted a laugh. They came in the back door of the house and washed their hands in the utility sink on the enclosed porch. The house had originally been a settler's cabin, but someone had expanded it, so it kind of rambled—a two-story Victorian with a big kitchen, a sunny dining room, a basement family room and spare room, one bedroom on the main floor, and three bedrooms upstairs.

They went into the kitchen, where Livie was just finishing setting the table and their dad sat reading the newspaper. He liked to read it when he got home from work. Their mom brought in the last of the dishes—chicken-fried steak and gravy, biscuits, and early garden peas.

"Will," Mom said to Dad, "did you hear that the Billingsleys are back in town? The gal who does my hair said."

Mom and Dad were regular-looking people. Dad wore jeans and Carhartt vests, even to his work as a wildlife biologist. He had a long mustache and always wore a ball cap. Slender, he had never gained that middle age weight. Mom was pleasantly mom-plump and curvy but not huge. She liked nice clothes, and so whenever she went to town she dressed up. At home, though, she wore a lot of capris and those stretchy sweatpants. Her brown hair was shoulder-length. She'd braid in into two braids onto her shoulders when she was busy, but she'd pull out the hot rollers when she went to town. Jenna definitely took after her.

Jenna stopped for a minute and then gave Elizabeth a significant look while passing her the peas. Elizabeth nodded that she understood—that was this Charlie's last name.

"No, I hadn't heard," Dad said from behind the newspaper, "but I'm sure you're going to tell me." He then carefully folded the paper and set it aside.

"They got in on Saturday," Mom said. She looked at Jenna and Elizabeth. "I don't suppose you remember playing with the Billingsley kids when you were girls? They've been summer people for years."

"Where are they from?" Elizabeth asked, trying to sound nonchalant.

"New York. The dad's a stock broker I think. They've got a dream house in Teton Village. I was there once, at a party with your dad." She turned to him. "Weren't we, Will?"

"If you say so," Dad said, cutting into his steak.

"Well, we were, and it was lovely. Not kitschy western. Real old-world décor, if you know what I mean. Oh, I would've killed for those chandeliers. European, Italian maybe. It was an old hotel that they totally redid when they first started coming here." Mom had her realtor's license, and though it didn't take up much of her time—she only sold a house or two a year—she followed who was remodeling and what was on the market. It was all part of her grand scheme to own fine things.

Then Mom's face opened up with an idea. Elizabeth glanced at Jenna, saying *oh no, now what*. Jenna shook her head. "We'll have a barbeque and invite them over! What do you think, Will?"

"Why?" Dad said. "They'll only ignore us. If you remember rightly."

"Will, they did not ignore us. They just had a lot of guests to take care of." She looked at Jenna. "They were the loveliest couple, and you kids played in the kiddie pool together. I can't believe you don't remember it—especially you, Jenna. You were only three, but you remembered it for a long time."

Jenna blushed.

"If you're playing busybody with our daughters," Dad said, "I'd put in a good word for Lizzy." He glanced at her and smiled. Elizabeth made a face at him.

"Oh, BS," Mom said. "Elizabeth's smart, but Jenna is beautiful and sweet. And Livie's got more spunk than any of us."

"So you think our fifteen-year-old should hook up, do you?" Dad raised his eyebrows.

"You know better than that, Will," Mom said. "You just like giving me a bad time. Doesn't he, girls?" Both Elizabeth and Livie smiled noncommittally, and Jenna put her hand on her mom's arm. "You're fraying my every last nerve, Will. You have no idea."

"You're wrong there, sweetie," Dad said, his face set innocent as an angel's. "I am very familiar with your every last nerve. Have been for twenty years."

"You have no idea," Mom repeated with a sniff.

Dad looked at Mom for moment with a slight smile and said, "You'll get over it. Who knows—maybe the Billingsley kid brought cousins. Then all your girls will have rich boyfriends."

"Wouldn't that be nice?" Mom said, without a hint of irony.

As soon as supper was over—and as it was Livie's turn to load the dishwasher—Elizabeth and Jenna went down to the family room in the basement with Elizabeth's laptop, ignoring the deep couch and sitting cross-legged on the carpet. They logged on to Elizabeth's Facebook account and typed in "Charlie Billingsley." Unfortunately, there was a huge long list of Charlie Billingsleys. The first one on the list, though, shared a mutual friend with Elizabeth, a rich local kid who split his time between Jackson and somewhere back East. Elizabeth clicked on that Charlie. "That's him!" Jenna said. His picture showed a good-looking guy—lively brown eyes, dark hair spiked blonde, a strong jaw with cleft chin, and a generous smile. The page said he was from Manhattan and went to the Dalton School. Luckily, he hadn't set his securities very high, and so they were able to look at his photos and check out his wall. He had 687 friends, a lot of them cute girls, but a whole raft of boys too. Under family, he had a pretty sister named Tiff, and his mom was there, but not his dad. A couple of cousins. He liked some cool bands and a number of what Elizabeth's best friend Mylie called prick flicks. His wall was full of simpering posts from girls and buddy posts from guys.

"Well," Elizabeth said, "he seems to be popular with the ladies."

Jenna scrunched up her face but didn't respond. Elizabeth immediately regretted her words, so she added, "But they're in New York and you're here where he is. That's something."

Jenna nodded but her mouth was set in a troubled line.

Chapter 2

The following Saturday was a street dance. All summer long, Jackson basically looked for any excuse to have a party. The locals mingled with the fake cowboys who hung around the real cowboys who drew all the pretty girls. The shorts-wearing tourist families eyed the summer theater actors dressed up like outlaws and the bikers who parked their Harleys outside the Million Dollar Cowboy Bar. The river rats and the granolas with their dreads sat at street cafes and drank chai. And everybody just hung out and got along.

When Elizabeth and Jenna asked to go to the dance, their dad grumbled a bit, as he always did when they wanted to go out, but it was because he worried about them. Elizabeth's ace in the hole was that Jenna was so responsible, and they all knew it. Livie, on the other hand, could be a pistol. She'd recently been caught drinking beer with a boy from school named Dennis and so couldn't go because she was grounded. Elizabeth was happy about that, since it would be up to her and Jenna to keep the wild child in line, which could ruin a whole evening.

It was early when they got there, light still in the sky, and so the kick-ass musician Jalan Crossland was up on the bandstand playing to a growing crowd who cheered, clapped their hands, and stomped their feet. Jalan's fingers flicked and strummed the banjo strings, his head bobbed and his lips twitched in concentration as he played "Trailer Park Fire." No one was dancing yet, though. Elizabeth wanted to stop and watch, but the determined look in Jenna's eye kept her walking on past. They made a circuit, trying to act nonchalant, but Jenna didn't see the guy she was looking for. They kept walking until it was near dark, and Jenna's face got longer and longer. Finally, they found a low wall under a street light near the crowd and sat, the cool air bringing up goose bumps. By that time, the music had changed, with the crowd careening around the makeshift dance floor to the country band Sawmill Creek.

Jenna finally leaned over and shouted in Elizabeth's ear, "He said he'd be here."

"His loss," Elizabeth shouted back, trying not to show her relief.

Just then, Elizabeth's cell phone buzzed with Indian flute music, her best friend Miley's notification tone. When she'd set it, Miley had raised an eyebrow and said, "Really?" but Elizabeth could tell she was secretly pleased. Miley's dad was Shoshone Bannock and was a representative to the state, while her mom was black and ran a barbecue place just off the town square. Miley always joked that she had to play basketball, as her genes gave her no choice in the matter.

The text said, *Howz trix?*

Elizabeth turned her phone sideways and with her thumbs typed, *Street dance. You?*

Me tooooooo, came the reply. Then, *Where you?*

Elizabeth told her.

"Who is that?" Jenna asked.

"Just Miley."

Jenna nodded.

Soon Miley showed up. She was wearing a white tank top and faded jean mini skirt that highlighted her beautiful skin, and her long dark hair was curled at the ends.

"Your mom let you out of the house in that?" Elizabeth said as Miley sat down. Jenna's mom was pretty religious and generally wouldn't let her out of the house with her knees showing.

"What she don't know won't hurt her," Miley deadpanned. "Besides, she's working tonight."

"Yeah, but what about the birdies?" When Miley was in trouble, her mom always said a birdy told her.

"Flew the coop, crossed the road, hit the hay," Miley said, one side of her mouth hinting a grin. "Hey, Jen," she said, looking past Elizabeth.

"Hey," Jenna said.

And so they sat and listened to the band. Elizabeth let her body sway to the music and Miley leaned back on her hands and crossed her legs and swung one flip-flopped foot. By that time, Jenna's face had settled back into her upbeat openness and she was nodding her head and smiling. But then a voice came from behind them, "Ho, there you are." They looked around and there was the guy Charlie in the flesh. They pushed to their feet and turned, Jenna flushed and smiled broadly. The guy was shorter than Elizabeth had expected, though he was still taller than she and Jenna. Shorter than Miley, though, of course. Pretty much everyone was shorter than Miley. The guy had an effortless look about him, easy and laid back. "I've been looking all over for you," the guy said to Jenna. This made Jenna's smile even brighter.

He just stood there for a minute, until Jenna said, "Oh! Charlie, this is my sister Elizabeth and our friend Miley." She waved in their direction, but her eyes never left his face. "This is Charlie," she continued.

"Nice to meet you," he said. "Well, come join us. We've scored a table." Then, waiting for Jenna to respond, he focused on her with a smile so white and wide and charming that, against her will, Elizabeth started to like the guy.

Jenna nodded and then nodded again and followed as the guy made his way through the crowd. Elizabeth took a deep breath and followed them, Miley behind her.

"Who's that?" Miley shout-whispered as they threaded their way through the crowd.

"Some rich guy," was all Elizabeth could manage.

He led them to some café tables near the bandstand. As it turned out, they were the best seats in the house—right next to the dance floor in clear view of the band, yet some trick of the acoustics let them talk easily. At the table was another guy and a girl. The guy was very tall with long limbs, dark hair, and an angular face with a sharp chin. He wore all black and sat kicked back in his chair, his legs loosely crossed, but he made no move to get up when they approached. The girl had piles of long wavy brown hair and the most beautiful peachy skin and freckles and wore skinny jeans and a beautiful black lacy shirt over a tank. She looked like she'd just stepped out of *Vogue*, but she didn't look pretty because she wasn't smiling. Her

14

chair was scooted right next to the guy's and she leaned over her armrest almost into the guy's lap.

"Charlie!" she said. "D'Arcy and I thought you'd been abducted by the *colorful* natives." She looked pointedly at the girls and said, "Well, perhaps you have." She made no attempt to lower her voice.

Charlie laughed, maybe nervously but also with good-humor, and said to the two at the table, "This is Jenna, the girl I was telling you about?" He smiled over at Jenna. "And her friends …"

"My sister and her friend," Jenna corrected. "This is Elizabeth and this is Miley."

The two at the table sat and looked at them through narrowed eyes.

Charlie looked at Jenna and said, "This is D'Arcy and my sister Tiff."

Jenna reached out to shake hands. The guy just nodded but didn't move otherwise, and the girl half rose and briefly squeezed her hand. Elizabeth and Miley nodded politely but didn't move either.

"Won't you sit down?" Charlie said to them all, but there were no extra chairs. He looked around but could only find one, which he placed next to his. He apologized that he couldn't find more, but he looked relieved when Elizabeth insisted that Jenna sit in it. It was uncomfortable to stand hovering over the people seated at the table, and so Elizabeth and Miley perched a little ways away next to the building wall on the short fencing around the enclosed café patio.

Charlie almost immediately asked Jenna to dance, and her face shone as she followed him out onto the dance floor.

Jenna's dancing was as always stiffly graceful, but Charlie's was fluid, like he felt comfortable and sure of himself. When the music switched from a rock beat to a country swing, he swept Jenna up in his arms and deftly swung her around. This loosened Jenna up, and she seemed to relax.

As the pair danced, the two at the table ignored Elizabeth and Miley, and Elizabeth and Miley ignored them and the two empty seats and chatted. Elizabeth noticed, though, that the girl Tiff kept leaning over the guy D'Arcy and whispering in his ear and touching his arm and laughing, while D'Arcy for his part did not respond. He didn't move away but just sat there and hardly cracked a smile. Soon, with a glance in their direction, D'Arcy asked Tiff to dance. Tiff was all too eager, and so they got up and moved to the dance floor. Even though Elizabeth and Miley hadn't been asked, they took the seats to save their places and to get off their feet.

"What a bunch of uptight assholes," Miley said, collapsing with a sigh into a chair.

"They can't help themselves," Elizabeth said. "It comes with the plane ticket."

Soon the set was over and the band took a break. The four came off the dance floor, and so Elizabeth leaned over to Miley and said, "Let's go to your mom's and get some sweet potato fries."

"Not looking like this we're not."

"Well, then, I got to pee."

Miley nodded and they got up.

"Where you going?" Jenna said as she came to the table.

"Going to hunt buffalo skulls," Elizabeth said with a smile.

Jenna nodded that she understood. "Don't be long," she said, her brow wrinkled. Elizabeth raised an eyebrow, and so Jenna leaned in and said, "Please?"

Elizabeth rolled her eyes but nodded. "Sure."

Elizabeth and Miley went and found one of those blue port-a-potties on a side street and took turns guarding the door. On their way back, Miley jerked to a stop and said, "Oh shit! Got to go. Meet up with you later," and ducked away into the crowd. Elizabeth glanced after her and then up to see the tall rounded frame of Miley's mom standing with someone and smoking a cigarette. Elizabeth paused and then smiled and walked right past her.

"Hey, Elizabeth," Mrs. Goggles said. "You seen my girl?"

"I thought she was home," Elizabeth said with an innocence she hoped didn't sound too exaggerated.

"Uh huh," Mrs. Goggles said. "When you see her, tell her I want her home by 11."

"I will do that, Mrs. Goggles," Elizabeth said. "If I run into her, that is." She put her head down and continued to walk.

"And tell your mom hi for me," Mrs. Goggles called after her.

Elizabeth nodded again and quickened her step. She came back to the café table through the alley behind, which smelled of beer and pee. When she looked around the corner she saw that Jenna and the girl Tiff weren't there, just the two guys. Thinking how awkward it would be, she popped back around the corner just out of sight.

Charlie and D'Arcy were talking, and because the band wasn't playing she could hear them. "Come on, D'Arcy," Charlie was saying. "Why don't you dance more?"

"I danced," D'Arcy said.

"Only because Tiff drug you out on the dance floor."

"Besides, I hate dancing. It's like the mating rituals of chickens out there." D'Arcy's voice became cartoonish. "*Duh-er.* Look at me, look at me." After a pause, he added, "The girls are all ugly, and I only like dancing with girls I know, especially in a place like *this*."

Just then, Mylie came up behind Elizabeth. Elizabeth raised her finger so Mylie wouldn't speak. Mylie stopped and nodded.

"You're crazy—this is great!" Charlie said from around the wall. "There are so many babes here."

"I think you've got the only pretty one," D'Arcy said.

"She is *fine*," Charlie said, "but her sister is pretty too. You could dance with her." His voice got louder, "She's right there around the corner behind you, you know."

As soon as she heard this, Elizabeth started and her ears began to burn, and Mylie took a quick intake of breath. Elizabeth didn't know whether to run away or stay put or what, so instead she let her body nonchalantly lean around the corner as if she'd been there the whole time, and damn them. They could decide for themselves what was true.

D'Arcy looked up just as Elizabeth glanced their way, and their eyes held for a split second before D'Arcy looked away. "She's okay, I guess," he said, as if he didn't know she was right there listening, "but it takes more than that to tempt me. Dance if you want to, but I'm not moving."

"You're an onion," Charlie said and laughed. Whatever that meant.

Just then, Jenna and the girl Tiff came back. Tiff's face was lively and animated and wickedly beautiful, and her hand was

18

on Jenna's arm. She was saying something to Jenna, something that made Jenna laugh, and Elizabeth decided right then and there that she did not like this girl.

Chapter 3

Of course, Miley came over the next day so they could do the post-mortem. She had had to run the night before when eleven rolled around, though Jenna and Elizabeth didn't have a curfew. In the morning, Dad had headed into town for supplies to work on the place, and so it was the girls and Mom for a lunch of fried egg sandwiches, chips, and fresh strawberries.

Jenna sat with a dreamy look on her face not saying anything, and so Elizabeth said, "At least somebody had a good time last night."

"What?" Mom said, and Elizabeth immediately regretted saying anything. "What?" Mom insisted.

"Remember how you were talking about the Billingsley kids?" Jenna cut in quickly. "We ran into them last night."

This made Elizabeth snort and Miley smile on one side.

"Mo-om," Livie said. "I told you it would be fun."

"Livie, it doesn't matter. You know what your dad said," Mom said as Livie sat there glowering. Mom then turned to Jenna. "Yes? Were they nice? A boy and girl, isn't it?"

"Yeah, they're nice," Jenna said, which made Elizabeth and Miley laugh out loud.

"What?" Mom said. "What it is?"

"Well, it's just that …" Elizabeth said. Jenna was mouthing *nooooooooo*, but Elizabeth couldn't help herself. "Jenna thought Charlie was particularly nice."

"Oh, that's great," Mom said. "She did when they were toddlers too. She talked about him for a long time."

Pink crept up Jenna's cheeks, and Elizabeth smiled broadly.

"And the sister?" Mom asked.

The girls shrugged. Only Jenna said, "She was nice."

Miley sat forward. "There was this other guy with them too. He sure was stuck on himself."

Elizabeth nodded and added, "He was moody and snooty and went out of his way to be rude."

Miley turned to Elizabeth. "Did you hear what he said later?"

"What?"

"Well, I said something to Charlie, *Are you enjoying your visit?* or something like that, and he said that he really liked the scenery, but when he said it D'Arcy laughed the way he does, under his breath, like it was a joke. When I looked at him, he said, *It's just okay.*"

"What an asshole," Elizabeth said, and then she added, "Sorry, Mom."

Miley turned to Mom and said, "He meant that the girls were ugly."

"What a brat," Mom said and then smiled. "You're lucky he didn't take a shine to one of you. That'd been even worse, I think." They all laughed at this.

"Oh, he's all right," Jenna said. "Tiff told me that with just them he can be a doll."

21

"Right," Elizabeth said. "And school shooters love their moms."

"But maybe he has the right to be stuck up," Jenna said.

"*What?*" Elizabeth said. They all looked at Jenna.

"I'm just saying," Jenna continued. "He's from a rich family too, right? Probably one of those really old families that have been around forever and their cousin was president or something. So maybe it's okay that he thinks he's better than us. Cause he is."

"I don't think so," Elizabeth said. "It depends on whether he's proud or he's conceited. Being proud means he's stuck on himself—it's about him—but being conceited means he wants to be better than everyone else. See what I mean?"

Jenna looked at her with her brow raised.

"I mean, maybe he's thinking about himself, or maybe he's wondering what other people think of him. It's either pride or it's vanity."

"I'm thinking both," Miley said.

"Well, if I were rich like him," Livie said, "I wouldn't come here for the summer. I'd go to Vegas or Europe or somewhere and drink and dance and gamble and have a good time."

"Not if your dad had anything to say about it," Mom said.

They finished their lunch, and it was Elizabeth's turn to load the dishwasher, and so Miley helped. Mom and Livie went out to work in the garden.

"Jenna's really head over heels," Miley said as she rinsed plates under the faucet and handed them to Elizabeth.

"She is," Elizabeth said.

"Well, she better not play hard to get, then," Miley said.

"What?"

"If anything, she should pretend to have an even bigger crush."

"What?" Elizabeth was distracted trying to get everything to fit in the already-stuffed dishwasher.

"Well, Charlie likes Jenna—you can tell. But if she wants to date him, she'd better really make it clear she likes him. Guys are dense that way."

"Well, if Charlie doesn't see how gaga Jenna is, he's not as smart as I give him credit for." Then she added, almost to herself, "I wish I knew a little more about him."

"I'm just saying," Miley said. "And anyway, it's a crap shoot whether they'll be any good together. Maybe it's better we don't know him at all. That she doesn't."

"Oh, that's bullshit and you know it," Elizabeth said, pushing Miley's shoulder. "You'd want to know all you can about a guy."

Miley smiled and shrugged and took a rag to wipe down the table.

Chapter 4

It was a couple of days later that Jenna received an email. Elizabeth had just gotten back from a run and changed out of her clothes and flopped down on the bed with a borrowed copy of *Mockingjay* when Jenna came into her room carrying her iPhone.

"Look at this," Jenna said, her voice a mixture of excitement and doubt. "What do you think?"

Reluctantly, Elizabeth set aside her book and took the phone.

The email was from TiffanyPrincess@hotmail.com, and it read:

If you don't stop by the house today, we could just end up hating each other for the rest of our lives, cuz you know how us girls are—catty to the very end. KIDDING! Seriously, can you come over today or tomorrow and we'll hang out and you'll have the honor of getting rid of my serious boredom. xoxo Tiff PS Charlie endorses this message. ☺

"Well?" Jenna said.

Elizabeth's first reaction was to laugh and tell Jenna exactly what she thought of this TiffanyPrincess, but one look at Jenna's face and Elizabeth couldn't bring herself to do it.

Charlie would be there, and what Jenna wanted more than anything in the world was to be with Charlie, and Elizabeth couldn't not let her have that.

"Well, what do you want from me?" Elizabeth managed, shaking her head.

Jenna looked at her with eyebrows raised—*huh? huh?* she was saying. *Should I?*

"Well, Charlie's not going to come to the house with a dozen roses," Elizabeth said with a smirk. "Too bad about the sister."

Jenna's face shone at her first sentence but then wrinkled at her second. "What do you mean—too bad?"

"She's a witch with a capital B, is what I mean."

"Oh, Elizabeth, she's not that bad. I kind of liked her."

"You would," Elizabeth said.

"So, will you go with me?" Jenna said.

"Not for all the tea in China," Elizabeth said. When Jenna frowned, Elizabeth said, "No, you go. You'll do great. You don't need me."

"You think so?" Jenna said.

"I know so," Elizabeth said. "Now get out of here and let me read my book before we have to do chores." Then she stopped and added, "Or *I* have to do chores?"

Jenna hugged herself, her shoulders to her ears. "Thank you, thank you, Sis! I'll just tell Mom you'll do mine." And before Elizabeth could answer, she was out the door.

Elizabeth shook her head and went back to her book.

It was early afternoon when Elizabeth's phone buzzed with a text from Jenna, the notification set to Reba McEntire's "My Sister."

25

It said, *Come bring ur and my swimsuits and stay overnight. No argue. Cleared with mom.*

Elizabeth shook her head. She'd rather muck out the stalls. *Skinny dip*, she sent back.

Her phone buzzed back. *Pleeeeeez, Lizard Breath?* Lizard Breath was Elizabeth's nickname. Then, after a second, *Plzzzz plzzz plzz plzzzz?*

Elizabeth ignored it, but then her phone kept buzzing with *pleez* until finally she sent back, *NOT staying!!!!*

Thank U, Jenna texted back.

Elizabeth gathered up Jenna's favorite swimsuit but then remembered that Jenna had the extra car. Ah well, she liked to bike, even though it was more than ten miles over to Teton Village. She stuffed the suit into her backpack. When she got there, she would just throw the bike in the trunk and make Jenna drive her home. That's where she drew the line.

When she confirmed it with Mom, Dad didn't say anything but instead gave her mom a significant look.

"She'll be staying overnight with Jenna," Mom said, smiling back at him.

"No, *she* will not," Elizabeth said.

They both looked at her surprised but didn't say anything. Just then Livie came in and saw Elizabeth.

"What are you doing? Where are you going?" Livie said.

"Nowhere," Elizabeth said.

"She's biking over to the Billingsleys to take Jenna her suit," Mom said.

Elizabeth winced as Livie said, "Can I come? Can I come too?"

Mom looked at Dad, who looked sternly at Livie.

Livie continued, "My time's up being grounded. Can I come?"

"Dad, I really—" Elizabeth started to say, but then Livie cut in.

"Just to Kum & Go? Please?" She was looking at Elizabeth as she said it.

Elizabeth sized up her parents. Her mom definitely would want to let Livie go, but the look on her dad's face said he could go either way. Which meant that he would probably give in after Livie's persistent whining.

"Whatever," Elizabeth said, "but only to the Kum & Go."

Livie hugged her enthusiastically, which made Elizabeth feel good despite herself.

"You come right back," Dad said to Livie. "And stay away from what's-his-name." They all knew he meant the boy, Dennis, she'd gotten in trouble with.

"You got money?" Mom asked.

Livie said she did.

It was one of those beautiful afternoons where the puffy clouds scudded across the sky and meadowlarks sang insistently from the creek bottoms, but it was just cool enough that a jacket was necessary. Bicycling warmed Elizabeth up in no time, as she skirted the busy highway and took the back roads. Livie followed her and was content not to talk, and so it was really nice. When they got to the Kum & Go, Livie peeled off, shouting over her shoulder, "Later, gator." She pulled up, her tires popping on the gravel, and hopped off in front of the store.

Elizabeth smiled as she continued on. When she got to her destination, she wasn't quite sure where in the village the house was, but Mom had given good directions—even though it was buried in pines, a rustic log monstrosity tucked up against the mountain, she found it easily. It looked like an over-the-top cross between a Swiss chalet and a log cabin kit, with white walls, brown crossbeams, log edging, green awnings, and a big wooden door. Elizabeth arrived mud-spattered, flushed, and windblown. She couldn't find anything to lock her bike to, so she hid it behind a bush near where their car was parked.

She was met at the door by a heavyset man with dark hair wearing pressed jeans and a sweater who said, "Miss Jenna is waiting for you out by the pool." Jenna tried to think where she knew the man from—he looked vaguely familiar.

"You're their butler?" Elizabeth said in disbelief. Was this really the twenty-first century?

"I'm the caretaker, but when the Billingsleys are here, especially just the kids, I help out."

She eyed him. "Hey, you're a friend of my dad's." Once when she had gone to the hardware store with her dad, he and this guy had talked for what seemed like hours, and she'd finally gone out to wait in the truck.

The man smiled slightly. "You're Will Banner's kid."

"Yeah."

"Well, say hi for me next time you see him."

He led her through the house. She glanced up and saw the chandelier her mom mentioned—a little flashy for her taste, but she could see why her mom liked it, as her mom was always going on and on about beautiful and expensive things. There were slate tiles and wood floors, built-in cabinets, oriental rugs, and overstuffed furniture in muted colors. In short, the house looked beautiful, very clean, and not at all lived in. The man led Elizabeth out some sliding doors into a spacious enclosed atrium that smelled of chlorine and had three walls and a sloping ceiling of glass through which you could see the pine-covered mountainside towering to the west. Lichen-rock walls supported the glass. The room held a large irregularly shaped pool, with a smaller shallow pool and a hot tub off to the side. The inside pool made sense—outdoor pools are impractical when you live somewhere it might snow in July.

"Here you are," the man said and turned and left.

"Elizabeth!" Jenna yelled. She sat on a deck chair along the side of the pool. She had changed into a beautiful shorts set that she must have borrowed, which made Elizabeth suspect that the swimsuit thing had been a lie to get her to come over. This did not put her in a good mood. Sitting in a deck chair right next to Jenna was Charlie. He was dressed in swim trunks but hadn't been in the pool yet. There was a third empty chair next to him.

In the pool on a floating lounge chair was Tiff. Tiff looked at Elizabeth, raised her eyebrows, and said, "Look what the cat drug in."

"What?" Elizabeth said, letting her irritation show.

"Did you *hitchhike*?" Tiff said.

"No, I biked."

"You rode a bike from *Jackson*?"

"A little farther actually," Elizabeth said.

Charlie called, "A little exercise does a body good, Tiff. Not that you would know." He smiled at Elizabeth.

Just then, Elizabeth heard someone come through the sliding glass door, and she turned and there was the tall drink of water that was D'Arcy wearing swim trunks and holding a couple of sodas. When he saw her, he stopped dead in his tracks and looked at her with such intensity that she stepped back and without meaning to ran her hand over the bottom of her face in case she had boogers and didn't know it. When she didn't find anything, she just assumed she looked so repulsive that he couldn't look away. In fact, he continued to look at her for a long time, until she frowned and turned her back to him. But even when she couldn't see him any more, the image of him stayed in her mind—his slender but muscled arms and chest, the way his belly was flat and hard, how extraordinarily long he looked.

Jenna jumped up and pulled another chair over beside hers and sat back down, holding her hand out for Elizabeth to sit. Elizabeth walked over, perched on the edge of the chair, unzipped her backpack, and tossed the suit into Jenna's lap. D'Arcy walked around behind them and sat in the other empty chair.

"There you go," Elizabeth said and zipped her backpack back up. She held it to her chest, looked around the room, and then stood up. "It's been fun," she said to Jenna. She leaned down and whispered, "Now take me home."

Jenna looked at her with a surprised expression. "You're not staying?"

Elizabeth just raised her eyebrows.

"Stay," Jenna said.

Elizabeth continued to look at her.

Charlie glanced at Jenna and then leaned over and said to Elizabeth, "You can swim. And George is putting some burgers on the barbecue." He glanced at the pool and continued, "And I promise that Tiff will behave herself." He raised his voice, "Isn't that right Tiff?"

"What?" Tiff said without raising her head from the cushion.

"You'll be less of a bitch than usual."

"I got to be me," she said, but then in one smooth motion Charlie stood and dove into the pool and surfaced right by her chair. He grabbed it and pushed and tipped it, while Tiff hollered, "Nooooo! No!" She grabbed him by his arms and tried to push him away, but when she couldn't, she clung to her chair and yelled, "All right! All right." Charlie shook her chair one more time, and she said, "An angel, that's me."

For her part, Elizabeth doubted her sincerity.

Charlie swam back to the edge and pulled himself up on the side. He sat for a minute and then shook his hair like a dog, and the spray caught Jenna and Elizabeth. Elizabeth stepped sideways.

Jenna grabbed her wrist. "No, stay, please?"

"I don't want to," Elizabeth said, but this made Jenna smile because she could tell that Elizabeth was giving in.

"Do I have to throw you into the pool too?" Charlie said with a grin.

"Just for a while," Jenna pressed. "You'll have a great time, eat some good food—they tell me George is a good cook. And you can even swim—you love that."

"I don't have a suit," Elizabeth said.

"Mom'll bring it. You know she will." They both knew she would.

Elizabeth stood there. She really wanted to get home and finish her book. She didn't feel social, but she didn't want to have to pedal all that way home. Her legs were tired, and she was hungry. As soon as she thought of it, her belly growled. She looked at Jenna, who was looking at Charlie with total rapture on her face, and then she looked at D'Arcy. He was watching her with an expression of amusement, a cocked eyebrow, but interested too. Something in his look was a challenge, as if he were daring her to chicken out and go home. Her anger flared. Who cared what he thought, but then she found she wanted to prove him wrong. The asshole. She looked back at Jenna and sighed.

"She'll stay!" Jenna crowed.

Elizabeth sat back down. "You get to call Mom," she said, pulling out her iPhone.

Jenna smiled, took it, and went over to the side to call.

It wasn't long before George led Mom into atrium, but they could hear her all the way from the hall: "My, what a lovely house! I just love those drapes. And the furniture. And a red wall. I didn't know you could get away with a red wall, but you do. So amazing. And lovely. I just love it. Love it."

By this time, Tiff had joined them at the poolside, and she looked at D'Arcy and mouthed *Loooooove it* and pursed her lips, just as Mom came in.

"Thanks, George," Mom said, smiling and nodding, and came over, craning her head this way and that. "For some reason, I had remembered the walls in here being wood. Did you redo them recently?" She looked at D'Arcy as she said it.

Jenna stood. She gestured to Charlie and said, "Mom, this is Charlie Billingsley and his sister Tiff."

Mom nodded and said, "Oh," and smiled.

"And this is their friend D'Arcy Pemberly."

"D'Arcy, what an unusual name," Mom said. "And Pemberly—an associate of mine recently sold a listing to a Pemberly?"

D'Arcy had a distant but polite look on his face. He sat forward on his chair. "Yes," he said, "My mom, Katherine Pemberly. She thought … well, she wanted to get away."

"How lovely," Mom said.

Tiff opened her eyes wide and her head jutted forward on her neck—*what a small-town bore*, she was saying.

"Well, I better go," Mom said, handing the bag to Elizabeth. "Your father will wonder." She pointed to the bag. "I've packed jammies for you both and a suit for you, Elizabeth." She looked at Charlie, "It's so kind of you to have them over." She smiled, nodded, and then turned and left.

She was barely out of earshot when Tiff said, "Oh, Charlie, I just *looooove* it."

Charlie got up and threw her into the pool.

Chapter 5

They ate supper outdoors on a side patio with a view of the steep mountain above them. Because the house was right next to the mountain, it was deep in shadow, but there were golden lamps all around. Elizabeth sat between Charlie and D'Arcy, with Jenna next to her and Tiff opposite. It was thick burgers with smoky cheese and grilled mushrooms and a spinach salad with walnuts and craisins and raspberry vinaigrette. Turned out, George was a good cook, and Elizabeth thanked him when he brought out the dessert of marble cheesecake. He didn't say anything but seemed pleased. "I'm lucky," Charlie said. "George is helping me learn my way around the kitchen." He liked to cook too, he said.

It was all too perfect. Elizabeth glanced at Jenna, whose face was glowing, and felt sorry for her. The way these summer romances went is the guy came, flirted, and then found another girl. Or they were only here for a week or two and then they were gone. You'd email them after but then never hear back. She'd seen it a lot in her sixteen years. And here was Jenna putting herself out there to be squashed like a bug.

Elizabeth made a show of looking around at the house and then said to Charlie, "A beautiful place. How long you here for?" She did not look at Jenna as she said this.

Charlie swallowed his mouthful and said, "Oh, I don't know."

"So, a week? A month? The whole summer?" She didn't want to let it go.

Charlie glanced at D'Arcy and said, "Definitely more than a week. A month?"

Elizabeth glanced between D'Arcy and Charlie. What did D'Arcy have to do with it? "Well, which is it?" she insisted.

Charlie shrugged. "Whenever we feel like it, we'll head back to New York."

"Boy, you really thought this thing through," Elizabeth said. She was starting to get angry for Jenna's sake, even though Jenna was giving her a look that said, *quit it, wouldja!* "Must be nice to just jump on a plane whenever you want, just quit everything."

Charlie shrugged.

"That's kind of shallow. Some people consider things more deeply."

"Elizabeth!" Jenna said.

D'Arcy said, "So you're one those thinking girls."

"Yes, I am," Elizabeth said. "People with a little depth are more interesting."

"Well, then, you must be pretty bored—around *here*," Tiff said.

When would city people get over themselves? "You'd be surprised," Elizabeth said. "Maybe if you had a little depth yourself, you might notice it."

35

Charlie said, "Well, when I'm here, I want to be here, and when I'm in the city, I want to be there. That's just the way I am."

D'Arcy laughed. "Fairweather Charlie," he said, "you go whichever way the wind blows."

"I like to think of myself as agreeable, yeah," Charlie said.

Elizabeth said to D'Arcy, "So you think it's better to argue for the sake of arguing?"

"No," D'Arcy said. "It's just that all someone has to say is, *hey, Charlie*, and he'll change his mind."

"So you think it's better to disagree with your friends just for the sake of some pigheaded idea?"

"To give in just because they're your friend is stupid," D'Arcy said.

"So friends aren't worth a crock of shit?" Elizabeth said. "And you think people who try to consider their friends are weak-minded?"

D'Arcy frowned. "It depends on what it is."

"You guys and your deep principles," Charlie said and then to D'Arcy. "We're on vacation—lighten up, Francis."

Throughout the dinner, Elizabeth caught D'Arcy eyeing her. After they had sat for a while, the patio getting darker and the lamps on the side of the house giving off an orange glow, she finally turned to him and said, "What?"

He looked startled. "Oh, uh," he said and paused. "Uh, do you want to go swimming?"

This irritated her to no end. "If I say yes, you'll think you're better than me because it was your idea, but if I say no, you'll hate me because I turned you down, so I guess I'll just say no so you can hate me with a clear conscience."

D'Arcy turned red. "I'm not that way," he said and seemed genuinely upset.

Tiff, who sat on the other side of D'Arcy and had been listening, said, "Oh, but your sister said you just *looooved* swimming. Didn't she, D'Arcy?"

D'Arcy didn't respond, and Elizabeth ignored her.

But then shortly everybody was back in the pool, so Elizabeth changed into her suit too. She immediately dove in and swam from one end to the other, executing her turns at each end, even though it was a short leg. When her shoulders were tired enough, she pulled herself up on the side. Because the house was in shadow a lot, whoever designed the place took that into account, and there was a big heater blowing warm air. It felt as good as lying in the sun. She lay back and rested, the murmur of the others' voices washing over her.

But then right in front of her was Tiff carrying things in her hands. Tiff sat down at Elizabeth's feet and dropped the stuff on the poolside. "Here, let me paint your toenails," Tiff said in a loud voice.

"Wha—?" Elizabeth said, but before she could pull away Tiff opened a jar of pale sparkly pink and dabbed at her toes. She didn't want her toenails painted, but *whatever*.

"I think pink really suits you," Tiff said.

Elizabeth did not think of herself as a pink person.

"My friend Charmine does people's color palettes, and pink is definitely you." Tiff wasn't looking directly at Elizabeth as she spoke. Then she launched into a story about Charmine and her and how they had crashed a pad in Manhattan and how they had been the life of the party—"And then James said to me, you know, James Franco? He said to me, 'Girl, where you been

37

all my life?'"—and on she went, dropping names along the way.

But there was something odd about the way Tiff was acting. She talked loud so that everyone could hear her and she held her body stiffly. Her shoulders were back so her boobs popped forward, even though she was leaning forward to paint, and her body was twisted oddly. She kept glancing over to where Jenna, Charlie, and D'Arcy were sitting. Charlie and D'Arcy were playing Battleship, and Jenna was watching.

Finally, after Elizabeth's toenails dried and Tiff finished her long story, Tiff reached down and pulled Elizabeth to her feet. Then she stepped between Elizabeth and the others and struck a pose like a model for a photographer, her shoulders back, hands on hips, one leg bent at the knee, foot turned out.

"Hey," Tiff said. When there was no response, she said, "Hey, D'Arcy, don't you think pink is Elizabeth's color? I was just telling her." But instead of stepping back out of the way, she continued to stand in front of Elizabeth.

D'Arcy glanced up and smirked. "You girls do that on purpose."

Tiff made of a show of being shocked. "Whatever could you mean?"

"You know, show off your … you know."

Tiff let out a shrill laugh and turned to Elizabeth. "How mean of him. Don't you think that's mean? What should us girls do to punish him?"

Elizabeth wanted no part of it. "You know better than me," she said.

"Not really," Tiff said. Then she leaned in and whispered, "Laugh. It drives D'Arcy crazy when you laugh." Tiff laughed again but all Elizabeth could manage was a weak smile. "D gets upset if you laugh at him," Tiff said so that D'Arcy could hear.

D'Arcy was no longer concentrating on the game and was looking at them, eyebrows raised. Catching his look, Elizabeth said, "That's too bad—because I love to laugh."

"Now who's shallow?" D'Arcy shot back.

"Not that kind of laugh," Elizabeth said. "I laugh at people who are full of themselves, people who should be laughed at."

"Maybe some people deserve to be proud of themselves," D'Arcy said. "Did you ever think of that?"

This made Elizabeth burst into real laughter, as she remembered the earlier conversation at home. She was chuckling when she said, "So which are you?"

Tiff said, "Yeah, D'Arcy, which are you?"

"I've got my issues," D'Arcy said, "But being full of myself isn't one of them. Like, if somebody pisses me off, I never forget it."

"And eventually everyone makes you mad, so you're just pissed at the world?" Elizabeth said.

"Well, at least my issues aren't twisting whatever people say to suit what I want," D'Arcy said and pushed himself up. "You want another soda?" he said to Charlie and Jenna.

Chapter 6

When it was bedtime, Charlie showed Jenna and Elizabeth to a big bedroom on the second floor decorated with lavender and green fabrics and dark woods, which had a great view of the valley. The girls would share the huge bepillowed bed. There were fresh toothbrushes in their own bathroom—which was good because Mom hadn't included those—along with soaps and shampoos and fluffy purple towels. Kind of like the hotel it used to be. They changed into their pajamas and got ready for bed.

"So," Jenna said, flopping on the bed, "what do you think?"

"'Bout what?" Elizabeth said as she rubbed in some rose-scented hand lotion.

"You know. Him. The house. Everything." Jenna's voice dripped with sappiness.

Elizabeth thought for a minute before answering. Finally, she said, "It's great. You know, fine." She didn't want to tell Jenna about her doubts, how she was sure they would all scoot out of there in a week or two and take Jenna's heart with them. She would bring it up later, after they were home.

There was a light tap on the door.

"Come in. We're decent," Jenna called.

40

"At least on the outside," Elizabeth said, but only so Jenna could hear.

"Shshsh," Jenna said, waving her hand at her.

It was Charlie, of course. "We thought we'd watch a movie. My mom is a movie buff, so we got a lot of old stuff." Then after a second, he added, "But it's all good. And we can always watch through the Xbox."

Before he finished, Jenna was up off the bed. "Sure. That would be great." She looked at Elizabeth. "You want to?"

"Nah," Elizabeth said. "I'll just hang out here." She'd had enough of the two-faced Tiff and grouch D'Arcy. "You kids have fun," she said with a smile.

But after they'd left and Elizabeth lay on the top of the covers for a while, she found herself wishing for her copy of *Mockingjay*, or any book for that matter. After all, it would be a while before Jenna got back to the room, and she wanted to stay up and make sure Jenna was all right. No books to be found in the room, so she decided she would go out looking.

The second floor was immaculate and beautiful—shining wood floors with oriental rugs, lamps along the corridors, and mirrors or beautiful paintings of Mount Moran or edgy modern subjects in off colors. Even though the house had been an old hotel, you could hardly tell, as the space had been opened up and was broken up at odd angles. Most of the doors were closed, and she figured they were bedrooms and so she didn't open them. Her best bet for books was downstairs—she thought she'd caught sight of some on the way in. The upstairs corridors wound around, and Elizabeth didn't get lost, but it took her a minute to find the stairs going down. The staircase came out in the front entry hall, and she could hear the TV from the back of the house. It was an old movie, she could tell by the forced dialog and the dramatic music. She didn't want to disturb them, and so she turned into the side room, a study, where she thought she'd seen the books.

Sure enough, there they were. She turned on a lamp and looked over the bookshelves. Except for a few cheap paperback mysteries, though, all the books were really old with odd titles. They looked expensive, so she hesitated to pull them off the shelves. About the time she decided to grab a techno-thriller, she heard someone behind her. It was Charlie.

"Sorry," Elizabeth said, "but I was just looking for a book."

"Well, good luck," Charlie said smiling. "These aren't books—they're museums. My dad collects old books and my mom collects old movies."

"Sorry to take you away from the movie."

"No problem. I've seen *On the Waterfront* a million times."

There was silence and Elizabeth decided she would just grab a book and be gone. "Well—" she started to say.

Charlie reached over and pulled a book from the shelf. "See this one? It's by Charles Baudelaire, my namesake."

"They named you after an old dead writer?" Elizabeth said and then immediately regretted it.

"An old dead poet," Charlie corrected and laughed. "This is a first edition of *Les Fleurs Du Mal*." Elizabeth suspected he was really good at French the way he said the words—easily, in the back of the throat. He continued, "Look, the illustrations are by Matisse." He flipped it open to a beautiful drawing of a woman's face. The lines were sure and fluid and the woman had a sexy look on her face.

Elizabeth blushed in spite of herself. "That's cool," she said.

Charlie put the book back on the shelf. "But Dad would probably kill me if I let you borrow it." He grinned.

"Well, what I was really looking for is a copy of *Mockingjay*, you know?"

"Well, we don't have much of anything later than the last millennium here, but we do have a Kindle. You'll have to come over to the family room though."

Elizabeth nodded.

They went back through the house and into a sunken living room with a large-screen TV and a glowing gas fireplace. The TV was paused and gave a white glow into the dark room. Elizabeth could just make out some couches where Tiff and Jenna sat and a bean bag where D'Arcy lounged.

"You didn't have to pause it," Charlie said as he crossed the room and flicked on a lamp.

"We were waiting for you," D'Arcy said.

"Sorry," Elizabeth said. "I was just looking for a book."

Tiff said from the corner of the couch, "There's a whole bunch in the library." She didn't sound like she said it out of kindness.

"You know better than that," Charlie said. "Dad would kill us."

Tiff said, "So you're a great reader, then, Elizabeth?"

Elizabeth didn't like her tone. "I wouldn't say I'm a *great* reader. I do all kinds of things."

Elizabeth could just see Charlie's smile. "Girls do everything," he said. "It used to be they ended up housewives, but now they do sports and are scientists and everything. I bet even here in … the country?"

"Yes," Jenna said.

"And they're good at it, I bet," Charlie said, looking at Jenna.

D'Arcy made a noise. "Girls aren't any better at things than guys. In fact, I can only think of one or two girls I know that are really good at more than, say, one or two things."

"That's true," Tiff said. "Girls aren't as good at things as boys."

There was silence in the room for a second, and then Elizabeth said, with more force than she meant to say it, "Really, Tiff?" Elizabeth hated women who were like that— always putting themselves down for men.

D'Arcy said, his voice deeper, "What I meant was, women should be expected to do all those things, but to be really thought of as exceptional, they have to do more. They have to be better, smarter, work harder. She has to be the top of her field, won a Nobel or something. Just like I would expect a guy to do."

"Well, then," Elizabeth said, "I don't expect you do know many girls like that. In fact, it's a wonder you know *any*."

"Oh, you're one of those," Tiff said.

"One of what?" Elizabeth said.

"Those women who hate women. Talk about your shallow."

Elizabeth could have killed her.

D'Arcy said to Tiff, "Unlike parading around in bikinis when guys are around?"

"Well, anyway," Elizabeth said, "you're not talking about a real person. You're talking about a mythical creature, like a unicorn. Most of us are pretty regular. No wonder you haven't seen any." It wasn't that she didn't believe there weren't any accomplished women. It was just that he seemed to hold the whole world to such a high standard. No one could reach it. No wonder he was a grouch.

By that time, Charlie had finished downloading *Mockingjay* and handed the device to Elizabeth.

"Thank you," Elizabeth said to Charlie, and meant it. She felt much better about Charlie and his kindness, but the other two hadn't changed her mind. With a glance at Jenna, she went back to the room.

It was late when Jenna came back to the room, but Elizabeth was still reading.

"So, how'd it go with Dreamboat?" Elizabeth said. *And the Snooty Twins*, she added in her mind. "Did he kiss you?" Elizabeth was of two minds on the subject—being kissed would make Jenna so happy, so she wanted it to happen, but then it would just make it harder later, so she hoped not.

"No, but he held my hand in the dark." Jenna hugged herself as she said it. "His hand was sweaty but cool, you know? But he just held it so gently."

"Well, congratulations," Elizabeth said. "You deserve to be happy."

Chapter 7

The next morning after showering, Elizabeth and Jenna went down to breakfast. The kitchen was a big room with lots of light and plants, a flagstone floor, black granite countertops, a large island with a butcher's block and an extra sink and stove, and a large table, where Charlie was playing a game on his cell and D'Arcy had a laptop open. Tiff wasn't up yet. Along the counter on the island was a small buffet with strawberries and bananas, muffins, French toast, sausages and scrambled eggs, and juice and hot chocolate—courtesy of George, no doubt.

Charlie stood when they came into the room. "Good morning," he said. "Hungry?"

"Good morning," Jenna and Elizabeth said together.

D'Arcy glanced up and said, "Hey."

"It's like a fancy hotel," Jenna said, with wonder in her voice.

"It's pretty nice," Charlie agreed and motioned for them to go ahead.

Elizabeth and Jenna helped themselves to the food. Elizabeth was particularly hungry from the biking and swimming the day before, so she heaped her plate with a bit of everything and topped it off with maple syrup. Jenna, who took just some fruit and a sausage, gave her a look. She ignored it.

The boys had already eaten, and soon after Elizabeth and Jenna sat down Tiff joined them. She had not changed out of her pajamas. She poured herself some hot chocolate and sat in an easy chair off to the side.

As they ate, D'Arcy typed away at the computer with a strained look on his face. He would think for a bit, type something out, and then tap-tap-tap erase it, shaking his head. Curiosity got the better of her, so Elizabeth said, "What you working on?"

Deep in his work, he didn't answer, but without looking up from his phone Charlie said, "His dad expects weekly email reports—in proper English with good grammar. Especially now."

"Why especially now?" Elizabeth said.

Charlie hesitated and then glanced at D'Arcy, who continued to focus on what he was doing. Charlie said in a low voice, "His mom and dad are getting a divorce. That's why his mom bought the house. She always liked it here." More loudly, he said, "And she thinks it'll keep her darling boy away from the corrupting influence of his father. Isn't that right?"

D'Arcy looked over at them and shook his head—not to disagree but just in general disgust.

From where Tiff sat curled around her hot chocolate, she said, "Well, I think it's great he writes his dad. Your dad will be happy to get it—won't he, D'Arcy?"

D'Arcy didn't say anything.

"I bet you're a good writer. Tell your dad hi for me. And your sister."

"Gaby is with Mom," D'Arcy said.

"That's okay," Tiff said. "I'll see her in person soon."

Elizabeth wondered whether that meant that the sister would be coming to Jackson or that they were headed back East. As much as she dreaded the thought of another snooty tourist, she didn't want them to leave.

"Leave him alone, Tiff," Charlie said. "He's trying to find million-dollar words to impress his father."

"*You* leave him alone," Tiff said. "You wouldn't know. You leave out half your words."

"It's cause my thoughts are so quick."

"Charlie," Elizabeth said, "that's just an excuse people use so that they can be sloppy."

D'Arcy sat back and pushed the computer away. He looked at Charlie. "You say things like that so that people think you're agreeable, but really you're bragging."

"Right," Elizabeth said, "like when you say you'll leave whenever you want to. You like to think it's devil-may-care, when it's really just a humble-brag."

"Whoa," Charlie said. "At least I'm not pretending I'm deep to show off." He looked at D'Arcy.

"Admit it," D'Arcy said. "If one of your friends said, *do this*, you'd do it."

Charlie rolled his eyes, and because he'd been so nice the night before, Elizabeth said to D'Arcy, "But it's what he wants to do, too. It's not that he isn't deep or smart or anything."

Charlie laughed. "You don't need to defend me, Elizabeth. D'Arcy is one of those guys who only likes you if you tell him to go to hell."

"He'd think it was all right if you told him off?" Jenna put in.

D'Arcy said, "If I thought he was doing it on principle, sure."

"So the idea is more important than the person—is that right?" Elizabeth said. "To me, friendship is more important."

"It's true," Charlie said. "D'Arcy likes ideas better than people."

To that, D'Arcy smiled and shook his head, but Elizabeth thought he also seemed upset, so she didn't laugh. It couldn't be easy trying to please your father when your parents were going through a divorce.

After breakfast, it was time for Elizabeth and Jenna to go. By that time, D'Arcy had turned back to his computer, and Tiff had disappeared upstairs, but Charlie walked them out to the car. Elizabeth made herself scarce by taking the keys to unlock the trunk and stash her bike, but she kept her eye on them.

Holding both of Jenna's hands, Charlie smiled into Jenna's face and then leaned in and said something into Jenna's ear. He didn't kiss her though. He held both of her hands in his for a long moment, then nodded his head and turned and left. Jenna stood there watching him, her hands clasp in front of her, until he disappeared around the corner toward the front door, and then her shoulders went up to her ears, her head went back, and she sighed.

"Here, lovergirl," Elizabeth said and gave her the keys. As soon as they got into the car, Elizabeth asked, "So, what did he say to you?"

Jenna had a huge smile on her face, but she shook her head and wouldn't answer.

Chapter 8

A few days later, Dad came in late to breakfast from chores before going to work. As he ate, he didn't say a word, didn't read the paper, and sat hunched over his plate staring at the center of the table and chewing his food.

Everyone else was almost done eating, when Livie hopped up from the table and grabbed her plate to clear it. Mom said, "Sit."

"But, Mom," Livie said, "I was …" At the look on Mom's face, Livie's words trailed off, and she sat back down.

Mom turned to Dad. In a tone the girls had never before heard their mother use, Mom said, "Are you going to tell them, or am I?"

Dad looked at Mom for a long time. Mom met his stare, her eyebrows raised and her jaw set. Elizabeth and Jenna and Livie glanced at each other with questioning looks, and each shrugged their shoulders. They didn't know what was going on.

Mom turned to them. "Girls," she began, "your father—"

"Holly," Dad cut in. "Don't make it harder than it is."

"I'm not the one making it harder," Mom said, "I'm not the one—" but then she bit back her words and was quiet.

Dad sighed and straightened his shoulders. He glanced around the table at the girls but then fixed his eyes back on the center of the table. "Before I met your mom …"

At that, Mom tilted her head down and looked under her eyebrows at Dad.

"*Before* I met your mom," Dad repeated, "I almost married someone else."

At this, Elizabeth took a quick intake of breath, Jenna's hands covered her mouth, and Livie straightened from her usual slouch and leaned forward.

Dad continued, "To make a long story short—"

"By all means," Mom said.

"—we had a son," Dad continued, "who is now all grown up and is coming to visit."

There was complete silence, and nobody moved for what seemed like a century. It was Livie who broke the silence. "We have a brother?"

"A half-brother," Elizabeth corrected.

"He's coming here?" Jenna said.

"Today," Mom said.

"He's an only child," Dad said quickly, "and he said he'd like to meet me." Then he added, "Meet us."

"What's his name?" Jenna said.

"Colin," Dad said.

"Colin what," Elizabeth said.

"Colin Banner," Dad said.

"He has our name?" Livie said.

"He is my son," Dad said.

"*And* our half-brother," Elizabeth said.

"How old is he?" Jenna said.

"He's eighteen," Dad said, once again looking at the center of the table.

There was silence again. Jenna was seventeen and Mom and Dad had been married for two years before she was born.

With a pinched look, Mom searched each of the girls' faces.

"Does this mean you two are getting a divorce?" Elizabeth said.

A quick intake of breath from Mom, but then Dad said, "No, I don't think so." He glanced at Mom, who avoided his look.

Again, silence around the table. Then Jenna said, "We have a brother."

When they were little, Elizabeth had wished that Livie had been a boy, and she had tried to persuade Mom and Dad to have more kids because she wanted a brother, but now it came as such a shock. She, Elizabeth, was her dad's favorite, and he had never told her she had a brother, even though he knew it had been her biggest dream for a long time.

The world had moved sideways somehow and left Elizabeth behind.

"And he's coming today," Mom said.

Nobody said a word for the rest of the meal.

All day, Elizabeth was furious at Dad for not telling, for lying all these years, but by late afternoon when Colin's flight came in, her head had cooled a bit. When he came home early to go pick Colin up, she went out to meet him.

"Hey, Little Bit," he said.

Elizabeth felt the urge to confront him, to ask him why, but then she didn't, not then. "Can I come to the airport with you?" was all she said.

He looked at her for a long moment and then said, "Sure."

They took the truck. Dad kept tapping the steering wheel with his thumbs, something he did when he was thinking about something, or when he was nervous.

The longer Elizabeth sat there not looking at him, the more spitting mad she got. He had never said anything. Not a word. He owed her that—at least. At the very least.

"When were you going to tell us?" Elizabeth began.

Dad didn't say anything, but his hands quit tapping.

"*Were* you going to tell us?"

Dad glanced out the window and then slowly looked over at Elizabeth. "Probably not," he said.

His honesty caught her off guard. What was she supposed to do with that? It was like he was a little kid who was trying to get away with something, only now he'd gotten caught. Elizabeth looked over at her dad. She'd never thought of him as a kid before. On one hand, she thought, she would've liked to've known him then, back when he'd been her age. He'd've been fun, that kid in class who always made everybody laugh but in a quiet way. She'd inherited her sarcasm from him.

She turned her back on him and stared out the window.

"You know," he said, "I wasn't that much older than you are now. What would *you* do?"

The first thing Elizabeth thought was that it wasn't fair, wasn't fair at all for him to ask that. Fathers shouldn't ask daughters. Some things were off limits.

"It's not the same," she shot back. It wasn't. He was a guy. She was a girl. Even if they were the same age, it was way different.

"Seriously, Elizabeth," her dad said. "What would you have done?" There was a note of pleading in his voice.

What would she have done? Well, she wouldn't have lied to her family—that was for sure. And she wouldn't have totally left her little baby behind. Had he even tried to be a dad? At all? Had Mom known? By the open wound that was Mom's face, Elizabeth was guessing the news was fairly fresh. She thought about her father's bent head at the breakfast table. He'd felt caught, just as he probably had all those years ago when he'd gotten married and then got some other girl pregnant. For just a second, Elizabeth felt sorry for him, but then she thought, *no, he's an adult. He's supposed to know these things.*

"I would've done the right thing," she said. There's no way she was going to make him feel better, not after he lied to her.

They didn't talk for the rest of the way to the airport.

Chapter 9

The small commuter jet was on time and had already
arrived from Denver as Elizabeth and her dad pulled up to the
tiny Jackson Hole Airport. Passengers ducked out of the door
and lumbered down the rolling stair clutching the rail, while
the baggage handlers whipped the cart out and around and
backed up to the hold to get the luggage. Elizabeth and her dad
walked into the terminal, and Elizabeth guessed right away
who Colin was. There weren't many people in the tiny
terminal. He stood over near the vinyl and chrome seats by the
large plate glass windows, head bent over his cell phone and
his other hand on his luggage, which was propped on the seat.
He glanced up and saw them coming toward him and his arms
dropped to his sides.

Colin was of medium height, pudgy, with black hair curling
around his ears and round glasses. He had a baby face but also
one of those five-o'clock-shadow beards, so that even though
he was 18 he looked 30. He was wearing wrinkled khakis,
loafers, and a pale-blue-striped button-down short-sleeved
shirt. He didn't look a thing like Dad—there must be a mistake,
Elizabeth thought—but then he did look like Dad in the way he

stood with his back curved and his hips tucked under, knees locked. Elizabeth hated that she noticed that.

Elizabeth hung back as her father stepped forward and put out his hand. "Colin?" he said.

"Yeah? I mean, yes, sir. I'm Colin." Colin extended his hand and the two men shook. Colin gripped Dad's hand like he was holding on for dear life, staring into Dad's face. Elizabeth couldn't decide whether Dad was excited to see Colin or not. It was hard to tell these things sometimes.

"Good to meet you," Dad said.

There was a long and uncomfortable silence as the two looked at each other. And though she hated herself for it, Elizabeth stepped forward to her dad's rescue. "Hi, I'm Elizabeth," she said and extended her hand.

Colin looked surprised as he extended his hand. He looked back and forth between her and her dad.

"I'm his daughter," Elizabeth said.

"Oh. Oh, of course," Colin said. "You're Will's—er, Mr. Banner's daughter." He glanced past them. "Are there more of you?"

"They stayed at home," Elizabeth said. "There's Jenna and Livie, my sisters. And our mom, of course." She eyed Colin as she said this.

"Of course, of course," Colin said. "I'm so happy to meet you." He said it like he really meant it.

"Well, Colin," Dad said as he reached over and took Colin's bag, "how was your flight?"

"They weren't bad," Colin said.

"Why'd you fly, instead of drive?" Elizabeth asked. "Gillette isn't that far."

Colin blushed as he said, "My mom wanted ... Well, she thought it would be safer." He glanced over at Dad as he said this.

Dad nodded. "She always was a mother hen."

A relieved smile broke over Colin's face. "Yes. Yes she is," he said.

Elizabeth frowned. She didn't like it one bit.

The trip home was really uncomfortable, and nobody said much. When they got home, Dad took Colin's luggage to the extra room in the basement. Colin was introduced around, and everyone was nice enough. Livie had moved on, so she just shrugged. Jenna went out of her way to give a wide smile and say, "I hope you have a good visit." What surprised Elizabeth the most was her mom. Mom had made a special dinner, which was on the table when they got home—her corn flake pork chops with mashed potatoes and gravy, melon, fresh greens from the garden, and cheese biscuits. Pecan pie and homemade ice cream for dessert. When introduced, Mom said, "Welcome, Colin," and bowed her head. Colin smiled in return. When everyone was sitting down at the table, Elizabeth saw him take a big shuddering sigh.

Everyone sat and the food was passed around. Colin hesitated at the pork chops, glanced at Mom, and then forked one off onto his plate.

There was silence until Mom said, "So, how was your flight?" She glanced at Dad.

"It was good," Colin said. "Those small jets are pretty smooth, though it was a bit bumpy coming into Jackson."

"Yeah, those mountains," she said. "Huh, Will?" She looked meaningfully at Dad.

Dad swallowed his bite and said, "That's for sure. They can be a real gut-wrencher. One time … well, not dinner talk, anyway." He smiled at Colin.

The table fell silent and pretty much stayed that way for the rest of the meal. Mom cut the pie and Jenna scooped the ice cream.

"This is very good, Mrs. Banner," Colin said. "You're a really good cook. Thank you for the nice dinner." His voice was so pushed and stretched, Elizabeth felt sorry for him. It couldn't be easy. Colin continued, "I appreciate you letting me visit like this."

"No problem," Mom said, "I understand a son wanting to visit his father."

It was still around the table. Colin froze but then nodded vigorously.

Mom continued, "You have to admit, it's a little awkward. Not that it's your fault. You can't help who your, er, being born. These things happen." Her voice took on a hard note.

"Yes," Colin said, "I know my being here is hard on everyone. I don't want to ruin anything, and I hope …" Colin hesitated. "Maybe if you get to know me, it won't be so bad?"

Dad cleared his throat. "It'll be fine, Colin. A little more male blood around here might balance things out a little." He glanced at the girls. "All estrogen and boy crazy, I can tell you."

They finished up their pie and ice cream and, thoroughly stuffed, cleared the table. It was Jenna's turn to load the dishwasher.

"I get the PlayStation," Livie called.

"Good," Jenna said. "You can play Colin."

"Mom, do I have to?" Livie said.

Both Mom and Dad were about to speak when Colin said, "That's okay. I *don't play* video games." He said it like they were bugs.

Both Livie and Elizabeth stared at him.

"They rot the brain," Colin said in a voice that sounded like someone else's.

Dad stepped forward. "How about I show you around the place?" he said.

Colin nodded vigorously. "Oh, that'd be great." His voice showed how eager he was. To be alone with Dad, Elizabeth thought.

As they left, Elizabeth turned to Livie and said, "Come on, Liv. Let's go rot our brains."

Chapter 10

The next morning after a quick breakfast, Elizabeth's job was to weed the garden. Already, the sky was impossibly blue, not a cloud in sight. Her mom had gone overboard this year and widened the garden, and the weeds were now tall enough to compete with the crinkly green of the potato plants and the smooth shoots of onions. It was a job Elizabeth hated and loved. She hated it because it was a lot of work in the hot sun, but she liked it because she was by herself with the birds chirping from the cottonwoods over the ditch banks and the smell of dewed grass or rain. It was going to be a hot day, so she went out after breakfast in cutoffs, gloves, and a big floppy hat to take advantage of the cool. Mom and Jenna and Livie were going to spend the morning canning asparagus—the stench of which Elizabeth was happy to get away from.

No sooner had she started to yank the big ugly weeds out by their roots, here came Colin. He wore the same clothes he had had on the day before, and he stood and watched her for a while with his arms crossed above the bump of his belly. Elizabeth knew she should say hi, but he was disturbing the one thing about this job she liked, so she ignored him.

She was on a particularly tall weed, bent over and grasping at its base with both gloved hands, grunting with effort, when he said, "You're good at that."

What did he mean by that? She continued to ignore him and yanked so hard that she almost fell on her butt when the weed gave way. Good at weeding. That wasn't even a compliment. She continued to weed, and he continued to stand there. He didn't even offer to help.

He wouldn't give up though. "Thank you for coming with Mr. Banner to get me at the airport. That was nice."

Well, she had to say something. "Thank you," she finally said.

"And your mom's nice." He said it like he was surprised. Well, he probably was. Elizabeth sure was.

"Uh huh," she said.

Colin stepped into the garden and stopped two rows away.

"Don't step on the beets," Elizabeth said.

"Oh!" Colin said. "Which are the beets?"

"Maybe you should stand back over where you were."

He did as he was told. Then he said, "Um, uh." He paused. Finally, he nodded and said, "Did Mr. Banner, uh, your dad, ever say anything about me?"

Elizabeth froze. She didn't like the way this was going. It was all wrong, and she hated being manipulated. "Like what?" It felt wrong to tell him that Dad had never said a word about him.

"I don't know, that I tried to get in touch with him?"

"Well, he told us you were coming."

"No, I mean years ago."

Should she lie? No. That would create this whole *thang*, and you never wanted to get into those kinds of places. She shrugged. Why the hell was he asking her anyway? Sure, it sucked to be him, but it sucked for everybody in one way or another.

"I hope he meant …" Colin said. Taking a deep breath, Elizabeth stood and faced him. She was about to tell him to go away and let her weed, but her facing him was all he needed. An intense look came across his face as he said, "I need your help. Will you help me?"

"What?" She took a step backwards. *He* was going to try to get *her* on his side? What was he thinking? This suck-ass boy comes and ruins everything, and now this?

"I want to put his name on my birth certificate. Do you think he'll let me do that?"

She stopped. "Wait. How did you get the name Banner, then?"

"I changed it. When I turned 18."

She just looked at him, her eyes narrowed. He hadn't even asked if he could use their name. He'd just barged in like he was doing now.

He stepped back into the garden, crushing some lettuce and beets as he tromped through. He put his soft, warm, sweaty hand on her arm. "You've got to help me," he said, his voice high and tight. "You're his favorite. If you help me, he'll do it."

That wasn't fair! No effing way! And now he was all up in her face and insisting. No way. She stepped forward and shoved him backwards. "*Get out* of my face," she said and walked past him. But then she turned back. "And get the hell out of my family." She turned and walked into the house.

As she came through the kitchen, her mother said, "Where's Colin? I thought he was out with you?"

Elizabeth stopped and looked at her mother.

"Well, where is he?"

Elizabeth shook her head. "In the garden where I left him, I imagine."

"You just left him there?"

"Well, there's not much of a fence around it, so I imagine he might've wandered off by now." Elizabeth kept her eyes on her mom's face.

"Elizabeth, have a little empathy for heaven's sake. He's, well, he's just trying to—" Just then Dad walked into the kitchen. He'd taken a day or two off from work—Elizabeth was sure Mom had insisted. "Will," Mom said, "tell your daughter to be a good hostess to *your son*. She just left him out there."

Dad looked between the two of them and then focused on Elizabeth. "You just left him out there?"

Elizabeth nodded once sharply.

"You seem to've disappointed your mother. Is that what you wanted to do?" Dad said.

"No," Elizabeth said, impatience in her voice. "I'm sorry, Dad. He's your son and everything, but he … Well, he's trying to ruin everything."

"Well, you seem to have a choice then," Dad said. "Disappoint your mother. Or disappoint me." He turned to Mom. "Do me a favor, Holly. Let Elizabeth work it out for herself."

At this, Elizabeth's whole body felt warm and grateful.

Mom made an *ahuh* sound and her chin jutted forward. "But he's *your son*!"

"Let me deal with that," Dad said and went out the door.

It was quiet in the kitchen for a full five seconds before Mom said, "Well, if you aren't going to weed the garden, you can help with the asparagus."

"I'm going to weed the garden," Elizabeth said and went back outside.

Chapter 11

Colin stuck close to Dad all morning, and Elizabeth could tell Dad was starting to get short tempered. Dad was used to having lots of space. By the afternoon, Livie had convinced Jenna to take her into town, and Elizabeth was roped into it too, and although it was not quite clear how it happened, Colin was invited along. As soon as Elizabeth heard that, she insisted they pick up Miley too. Then she'd have someone else to focus on—"moron support" as Miley called helping each other put up with guys they didn't like. Both Dad and Mom seemed happy with the idea.

"Colin, why don't you ride up front with Jenna?" Elizabeth said nonchalantly. She calculated that there was no room for Miley in the bucket seats up front if Elizabeth called shotgun, but if she didn't call it Livie would. But if Colin sat up front, Elizabeth would not have to sit with Colin and would be able to sit next to Miley, with Livie on the other side. Livie's glares would be a small price to pay.

"Aah!" Livie said.

Elizabeth motioned to Colin's back and frowned, saying Livie should let the guest have the good seat. Livie shook her head but gave in. She had bigger fish to fry, and she needed

Elizabeth's cooperation—and Elizabeth knew it. Livie pushed the whole thing because she wanted to see Dennis. Mom and Dad knew it too, but they counted on Jenna and Elizabeth to see that she didn't get in any trouble. And of course, Jenna was on the lookout for Charlie. Elizabeth just hoped they didn't find them both, because in that case it would be up to her to entertain Colin. At least Miley would be there.

They stopped in the burbs to pick up Miley, Elizabeth scooting to the middle so Miley's long legs didn't have to fight with the hump. Once they were settled in again and driving to the square, Miley looked at the back of Colin's head and then at Elizabeth and raised an eyebrow.

"Oh, yeah," Elizabeth said. "Miley, this is Colin. He's our *half-brother*." Colin turned in his seat and smiled pleasantly at Miley.

"Huh?" Miley said, her forehead squinched.

"This is Miley, my best friend," Elizabeth said to Colin.

"Since when?" Miley said. "Half-brother, not best friend."

"Since yesterday," Elizabeth said. Then, after a pause, she added, "Well, technically all our lives."

"Welcome to the family," Miley said.

Not hearing the sarcasm—or ignoring it—Colin said, "Thank you. I, well, I've always wanted sisters or brothers."

"Well, now you got a whole armload," Miley said, a smile creeping over her face. "Good luck."

They found a parking spot off the Town Square and piled out, stretching their cramped legs and adjusting their clothes. The plan was to walk around the square, maybe stop for ice cream, and eventually end up at bookstore slash café, the Deckled Edge, run by their Aunt Geri and her partner Patty.

Geri and Patty always had their music buddies over on Friday afternoons. Patty played a mean dulcimer, and there was a banjo and a guitar and some bongos. People in the audience would pick up tambourines or maracas and join in. There was always free chai and fresh hummus and pita warm from the oven, or toasted soy beans, or sesame crackers, or something else. Aunt Geri was the chef, and she could take the grossest of ingredients and make it taste heavenly. Somehow, it had become cool for high school kids to hang out there, and so there was always a few friends. Or cute guys.

They began to walk, Jenna and Livie out front trying to make it look like they weren't searching the crowd, Colin in the middle, and Elizabeth and Miley taking up the rear. Colin craned his neck, taking in the huge arches of elk antlers at each corner of the square, the shops selling overpriced artwork and pottery and plastic Indian relics, the Million Dollar Cowboy Bar and the yoga center, the kiddie Gap and outdoor store with its decapitated mannequins in bulging speedos. They dodged large families of large tourists in brightly colored shorts who wandered around. "Like a herd of elk with the lead cow shot out," her dad would've said.

"What you think?" Miley said loudly to Colin.

"It looks great," Colin said, but it didn't sound sincere.

Miley walked ahead so that she was even with Colin. "I know, right?" Miley said. "More plastic than Barbie's boobs."

"No, it's great," Colin said. "A lot of money around here?"

Miley snorted. "You'd think so."

Elizabeth thought how odd they looked together—Miley edgy and beautiful with rich brown skin and hair that wouldn't quit, Colin short and wrinkled and pudgy and earnest.

"I'm going to make a lot of money someday," Colin said. "I'm headed to U-dub in the fall to get a degree in computer science. Then I'm headed to Silicon Valley. I have this idea."

"Yeah?" Miley said.

Why was Miley being so nice to him? It didn't make sense. He was Elizabeth's so-called brother, not hers.

"Yeah—I mean yes," Colin said. "You know how you always lose the remote? Well, I think I've figured out a way that you can use hand gestures to control the TV. You don't even need a remote."

"Wow," Miley said. "That's amazing."

Wow? Miley never said *wow*. What was up with that?

They hadn't walked halfway along the square when Livie ran ahead to where Dennis sat on a bench. A sophomore like Livie, Dennis was short and wirey, with brown hair down past his shoulders and a smiling round face and eyes that seemed to slowly take things in and accept them with a blink. He always wore unlaced sneakers, baggy cargo pants, and a t-shirt—today it was tan with a white marijuana leaf on the front. Dennis sat with his elbows hooked over the back of the bench, his butt scooted forward, and his knees relaxed wide. When he saw Livie, though, he sat forward.

Sitting next to Dennis was the most gorgeous creature Elizabeth had ever seen. He was tall and slender, dressed like a jock in long shorts and one of those shirts that pulled the sweat away from you and sneakers with individual toes. He had brown skin and high cheekbones and full lips like a girl. When they walked up, he and Dennis stood, and Elizabeth felt like the guy's eyes were liquid caramel—warm and soft and enveloping. She took an involuntary breath.

"Hey girl," Dennis said as Livie threw her arms around him.

Jenna glanced over at Elizabeth, and they nodded their heads—they were going to have to watch Livie like a hawk. The next thing you knew, she'd ditch them and be off with Dennis getting into trouble.

"Hey, Dennis," Jenna said.

"Who's your friend?" Elizabeth said.

"Yeah, man," Dennis said. "This is Teo, Teo Wick." He nodded for a minute and then said, "Teo, everybody." Teo's smile seemed to be just for Elizabeth, though he nodded to everyone else.

Elizabeth stepped forward. "I've never heard the name Teo before." She smiled at him.

"It's Persian," Teo said, in a full voice that smoothly drew out the *purr* in Persian.

There was silence for a moment, and then Dennis said, shaking his head, "No way, dude. Teo is Greek, like Theo. It means Greek god or something like that."

Teo flushed a little. "It's Persian too."

"Greece and Persia were right next to each other anyway," Elizabeth said.

Livie gave Elizabeth a mean look, but Dennis shrugged his shoulders. "Chillax. If he wants to be Persian, he's Persian. You can be frigging Xerxes." Dennis put his hand on Teo's shoulder and bobbed his head.

"Teo was *born* in Jackson," Livie said.

"You grew up in Jackson?" Elizabeth said. It didn't make sense, since she'd never seen him before.

"I was born here, but I grew up mostly over by Pinedale. My dad was in the oil fields," Teo said. His voice still had that honey quality.

Just then, the roar of motorcycles overtook them. It got louder and louder until around the corner came two big bikes that looked like something out of a post-industrial horror movie.

Jenna said, "Oh, oh!" under her breath.

It was Charlie and D'Arcy. They pulled right up next to the group and let the bikes idle, so that the roar died down to a soft burbling.

"Jenna!" Charlie said. "How's my favorite babe today?" His smile through his helmet was wide and warm and sweet.

Jenna glowed. She stepped over to the bike and put her hand on his shoulder. "Nice bike," she said.

It was about then that Elizabeth lost track of what Jenna was saying. She'd glanced over at Teo, whose face drained of color. He was staring directly at D'Arcy. It was hard to see with the helmet, but she was sure that D'Arcy's face turned bright red, and his jaw clenched. He narrowed his eyes and stared back at Teo until Teo looked away.

D'Arcy revved his bike and pulled up with a jerk right next to Charlie. "Sorry, Charlie, but my Mom's waiting," he said before he revved the engine again and took off without a look backwards. Charlie looked after him, turned to Jenna and shrugged. "I'll be seeing you," he said.

"I hope so," Jenna said as Charlie nodded and then revved his engine and eased away from the curb.

What was that? Elizabeth wondered. "Well," Elizabeth said, "I'm hungry. Let's go over to Geri and Patty's."

"Ah, I was thinking," Livie said. "You guys go on ahead. Dennis and Teo and I were going to, ah, go over and—"

"NO WAY," Elizabeth and Jenna said in unison. They'd been expecting just that.

"You know better," Jenna said. "Dad would kill us."

Livie looked at Dennis and good-naturedly shrugged her shoulders.

Jenna must've felt sorry for her because she said to Dennis and Teo, "Come with us. It's always a good time."

Livie raised her eyebrows at Dennis. "Want to?"

Dennis glanced at Teo and then nodded. "Sure," he said. "Whatever."

Chapter 12

On the walk over to the Deckled Edge, Jenna had a faraway smile on her face.

"Psst, Jenna," Elizabeth said, speeding up so that Livie and the two guys were left farther behind. Miley was still talking to Colin, which bugged Elizabeth a little. "Jenna," Elizabeth said. "Did you see that?"

"What?" Jenna said.

"Did you see that? The way D'Arcy and Teo looked at each other?"

"What? Like how?"

"Like they were ready to kill each other," Elizabeth said. "You didn't see it?" She paused. "Of course you didn't see it," she added, mostly to herself.

"Are you sure?" Jenna said. "How would they even know each other?"

Elizabeth glanced back at Teo. "I don't know," she said, "but there's something there."

"I don't think so," Jenna said. "Not that I doubt you," she added.

"Yeah," Elizabeth said.

Just then, Miley caught up with them. "Colin's interesting," she said, half to herself.

Elizabeth opened her eyes wide, jutted her chin, and shook her head. "And what's up with that, may I ask?" She looked at Miley.

Miley smiled sheepishly. After a second, she said, "Well, he is."

"Right," Elizabeth said.

"'Sides, I got him out of your hair. You looked like you'd chew him up and spit him out."

"I did not."

"Yes you did," Jenna put in.

"Well maybe," Elizabeth said.

The front of the Deckled Edge was warmed by the yellow afternoon sun, and as they walked in through the open door, the heavenly smell of baked cookies and the mellow sound of stringed instruments filled the air. Patty and two of her friends plucked away in the area cleared for the band. Patty had curly blonde hair escaping from a bandana, prismatic blue eyes, and a comfortable plumpness that encircled her dulcimer. There were also couches with low oblong tables and small round tables with chairs and a counter with stools. There were off-beat book classics on a shelf, and the red brick walls were lined with artwork of mountains and elk from local artists. The place had a fair crowd—not packed but enough people to feel good. Some older hippy types, a family with young kids, and some other teenagers that Elizabeth knew just enough to wave to. On a low table to the side were huge monster cookies, a pitcher of warm chai, and cups and napkins.

Aunt Geri came out from the kitchen holding some plates of food, which she delivered to the family in the corner on a couch. She was tall and wirey, with a husky voice and spiked gray hair cut above her ears with their large gold hoops. A butch female version of Dad, which did not come off as weird as it sounded.

Aunt Geri saw them and nodded. They pulled two tables together toward the back and gathered chairs and sat. Elizabeth and Miley sat together, and Elizabeth was happy to find the hunky Teo on her other side, though she tried not to show it.

Once Aunt Geri had taken care of the other people, she came over. She smiled, but in her very quiet way—some people might not even notice. "Thanks for coming," she said. "Can I get you kids anything?"

Jenna stood and gestured to Colin. "Aunt Geri," she said, "have you heard about, I mean, met Colin? This is Colin Banner." Colin stood and clutched his hands in front of himself. At the last name, Aunt Geri's brows lowered, but otherwise her face stayed pleasantly blank. "He would be your nephew." Jenna turned to Colin. "Colin, this is your Aunt Geri, Dad's sister."

Colin tightened like a plucked wire. He held out his hand and said, "It's so nice to meet you." He paused and then added, "Aunt Geri."

Aunt Geri looked at him for a minute and said, "You're Will's son, then? By Judy, no doubt." She shook his hand.

"Yeah, my … yeah," Colin said. "My mom is, uh, was Judy Meyer."

"She would be," Aunt Geri said, nodding, her head tilted to the side. "You just never know who'll turn up." She waved her hand. Elizabeth knew her well enough to see she was taking it in stride. Elizabeth wasn't sure if Colin could tell, and she didn't really care. Let him stew.

Elizabeth introduced Dennis and Teo. Geri already knew Miley.

"Well, help yourself to the chai," Geri said. "Can I get you anything else?" She glanced around at all of them. Livie ordered some hot chocolate, Dennis ordered a cinnamon roll heated with butter, and Teo ordered an Americano. Elizabeth ordered a cherry Italian soda for herself and for Miley. Jenna said she'd just have the chai. Geri went to get the drinks, and they all talked together over the music. Geri brought their orders, nodding and saying, "Just holler if I can get you anything else." Livie started talking to Dennis, and Colin said something to Miley, and so Elizabeth was left to talk to Teo. Not that she minded.

As they chatted, Elizabeth wondered again what it was between Teo and D'Arcy. She was trying to figure out how to ask when he brought it up.

"So, how long has D'Arcy been in town?" Teo said.

"A week or two, I think," Elizabeth said. "Apparently his mom bought a house, though he spends a lot of time at the Billingsleys." She thought of D'Arcy's sour face and added, "His parents are getting a divorce."

"That's too bad," Teo said. "His dad's a nice guy. My dad worked for him."

"Your dad ... Oh, D'Arcy's dad is in the oil business? I thought he lived in New York?"

"He does. They do. But they have things going on out here too. Mr. Pemberly owns an oilfield services company, and my dad worked for him. We'd have barbecues at his house sometimes when I was a kid."

Elizabeth couldn't keep the surprise off her face.

"Yeah," Teo continued, "I've known D'Arcy all my life. We used to hang out together when we were kids and they were out here on business trips." His face had the faraway look of remembering. Then he looked at her. "Are you friends?"

"Uh, friends? No." Elizabeth couldn't keep her disgust from her voice, and she didn't really want to. "He's not a very nice guy."

"I guess I shouldn't say anything," Teo said, biting his lip. "I've been around him too long. But a lot of people think he's the cat's meow."

"Well, I'm not one of them."

A relieved smile came over Teo's face. "That's good. Me too. I think cause he's rich and polite everyone gets fooled. Is he here long, do you know?"

Elizabeth shrugged. "I don't know. They didn't say."

Teo smiled. "His dad's cool. He kept my dad on, even when oil was really cheap and he could've bolted. I'm sure there were things that could've made him a lot more money." Teo's expression flattened. "But then, for some reason D'Arcy decided he didn't like me, and so he got my dad fired." His eyes widened and he looked younger for a minute. "I could almost forgive D'Arcy because his dad is so cool."

"He had your dad fired?" It sounded just like a shitty thing D'Arcy would do.

"Well, that, and he was going to give me a good summer job so I could save money to go to college. Now, I think I'll have to go the ROTC route, if they let me in." He sipped his coffee and watched the musicians for a minute. "Mr. Pemberly could've given me a summer job anyway, but then there was D'Arcy spouting off. Maybe I shouldn't have stood up for my dad and told D'Arcy what I thought of him. He hates me because of that."

"That's not fair," Elizabeth said. "Couldn't you just go to Mr. Pemberly and explain it all?"

"There's no way he's going to take my word over his son's, you know?" Teo shook his head.

"Well, that's horrible," Elizabeth said.

"All I can think is that D'Arcy was jealous that I got along so well with his dad."

"What an asshole," Elizabeth said. "I knew he wasn't very nice to be around, but ..." Some people just went out of their way to make other people miserable. "In fact, the other day, he even said he held grudges and valued his *principles* over people."

"Yeah, that's him," Teo said.

"Well, that's just awful," Elizabeth said. "You're so nice"—she blushed as she said it, but continued—"and he's such an asshole. And stuck on himself."

"Well, his family's great, and he's definitely proud of his family and wants to please his father." A weird expression came over Teo's face—Elizabeth wasn't quite sure how to take it—and he added, "And his sister too. He's touchy about her, too."

"What's—Gabby, is it? What's she like?"

"I wish I could say she was nice. She is nice to most people—I hate to talk bad about her. But she's like D'Arcy—stuck on herself. She really liked me when she was a kid, but now, well. Anyway, she spends most of her time in New York."

"Do you know Charlie? Or the Billingsleys?"

"Naw, not really," Teo said. "I've heard the name." He thought for a moment. "Wait, I think D'Arcy's mom was a Billingsley. Maybe they're all cousins."

"Hmm," Elizabeth said.

"Yeah, D'Arcy's mom, well, I hate to say anything, but she can be a real bitch."

"She just bought a house, they said."

"Makes sense. She always loved it here."

Dennis and Teo had to leave soon after, and as Teo stood, Elizabeth put her hand lightly on his arm, smiled her most winningest, and said, "See you round?"

He leaned in, as if he was going to kiss her, and she froze, but instead he whispered, "Count on it." Then he winked at her as he pulled back.

Elizabeth decided right there that he was the most delicious guy she had ever come across.

Livie hugged Dennis enthusiastically. "Dude," she said.

"Pixie," he said, hugging her back with one arm.

He and Teo slouched toward the door, just as two more high school girls came in. Elizabeth knew the girls a little. Karissa Montgomery and Brittany King. She'd played with Karissa when they had been in grade school, but she didn't know Brittany well—only the rumors about her and what she did with the boys. Brittany looked Teo up and down and leaned forward and said something to him. Teo smiled at her but then he and Dennis left. Elizabeth felt herself blush as jealousy bubbled up inside her. The girls joined the high schoolers at the other table.

The rest of the group stayed for a bit longer. Then they stood, waved at Patty who nodded her head and smiled wide, said goodbye to Aunt Geri, and left. On the way back to the car, Colin fell in beside Elizabeth and Miley. This time he focused on Elizabeth and talked on and on about housing prices in Silicon Valley, which companies might be interested in his idea, and so on. At one point when Elizabeth unconsciously let out a deep sigh, Miley pinched her. Elizabeth jumped but smiled at her and rolled her eyes.

When they got home, Mom had supper waiting for them. They ate and talked about their day in town. At the mention of Dennis's name, Mom frowned and Dad said, deep and low, "You promised, Olivia."

"I didn't do nothing," Livie said.

Elizabeth just shook her head. Livie was the youngest and got away with murder, Elizabeth often thought. Mom generally let them all get away with a lot, and it was Dad who laid down the law, but for some reason, he seemed to let Livie get away with a lot more than he'd let Elizabeth get away with. Even and especially when they were little. Elizabeth and Jenna had not been allowed to take food to their rooms, for example, and if candy was found up there, they got in big trouble. Livie, though, had thrown such a fit one day because she wanted to take a candy bunny to nap time, she literally lay down on the floor and flailed, her little fat arms and legs waving and pounding. Dad had just caved. Caved. The unfairness of it still made Elizabeth grit her teeth. Deep down, Elizabeth knew, actually, that she was her father's favorite, but there was something about Livie—whether he'd just given up or her personality was strong enough that she overran his will. Definitely some of that going on.

When they were alone, Elizabeth told Jenna what Teo had said.

"Well, I don't believe it," Jenna said. "Maybe it's just a misunderstanding." Her forehead wrinkled, trying to put it all together. "Maybe they're both in the wrong, just a little bit, you know? We can't know what went on. Maybe neither of them did anything wrong."

"Right," Elizabeth said. "So nobody did anything. Nobody's at fault." She tried to keep the smirk off her face. "Heaven forbid we think badly of someone."

Jenna shook her head but smiled. "You're so determine to." She thought for a minute and continued, "People don't just treat others that way on a whim. If D'Arcy's father did what Teo said he did, then he must've had a reason. We only have Teo's word for what went on. And I can't believe that Charlie and his family would be such good friends the Pemberlys and D'Arcy if that was the case."

"Well, I heard they might be related," Elizabeth said, "and that's why. Besides, Teo's story sounded true, and he told me particulars that he couldn't have just made up. All without me even asking. I'd also say, the way they looked at each other— it's true."

Jenna continued shaking her head. "I don't know what to think."

"Well, I do," Elizabeth said.

Just then, Jenna's phone buzzed with a notification, a new tone Elizabeth hadn't heard. It was the song "The Wind Beneath My Wings," and Jenna blushed when it came on.

"Who—?" Elizabeth said, but Jenna waved her hand and didn't answer as she looked at the text. "You *didn't*," Elizabeth added, with a big smile on her face.

"They going to the powwow down in Alpine tomorrow," Jenna said.

"Who?"

"You know who," Jenna said.

"Well, I better come too," Elizabeth said shaking her head. She knew Jenna wanted her to come, and she had a fierce hope that they would run into Teo, unlikely though it was. "If only D'Arcy wasn't coming," she said mostly to herself. *And Tiff,* she didn't say but wanted to.

"Oh for heaven's sake," Jenna said. "He's not that bad. You'd like him if you gave him half a chance."

"God no! That would awful—to like someone you're trying so hard to hate."

Jenna snorted.

Mom said they could go as long as they were back in time for chores. Elizabeth spent extra time getting ready. Instead of just letting her short hair air dry, she used a blow dryer on low and moussed it so it curled on the top. She wore her usual jeans, but then she put on a turquoise top with no sleeves and slid on some bangles. She also put in her diamond studs and her turquoise sandals. When she came out, Jenna smiled knowingly but didn't say anything.

They heard the drums as they pulled up to the powwow, and when they stepped out of the car, they could hear singers' distinct voices: "Hey-ya, hey-ya, hey-ya, hey-ya." They'd missed the Grand Entry. Cars were all parked off to one side in a field, and tents and awnings were set up around the outside of a big circular open area. People stood around the edge of the area and watched and clapped as the dancers danced in the middle. Some of the dancers wore regalia—brightly colored beaded shirts and leggings and moccasins with large headdresses that swayed as they moved. Others wore more traditional clothing with few ornaments, just a tanned wolfhide headdress and a bare torso that showed off Sun Dance scars on their chests. These dancers were less showy in their movements, smaller but more powerful. The First Nations community is like an organism, Elizabeth had been told, and the drumming is the heart of the whole thing.

Jenna and Elizabeth had skipped lunch on purpose so they could get Indian tacos—fry bread topped with taco burger, cheese, lettuce, salsa, and sour cream. They got their tacos and sodas and found a bit of grass off to the side, but all the while keeping an eye out on the road. There was no sign of either Charlie or Teo, and so they finished their lunch and watched the dancers. They saw a few people they knew, who nodded hello.

Then there came the pa-ta-ta roar of motorbikes, low at first but then loud as they pulled up into the makeshift parking lot. It drown out the voices of the singers, and some of the elders looked annoyed.

"Come on," Jenna said, pushing herself to standing.

"What?" Elizabeth said.

Jenna held out her hand and tipped her head toward the noise.

"Oh," Elizabeth said. She hadn't been thinking about Charlie and D'Arcy on bikes—she'd been scanning the crowd for Teo. She tried not to let the disappointment show on her face.

Sure enough, it was Charlie and D'Arcy. The attendees were eyeing them as Jenna and Elizabeth walked up. Elizabeth didn't blame everyone—the two guys wore a combination of guys' athletic clothes and bike leathers, all obviously very new and very expensive.

"Charlie!" Jenna said.

"Hey, girl," Charlie said, removing his helmet and taking Jenna's hand. "Glad you came."

Jenna beamed.

Charlie and Jenna were so focused on each other, that left Elizabeth and D'Arcy standing uncomfortably off to the side. They glanced at each other at the same time but then looked away, uncomfortable.

"Hi, Elizabeth," Charlie said cheerfully.

"Hi, Charlie," Elizabeth said, and then out of shame she added, "Hi, D'Arcy."

D'Arcy nodded, an unreadable look on his face.

Jenna suggested they go over and find a seat to watch the dancers, and so they did, the couple in the middle and Elizabeth and D'Arcy firmly on either side. They hadn't sat for five minutes before Charlie offered an excuse and he and Jenna were off walking by themselves, which left Elizabeth and D'Arcy sitting too far apart but too close together.

Elizabeth began to fume to herself. How dare he? How dare he what, she wasn't quite sure. She also decided she wasn't going to speak to Jenna for a week. Then she thought how rude

D'Arcy was, just sitting there twiddling his fingers and not saying a thing, until she realized she hadn't said anything either.

"Well," she said, "the dancers are always pretty cool."

D'Arcy glanced their direction and then nodded.

"This is where you say something," Elizabeth said. "You know, that's how conversation works. I say something, and then you say something, and that's the way it goes."

He smiled in spite of her tone and said, "Just tell me what I should say, and I'll say it."

She lowered her voice. "*Yeah, those dancers. Yeah.*" Then she let her voice go back to normal. "And the weather today is cooperating. A nice day." Again, her voice low. "*Yes, the weather is nice today.*"

"Well, there you are," he said.

"It's only polite." She didn't want to sound like a prude, but he was being an asshole.

"So we're all about being polite, are we?" he said.

"If you weren't raised by wolves, yeah. Otherwise, you can just shut up."

"Are you saying that to shut me up or because you don't want to talk?" D'Arcy said.

"Both, and I don't think I'm alone." She looked straight into his face and found it full of amusement. "You and I are both antisocial—that is, unless we can amaze people with some smart remark."

"So you think you know me?" he said.

At that, she shrugged. After a second, she said, "You think you know someone, and then you see them when someone else walks by and they turn the color of a beet. So, yeah, maybe I'm getting ahead of myself."

D'Arcy turned red again, and his eyes narrowed. After a pause, he said, "Yeah, that Teo. He's all spit and polish on the outside. But give him time. It wears off."

"It wore off for you, didn't it? And then you had to grind him into the dirt, didn't you?"

At that, D'Arcy didn't answer but his jaw clenched. Luckily, they were saved by Charlie and Jenna coming back.

Charlie took one look at their faces and laughed. "Come on, guys," he said. "We've only been gone a few minutes. You can't have had your first lovers' spat in that amount of time."

"I'll give it to D'Arcy," Elizabeth said. "He's true to his convictions. Once he makes up his mind about someone, he doesn't change it."

D'Arcy nodded and lifted his hands, saying *yeah, so?* or maybe *whatever*.

"Well, it's important if you're pig-headed like that that you take the time to have the right idea about someone," Elizabeth said.

"Yeah, you've got me figured out," D'Arcy said. "Come on, Charlie."

Charlie pulled his head back, saying *wait, what?* "We just got here."

"You thinking that shows more about you than it does me," D'Arcy said to Elizabeth. "Right now, neither of us are on our best behavior."

"Then what better time to find out about you," Elizabeth said.

"Well, I wouldn't want to disappoint you," D'Arcy said.

Jenna glanced between them and said quietly, "Maybe you better go, Charlie?"

Charlie sighed. "Yeah, maybe so."

Jenna walked Charlie back to the bikes, and so Elizabeth trailed along behind. Charlie and D'Arcy got on their bikes and started them up, drawing angry glances at the noise from the people around. Charlie waved as he pulled away, D'Arcy behind him.

"*Eee-lizabeth*," Jenna said.

"WHAT," Elizabeth said.

"You're hopeless."

Chapter 13

That evening, Mom decided she didn't want to cook. It was late and everybody was hungry. "We're going to Hopping Johns," she said. Hopping Johns was the restaurant that Miley's mom owned. It was really good Southern food— barbeque, to-die-for cheese biscuits, rice and beans, collards, pie, and much more.

"I'm having pecan pie," Livie shouted.

"I'm having sweet potato pie," Jenna added.

"Apple pie with cheese," Elizabeth said.

"I think I'll stick to my ribs," Dad said.

Mom just smiled. Everyone knew that she was getting the coconut cream pie.

Livie had already changed into her pajamas, which had Teenage Mutant Ninja Turtles, of all things. As they got ready to go out to the car, Elizabeth eyed Livie. "You're going to change, right?"

"What?" Livie said. "Why?"

"Really?" Elizabeth said. "We're going out in public. You're actually going to wear Mutant Ninja Turtle pajamas out in public?" She let the disgust drip through her voice.

"Sure," Livie said, shrugging.

"Dad. Make Livie change."

Dad had an amused look on his face. "If Livie wants to look like a four-year-old boy, that's no skin off your nose."

"Really? Really?" Elizabeth said. There were times when she truly believed she'd been born into the wrong family. This was one of those times. "Maybe she should put on a bathrobe. You know, to really set off the outfit."

"I have that leopard print one," Livie said.

Elizabeth snorted and Dad laughed. "That'd be just the ticket." But to Elizabeth's relief, Livie did not go to get the bathrobe.

They all piled into the car and drove into town. Because Elizabeth was generally a pretty upbeat person, by the time they got to town she'd quit obsessing about Livie. *It's her own embarrassment*, Elizabeth thought, *not mine*.

The parking lot was full when they pulled up, so they had to park two blocks away and walk. They went in, and who should meet them but Miley, who was the acting as hostess. When Mrs. Goggles was short-handed, she'd pull Miley in. Miley didn't mind because she made extra spending money.

"Well, if it isn't the lovely Banner family," Miley said with a smile.

"Well, if it isn't the magnificent Miley," Jenna said.

Miley glanced back toward the kitchen. "We're actually booked up tonight. A big party, plus loads of reservations."

Everyone looked disappointed.

"But," Miley continued, "I think I can do something. I know people." She lifted a finger, telling them to hang out for a minute. She walked across the dining room and into the kitchen.

"I hope they can get us in," Mom said. "I was really looking forward to that pie."

Elizabeth stepped forward to watch for Miley to return and glanced around the dining room. Guess who was sitting at a booth in the corner? Charlie, D'Arcy, and Tiff. *Oh my god*, she thought. She glanced at the offending Mutant Ninja Turtles and then waved Jenna forward and pointed. Jenna glanced at them and then flushed to the roots of her hair. Her eyes got really big.

After a short wait, Miley made her way back across the floor. "You're in!" she said. "Got some cousins who were just leaving. Give us a minute to clear."

Jenna grabbed Elizabeth's arm and pulled her back into the entry. "They're here," she whispered with a strangled sound. Elizabeth nodded.

"Who's here?" Mom said.

"Uh, nobody," Jenna said.

"Oh, don't give me that. Who's here?"

Elizabeth glanced at Jenna and said, "The Billingsleys."

"Oh really?" Mom said and walked over to look into the dining room. She spotted them. "Hi," she practically yelled across the room and waved. Tiff seemed to be the only one looking, and, with a pained look on her face, she didn't return the wave.

"Mom!" Jenna said.

"Well, how do you think you do it?" Mom said.

"Do what?" Dad said.

"Get to know people. You know," Mom said.

"Holly," Dad said, "there are some people you don't need to make the effort for."

Mom fixed Dad with a look. "Will, in case you missed it, one of your daughters actually has the hots for that boy."

"Well, let me just trot out the silver," Dad said.

Mom sighed. "Hangry, much?" she said in a flat voice.

Dad laughed. "Better hangry than hinky, I always say."

Mom smiled.

Elizabeth stood there listening to them and wanted to turn right around and go out the door, pie or no pie. "Really, Dad? Really, Mom?" she said.

"Elizabeth," Dad said, "you really need to get over yourself."

Sure enough, the table that was cleared was out on the floor right next to the booth where the three sat. *No, no, no, no,* she said to herself, but sure enough, Miley lead them right to it. As they walked over, Tiff whispered something to D'Arcy, and all three of them turned to look. Charlie got a bright look on his face and raised his hand to Jenna, but Tiff and D'Arcy both frowned. Even so, D'Arcy looked directly at Elizabeth. He kept glancing at her, and even as they were seated and ordering their food, he stared at her when he didn't think she was looking.

It was truly the most mortifying meal Elizabeth had ever eaten. Dad did what he always did when he ordered ribs. He took three or four napkins and tucked them into his shirt and laid them onto his lap, and by the time he was done, barbecue sauce was everywhere. He looked like a surgery patient. Even though she was busy, Mrs. Goggles came out, pulled up a chair, and chatted with Mom for a while. Mrs. Goggles was a tall comfortable-looking woman with beautiful dark skin and a no-nonsense attitude. Her hair was pulled back in a bandana, and her apron was sprinkled with flour and smeared with grease. They gossiped about the women they played Boggle with, and then they talked about who was moving to town and what houses were being sold.

"Oh," Mom loudly said at one point. "Do you know the Billingsleys? You know, they've remodeled that old Ramshorn Hotel over in the Village. These are their kids." She gestured to the three in the booth. All three looked up. "My Jenna and Elizabeth have been hanging out a lot with them. Particularly Jenna." She said it loud enough for the three to hear. Charlie gave a smile, but for some reason D'Arcy's eyes got really wide and glanced back and forth between Charlie and Jenna. Tiff just shook her head.

"Mom!" Jenna said.

"What?" Mom said. "It's true."

Jenna widened her eyes and clenched her jaw and shook her head slightly.

Mom turned back to Mrs. Goggles. "Well, anyway," she said. They talked for a bit more and then Mrs. Goggles went back to the kitchen. They'd just been served their pie when the three at the table got up to leave. Tiff was talking to D'Arcy, and both ignored the Banner table, but Charlie walked over.

Jenna pushed up to standing. "Hey," she said.

"Hey," Charlie said.

"Oh," Jenna said, glancing between Charlie and the table. "Charlie, this is my family. Family, this is Charlie."

"Nice to meet you," Charlie said.

"Charlie, let's go," Tiff said loudly from halfway across the room.

"Right," Charlie said. "Nice to meet you." He smiled once more at Jenna, and Jenna smiled back at him.

Charlie walked back over toward the other two, but he hadn't taken two steps when Livie turned to Jenna and said loudly, "I don't see why you like him. He's not all that."

Jenna turned white, and Elizabeth decided right then and there she was going to run away and join the circus. Or at the very least she was never going out into public again with her family.

That night, Elizabeth got an email—from Tiff of all people.

You're such a little idiot, Tiff wrote. *Teo's a lying asshole. D'Arcy and his family have always treated him well, and he was the one that did things wrong. I'm sorry you have to hear this from me, but he's slimy as a snake, maybe cuz of where he's from. You westerners see things a little differently.*

Elizabeth shot back: *Yeah, TIFFANYPRINCESS, we do see things differently. Thank God!*

Don't say I didn't warn you, Tiff texted back.

It was a couple of days later, a Sunday, that they made plans for Miley to come over after supper and bring a movie.

But before that. A supper of herb-baked chicken and mashed potatoes and gravy and home-made rolls—made by Jenna—and strawberry shortcake for dessert. Afterwards Dad suggested he and Colin play some horseshoes. "Ever played horseshoes?" Dad asked Colin.

"Not a big horseshoe crowd, where I'm from," Colin said, "but sounds like fun."

Livie helped Mom with the dishes while Dad and Colin got set up. Then Mom and the girls sat in lawn chairs to watch. They played a couple of rounds, Dad showing Colin how to hold and throw the shoe and how to score points.

"So, Dad," Colin said, his voice still stretching over the name, "there's something I've been meaning to ask you."

"Um hmmm," Dad said. Dad took his horseshoes seriously. Mom, on the other hand, was listening and sat forward in her chair.

Elizabeth knew what was coming, she was pretty sure.

"The reason I came was to get to know you. And everybody." He looked around, aware that they all were watching. "You know that I changed my last name, legally that is. But that isn't what's on my birth certificate. I was hoping to change that."

Dad's shot went wide, but he didn't show any emotion. After a pause he said, "I don't see a problem with that." Elizabeth thought she sensed him tense, something about the shoulders. But what she was sure of—Mom did tense and her eyes narrowed.

"That's very generous of you," Colin said. "Thank you so much. I was expecting … Well, I've been pleasantly surprised with you all. You've all been so kind and generous." His eyes skipped over Elizabeth as he glanced around. He hesitated and then continued, "But there's just this one thing." He turned to Dad. "You have to get a swab test, swipe the inside of your cheek. In order for me to put my name on the birth certificate, we have to get our DNA done."

Dad stood looking at Colin, his head to the side, thinking. It was Mom who spoke up. "Will. I don't think that's a good idea, Will." She seemed fairly calm, but Elizabeth could tell she was shaking with anger.

Dad looked at Mom and then back to Colin. "I don't ..."

Colin stepped forward, between Dad and Mom, and turned to Dad. "It's really no big thing. I already got my part done. All you have to do—"

Mom pushed herself out of her chair. "Will," she repeated, "I don't think that's a good idea."

Colin turned to Mom and held out his hand. "Mrs. Banner, I understand it might be a little strange—"

Mom stepped forward so she was standing next to Dad. "A little strange," she said under her breath. "Colin, you have no idea. Look. I've done my best to understand where you're coming from. I've opened my home to you and have been as welcoming as could be expected. But I don't think this is a good idea." She looked at Dad. "Will."

Dad looked at Mom and then at Colin. He shook his head. "Holly, I really don't think—"

"Don't you dare say this is none of my affair. Don't you dare," Mom said. "It damn well is my affair."

"That's not what I was going to say," Dad said. "I was going to agree with you." He turned to Colin. "I don't think that's a good idea, son."

There was a moment of silence when anything could happen. It felt as if the world stood on a precipice, and it could plummet to the ground or just as well fly into the sky. Elizabeth held her breath.

Colin puffed his shoulders and glared at Dad. "Son? Son?!" He stepped forward so that he was standing right in front of Dad. "You have the chutzpah to call me *son*? After all these years of nothing? I wrote letters. Everything. I hung my whole world on you. But nothing from you. Not even a … I ask one simple thing, and you can't even—"

Dad clenched his jaw. The anger was building in him, and Elizabeth was afraid of what was going to happen. "Colin, you're way out of line here. Yeah, you are my son. I've said as much. But there are some things—" Mom stepped behind Dad and put her hand on his shoulder in support. Dad shook it off and stepped forward. "You can't just come here and put yourself into our lives. It doesn't work like that."

Colin's face had turned beet red, and his hands were clenched at his sides and his jaw thrust forward. "You! You!" He unclenched his hands and then clenched them, unclenched and clenched. He looked around as if the answer was on the ground. Then he looked at Dad again. "You know what. I don't have to take this. All I wanted was this little thing, a token after all these years, and you won't even give me that. You bastard. You fucking bastard." He turned and looked at Elizabeth with such an expression of pain and anger. He held her gaze until she looked away and then turned and walked across the lawn and around the corner of the house. Elizabeth took a shuddering breath.

They all stood frozen for a minute before Mom said, "You better go see—"

"I will," Dad said, cutting her off and slowly walking after him.

With all the uproar, it wasn't until Elizabeth was getting ready for bed that night that she realized Miley hadn't stopped by.

Later, Jenna tapped on Elizabeth's bedroom door and came in carrying her laptop. Jenna's sad expression was made worse by the eerie light under her chin from the laptop. "Is Dad all right?" Elizabeth asked. Jenna didn't say anything, just handed Elizabeth the computer.

There was an email from TiffanyPrincess. *Whew*, Elizabeth thought. *Is that all?* She glanced up at Jenna and shook her head. "What's she done now?" Elizabeth said.

"Just read it," Jenna said and fell backwards on the bed and lay looking up at the ceiling.

The email was from earlier in the day. It began: *We're outta here, all of us, back to the city. A flight this afternoon.*

"Oh, Jenna," Elizabeth said. "I'm so sorry."

"I don't understand," Jenna said. "They could do whatever they wanted, and they wanted to leave."

"Maybe they'll come back?

"No, they won't. Read the rest of it."

The email continued:

Girlfriend! I won't lie and say I'll miss Jackson, but because you're cool I wanted to email and say goodbye. Will miss you!!!! Maybe we can hang out sometime in the future or maybe we can keep in touch by email. Anyways. We were just going to go back for a few days, but you know Charlie. Once he's in NYC, he never wants to leave. Not only that, but we get to hang out with Gabby and all our best buds. Gabby's so great. Charlie really likes her. We all grew up together, you know. He specifically said he was looking forward to seeing her. Anyways. It was nice knowing you.

XOXO

Tiff

Elizabeth pushed the computer away.

"Well," came Jenna's voice.

"Well, what?"

"See, he didn't like me after all. He likes Gabby."

"Oh, bull pucky. You'd have to be blind not to see how much Charlie likes you."

Jenna didn't say anything.

"Not only that. Consider the source. Tiff sees it too, how much Charlie likes you, and so she's going with him to make sure he doesn't come back. Then she *just happens* to mention he's in love with another girl. Oh, offhandedly by accident. She's not that dumb. We're not *her kind*, and she doesn't want us around anymore. Not only that, she's so lovesick for D'Arcy you'd think she was a cat in heat, yowling and carrying on the way she does."

"Oh, Elizabeth. It'd be easier if it was true. But she's not like that. You may think she's mean and sneaky, but I like her."

"You would."

Jenna sighed. "I hope it's not true, that they're not coming back."

"Well, we'll just have to show her and get you and Charlie back together," Elizabeth said.

"How? If he's not here."

"Oh, he'll be back." Elizabeth was sure of it. She'd seen how much he liked Jenna, and she'd also seen how much of a liar and manipulator Tiff was.

Chapter 14

Early the next morning, when Colin hadn't returned, Dad and Mom talked about what to do. He was an adult so really not their responsibility. Dad wanted to contact his friend who was a cop but Mom thought he should call Colin's mother. "She'll be worried, and who knows, maybe he flew back. Or called her." At that Dad just glowered.

To avoid the tension, Elizabeth went up to her room and texted Miley, *What happened to you last night?*

Almost immediately her cell rang with Miley's ring.

"Hey, girl," Elizabeth said.

"Hi," Miley said.

"So, where were you?"

"I, well … Sorry I didn't make it."

"No biggie. So what you up to today?"

"Well, the reason I didn't make it …" Miley's voice had none of its usual snark.

"What's the matter? What's wrong?"

"I did start to come, but then Colin was walking along the road, and you just don't leave people walking along a road, especially people you know, and so I stopped to see what was the matter and—"

"Slow down. Breathe. I can't understand you."

"—and he was really mad and so we drove around and talked for a while—"

"You picked him up?" Elizabeth tried to keep the snottiness out of her voice.

"Of course I picked him up, Elizabeth. He's your brother."

Elizabeth felt the flush of shame rise in her cheeks. She hadn't thought of that.

Miley continued, "Long story short, he's staying in our camper trailer. Mom insisted. I thought I should let you know, even though he says not to."

"My parents—my dad has been going a little ape-shit. Thank you." She got up from her bed to go downstairs to tell her parents, her phone at her ear.

There was silence on the line for a minute. Then Miley said, "Sorry I didn't come over. It just happened. I didn't choose to be with him or anything."

Which made Miley think that maybe that was it exactly, that Miley wanted to be with Colin and was feeling guilty about ditching her. The silence stretched out and hung between them and became this *thang*, just exactly what Elizabeth didn't want. She said, "I know, Miley. It's fine. No problem."

"I just know how much you *like* him," Miley said. "I didn't want to interfere but I couldn't do nothing, you know?"

"It's fine, really, Miley."

"Really?"

"Yep," Elizabeth said. "Now I better let my parents know before they have a conniption."

"Okay," Miley said, though her voice quavered like she didn't think it was quite okay.

Elizabeth didn't think it was quite okay either, but she wasn't going to say anything. "Bye."

"Bye. I'll let you know if, well, I'll keep you informed."

"Sounds good. Bye." Elizabeth ended the call. She was at the bottom of the stairs. "Dad," she hollered, coming into the kitchen, "Mom."

"Shshshsh," Mom said, waving a hand, "I'm on the phone."

"I know, but, where's Dad?"

"Elizabeth! Shshsh," Mom said. "Yes, Dorothy. Uh huh." Miley's mom was Dorothy.

Oh. Mom knew. Good.

Mom put her hand over the phone and whispered loudly, "Go get your dad. He's just about to leave." She waved her hand toward the door.

That afternoon, Elizabeth came into the den where Jenna was watching TV, some old cartoon, only she wasn't watching it. She was staring at her hands. Elizabeth shook her head and then flopped down right next to her.

"Bastards," she whispered to Jenna and bumped her shoulder with a friendly push.

"At least I didn't make a fool out of myself," Jenna said. "I thought he liked me, but he didn't and that's that."

Elizabeth looked at her.

"No big deal," Jenna added.

Elizabeth let out a snort. "You're just too sweet for words." She put her arm around her. "*No big deal*—it is a big deal. He liked you, for heaven's sake."

"Apparently not."

"Oh, he liked you, and if you can't see that you're blind. But because you're the sweetest thing on earth, you don't blame him for just running off without so much as saying goodbye." She shook Jenna gently. "I look at the world and I see idiots who couldn't find their butts with both hands. People who can't see the wonderful thing right in front of them. You look at the world and see nothing but good people. And that's why I love you."

Jenna smiled and took Elizabeth's hand in hers and patted it. "Because that's what you're looking for. You act like Charlie did this on purpose, that Tiff did something. He was being friendly, that's all. He didn't mean for me to think anything else, and so it's my own fault."

Elizabeth snorted again. "If anything, that's what guys want you to think. That way they have plausible deniability when they drop you like a hot rock." She deepened her voice, "*Oh, did you think that? I didn't mean that and it's just your stupid girlyness that made you think that.*"

"If they did it on purpose then, yeah, it would be wrong, but you give people too much credit for being devious."

"Well, for what it's worth, I think you're right that Charlie didn't do it on purpose. I don't give him that much credit, but the effect is the same, isn't it?"

"So you think it was Tiff?" Jenna looked doubtful.

"Well, Tiff and D'Arcy, yeah," said Elizabeth.

"Well, I don't think so. Why would they do that? They want him to be happy, don't they?"

"Yeah, but that's not the only thing they want. It's obvious Tiff has the hots for D'Arcy, and she feels threatened by us, so she'd want to get away as quick as possible. D'Arcy's just a misanthrope. He doesn't like people on general principle."

"Maybe Charlie actually does like D'Arcy's sister."

"I highly doubt it. Pretty convenient for Tiff to say, not to mention it being mean."

Jenna shook her head. "Well, I don't think they're trying to be mean. Whatever the reason. That's what I want to believe and so that's what I think."

Elizabeth shook her head but didn't say anything else. Jenna wanted to believe it, and as much as Elizabeth knew better, she didn't want Jenna to feel any worse than she already did.

That night at supper, Mom glanced at Jenna and said, "Hey, did I hear that the Billingsley kids flew back to New York?"

Jenna's face fell, so Elizabeth leaned forward and said, "I don't know. I heard they're coming back."

Jenna opened her mouth to say something but then shut it. Mom paused for a bit and then said, "Well, at least they're coming back. You kids were having such a good time."

It was later, after supper, when Elizabeth was helping her dad graining the horses that he said, "So, that Billingsley kid is quite a flirt?"

"What makes you say that?" Elizabeth said.

"Well, seems like Jenna got her hopes up, and now he's left town."

Elizabeth shrugged.

They worked beside each other a little longer, and then Dad said, not looking at her, "You'll be next."

"What?"

"I said, you'll be next."

"I heard you."

"Girls like a good romantic heartbreak every now and then. Looks like Jenna got hers. And she's your sister. And you got to one-up your sister."

Elizabeth shook her head but then couldn't help smiling. "We all can't be as lucky as Jenna."

Chapter 15

It was a couple of days later that Elizabeth's phone range and it was Miley.

"Hey," Miley said, after they chatted for a bit, "I was thinking. You haven't been over for a while. Why don't you come and stay a few days, a week maybe."

The first thing that came to Elizabeth's mind was, why would I want to do that, what with Colin right there, but she didn't say it, of course. Instead, she said, "I'm not sure Colin would want me there. He's still staying with you, isn't he?"

There was silence on the line. "Yeah. Yeah, he's still here." There was another pause. "But if you come over, you won't hardly see him. He's been helping Mom get a Facebook page set up for Hopping Johns and some other computer stuff, so he's not here much, really." Then she was silent again. Elizabeth got the feeling that there was something else, but it didn't seem right to push it.

"I don't know," Elizabeth said.

"Besides, I want you to come," Miley said.

"Oh, I want to, definitely," said Elizabeth. "But it's just ... well …" The last thing in the world she wanted right now was to be around someone who seemed bent on destroying their family. "How about in a couple weeks, when Colin goes back to wherever?"

"I don't think he's going anywhere until fall, till college." Elizabeth didn't say anything.

"Elizabeth, you aren't going to abandon me, just because I did the right thing?" Miley's voice was quiet. Elizabeth heard the rest of the sentence without Miley saying it: *Because I cleaned up your messes*.

"We've been going to have you stay all summer, and now's a good time. Why don't you come? It'll be so fun." There was a wheedling tone in Miley's voice.

What could she say? She certainly didn't want to, but she couldn't say no, and so she agreed.

It was settled. Miley said she would to drive over and get Elizabeth that afternoon, and Elizabeth went right away to ask Mom. Mom called Dad to coordinate. Then Mom said, "You sure?"

Elizabeth shrugged.

"Well, all right then," Mom said.

Elizabeth threw some clothes into a bag and Miley stopped by shortly after in her mom's car.

"Hey," Miley said, smiling broadly. "I'm so glad you came."

"Me, too," Elizabeth said, and she meant it. Miley was such a great friend, and she resented the idea that Colin would get between them in some way. "BFFs, even if idiots get in the way."

Miley smiled. "Yeah," she said. She glanced out of the corner of her eye at Elizabeth and continued, "You know, you're a little too hard on Colin. He's not a bad guy if you get to know him."

Elizabeth raised her eyebrows and looked at Miley.

"Really," Miley said. "I understand why you don't like him, but you got to get past the crap of his barging into your family like a herd of buffalo—but now that I think about it, he is a little buffalo-ish." She giggled. Elizabeth laughed at the image of the lumpish Colin growing dark hair all over his body. "But he's really not that bad, if you put that aside. And you really can't blame him. If I didn't know my parents, I'd want to find them, and I'd want them to welcome me, even though that's stupid to think it'd happen."

"Yeah, what my dad did way back then does kind of suck." Elizabeth felt better saying it out loud.

"I'm just saying, don't just go all ninja death ray on him, okay? You owe him that."

Why was Miley all defensive about him all of a sudden? But she supposed she had it coming. He was her relation, and here Miley and her family had stepped in and saved him— saved them, really. That was so nice, very much in keeping with Mrs. Goggles's ideas about how you help other people.

Elizabeth nodded. "Yeah, you're right," she said.

They spent the afternoon playing Minecraft. Miley was a bit of a gamer geek, and Elizabeth loved making her happy and like the games. They built a city with a garden, demolished mobs of zombies and creepers, and created new skins for their characters.

It was suppertime before Elizabeth heard someone come in the kitchen door.

"Want something to eat?" Miley said. "Mom said she was going to send home some Cuban pork mojo and deep fried plantains."

"Would a hobo eat a ham sammy?" Elizabeth said with a grin. Mrs. Goggles cooked a mean dish, no matter what it was.

But when they went into the kitchen, it was Colin who was standing there unloading the bags. "Hi, Colin," Miley said and glanced at Elizabeth and then at Colin, who raised his eyebrows. Miley shook her head slightly side to side before going to the cupboard to get out plates.

Elizabeth tried keep her thoughts off her face as she looked at Colin, who, when he saw her looking, smiled broadly. "Hello, Elizabeth," Colin said. "It's nice to see you, in spite of, well …" He let his voice trail off. He smiled again, his face open.

He was trying, Elizabeth could tell. So she said, "Yeah, sorry about Dad." She wasn't on Colin's side but she was still mad enough at her dad to let it show.

They sat and ate, just the three of them. Mr. Goggles was off on a business trip, and Mrs. Goggles was working. Miley didn't have any siblings. The food was heavenly, as always. The pork was tender and fall-apart with its garlic and lemon dressing, and the plantains were sweet and crunchy. There were crusty bread rolls too.

"Colin's been working on Mom's computer," Miley said. "She's really happy with it."

Colin nodded. "Yeah. I set up a Facebook page, and I had this idea for a contest. Everybody sends in their pictures of their Southern memories, especially if they're about food, and they get a coupon. We've got a few entries already. One guy talked about shooting squirrels with a slingshot and making squirrel pie."

"You should have seen it," said Miley. "He had a picture of squirrels on a stringer, just like they were fish."

They continued to talk about Miley's mom's restaurant, and Colin had all kinds of ideas. He changed where the checkout stand was to make the flow better coming in and going out. He suggested redecorating with green and red because it was supposed to make people eat more. And he went online and found free ways to advertise.

Just when Elizabeth thought she might even like him a bit, though, he said, "I'm really good at these kinds of things." He did have some smart ideas, but to say it like that sounded like bragging. And then there was Miley nodded along with him.

Shortly after, Colin said that he was going to turn in. He was beat. "Uh, could I talk with you for a minute, Miley?" he said. "Uh, alone?" He jerked his head, indicating she should follow him to the other room.

Miley said to Elizabeth, shrugging her shoulders but smiling, "I'll be right back."

"I'll see you tomorrow, Elizabeth," Colin said.

They went around the corner into the mud room. There was a smacking sound, what sounded like a smooch, and then two seconds later Miley was back. They hadn't had time to say two words. Elizabeth let the surprise show on her face.

"What was that?" she said as she heard the outside door close. The idea that Miley and Colin were dating had briefly crossed Elizabeth's mind, but she had instantly dismissed it on account of how repulsive Colin was.

Miley looked sheepish but a little defiant too. "We're a thing," she said simply.

"NO WAY," Elizabeth said.

Miley narrowed her eyes and gave her a hard look. After a pause, she said, "You're being a bitch. Just because he came and made things messy. He can't help who his dad is. And he's smart and funny. And he's a good kisser." She smiled when she said this. "Even my mom likes him."

Colin. And Miley. He was short and dumpy and boring and she was tall and gorgeous, a knock out. And smart. It just did not compute. How could that be? She realized she had a look of revulsion on her face and Miley was getting angry, and so she smiled and said, "Cool." She couldn't think of anything else to say.

That put a distance between them for the rest of the week. It was still great to hang with Miley, but Elizabeth felt uncomfortable too, especially when Colin was around. They didn't do any PDAs or anything but they looked at each other like they had a secret.

When Elizabeth was leaving after the week was up, Miley hugged her and said, "Please don't stay away. Promise me you won't do that thing that girls do." When Elizabeth hesitated, Miley added, "Even if it's kind of weird."

"It's you who's *occupied*," Elizabeth said.

"You know what I mean. Promise me."

Elizabeth gave her a hug. "Of course." She wasn't sure she meant it, though.

Chapter 16

Elizabeth's phone beeped with a text message while she was currying the horses. She'd been working on the blue roan, Fancy Dancer, and he loved it. If she stopped, he'd turn his head and look at her. "Man, you're high maintenance," she told him.

The text said, *I was thinking about you*, but the number was not anyone she recognized. She hadn't entered the number on her phone, so there was no picture or identification.

It creeped her out. Who would be texting her that they're thinking about her when she didn't even know who it was. A little too stalkerish. She text back immediately, *WHO IS THIS?!*

A text popped back, *O! Sorry. This is Teo.*

Wow. It was Teo! She couldn't believe it. *Cool!* she texted back, immediately regretting the exclamation point. *What you up to?*

Just hanging. You?

Wait a second. How did he get her number? She didn't want to sound weird, but how did he get her number? She texted back, *Same. taking care of horses.* She hit enter, hesitated, then typed, *Say, where did you get my number?*

You gave it to me, he texted. *Don't you remember?*

For the life of her, she didn't remember giving it to him. But he had it—that was all that mattered. Her insides flip-flopped. He went to the trouble of texting me! Ignoring his question, she texted, *So, howz it going?*

Gr8! So, you want to do something?

He was asking her out! She gave a little squeak. The blue roan turned his head and looked at her. She absent-mindedly patted him and then texted back, *Sure. Whatya want to do?*

It's a surprise. Pick you up at 3?

Yeah, but I can't be out real late.

Stoooopendous. See you then. A minute later, *Oh. Where are you?*

She sent him directions, a wide grin on her face.

When she got back to the house, she ran into Jenna's room and flopped on the bed. Jenna was at her desk on her computer. "Guess what, guess what!" she said.

Jenna glanced at her, finished typing, and then turned. "What?"

"Teo's picking me up this evening. We've got a date!"

Jenna's face darkened for second but then she smiled. "That's great, Elizabeth."

Dang. Elizabeth had forgotten that this might make Jenna feel bad, and she hadn't in a million years wanted that. "Oh, I'm so sorry, Jen! I didn't mean ..."

Jenna shook her head. In a deep voice, she said, "I insist you never date just so that you don't hurt my feelers." She smiled. "No, that's great. Teo is good looking."

"Oh, isn't he?" Elizabeth couldn't help herself. She was so excited she felt like she would burst.

"Have fun," Jenna said and turned back to her computer.

Elizabeth went to clear it with her parents. Her mom was out, and since her mom would call her dad anyway, she called him at work. She told him about Teo.

"Who is he?" he asked, his voice clipped.

"Oh, he's from Jackson, but apparently his grew up over by Pinedale. A nice kid."

Her father paused and said, "Okay, but if you need anything, you make sure to call, right? You know how it works." Her parents had insisted many times that if she ever needed them, whether it was two in the morning, that she should call and keep calling till they answered. Not that it would be that late. She didn't have a set curfew, but she knew if it was much after 10 they would get worried.

She grabbed an apple and some cheese for a snack and then ran upstairs to change. She put on blue jeans, a white sleeveless shirt, and a jean jacket and spiked her hair. She put on a little makeup, and as an afterthought she put hoops in her ears. It'll have to do, she thought.

Teo pulled up in a cherry red short box Dodge Ram pickup. Elizabeth was sitting at the kitchen table talking to her mom when he pulled up. Livie dashed through the kitchen and out the door, letting it slam behind her, and ran out to meet him. Elizabeth and her mom exchanged glances. Elizabeth went outside to meet them as they came up the porch.

"Come on in," Livie said as she held the door for Teo.

"Hi," Teo said to Elizabeth. "Thanks, kiddo," he said to Livie. "She was just asking after Dennis."

"Shshsh," Livie said. "It's supposed to be our little secret."

"You know what they say about secrets," Teo said, smiling at Livie.

"What?" Livie said.

"It's a secret." Teo's eyes crinkled in amusement. Elizabeth couldn't help herself—his golden eyes just made her melt.

Livie made a disgusted sound and went in the house.

"Don't mind Livie," Elizabeth said. "She's a wildcat in a girl's body."

"I don't mind Livie," Teo said.

"Well, that's kind of you."

They went into the kitchen, and Elizabeth introduced Teo to her mom.

"In from out of town, are you?" Mom said.

"No, I'm from here. Kind of."

Mom looked at Elizabeth and raised his eyebrows.

Elizabeth said, "Well, he didn't go to school here, but he spent a lot of time here. He was mostly over by Pinedale."

"Ah," Mom said. "What grade are you in?"

As Mom was talking, Dad came into the kitchen and poured himself a glass of ice tea and leaned back against the wall nonchalantly. Too nonchalantly. Teo glanced nervously at him as Teo said, "I just graduated. I'm headed to U Dub. ROTC. And I'm thinking of majoring in finance, maybe."

"That's nice," Mom said. She looked at Elizabeth and nodded, saying *He seems good.*

Dad didn't say anything, just stood there with his arms crossed.

Elizabeth glanced at Dad. "Well, we better be going," she said. "You ready?" she said to Teo.

He nodded. "You have a wonderful place here, Mr. and Mrs. Banner." He was looking at Dad. "I'd like to own a place like this some day. As a summer home maybe." Dad raised his eyebrows at that, but Teo didn't seem to notice. It was kind of an insult to say their property that Dad had worked years on would just be this summer plaything, even if Teo meant it as a compliment.

Elizabeth looked at her dad and shrugged her shoulders, saying *What can you do?*

Dad just looked at her. Elizabeth would have to talk to him later about Teo. He didn't seem to like him at all. "I'll call you," she said, meaning if she needed anything, and he nodded.

"Have a good time," Mom said.

Elizabeth and Teo went out to his truck, and he held the door for her as she climbed in. Very romantic. Elizabeth couldn't help but smile. It felt old fashioned but in a good way. It was a really nice truck. The seats were leather and it was really clean on the inside and smelled nice.

After Teo got in the driver's side, Elizabeth said, "Nice ride."

Teo nodded and smiled. "Isn't it?" he said as he turned the key and it started up. "Seat belt," he said and winked at her.

How sweet, she thought as she clicked in her seat belt. She would have put it on anyway, but it was great that he cared enough to remind her.

"What should we do?" Elizabeth asked. "Go to a movie later, or grab something to eat? Or both?" Elizabeth realized she was starting to get hungry.

"Well, maybe we could drive around for a bit, maybe grab a bite after. Then go up to this cool place I know in the hills. It's a really nice place."

"Sounds great," Elizabeth said. As long as she got to hang out with him, that's all she cared.

He revved the engine a few times on the highway, but then as they drove through town he was very legal, stopping completely at all the stop signs and using his blinkers. They talked. The first thing Teo asked was about her plans for the future, which was really sexy. She told him about running track and how she thought she'd go to junior college for a while, but if she could get a track scholarship she might go straight to the university, maybe in Idaho, maybe in Wyoming. Something in the sciences, she was thinking, because she was good at math. Possibly wildlife biology like her dad. "What about you?" she asked. He explained that he'd always been impressed by the amount of money Mr. Pemberly had, and Mr. Pemberly was in finance, and so he was thinking that was the way to go. "People like you and me know how important money is in a way that guys like D'Arcy don't because they've always taken it for granted," he said as he turned off the highway onto a gravel road.

It was true, though she hadn't thought about it that way. Teo was pretty smart. Chalk another one up to him. She glanced over at him and thought how lucky she was to be sitting here in the truck with him. He was just so dang good looking. He took care of himself. He'd recently had a hair cut, and he wore clothes like athletes wear that really made him look good. She wasn't sure if he was an athlete. He seemed put together, though—impressive, like he was going places. And it didn't hurt that he smelled really good too. Elizabeth wanted to scoot over next to him and put her nose in his neck and feel his warmth. I've got to stop this, she thought, but she didn't really mean it.

Just then the gravel road topped out on a tall hill, and they could see all of Jackson Hole spread out below them. It was beautiful, the way it was cupped in the valley, this settlement on a grid surrounded by mountains. Teo pulled off to the side of the road and parked the car and turned the engine off. He flipped the steering wheel up and propped one arm on the door and the other on the back of the bench seat and took a deep breath. "What do you think?" he said.

Elizabeth didn't quite know what he was asking so she said, "I'm really glad to be here." And she was. She glanced at him and smiled, unclipped her seat belt and slid across the seat to sit next to him. Not so close as to give him the wrong idea but close enough that he got the message loud and clear: *I really like you.* "Girl," he said and smiled broadly at her. He kept his arm across the back of the seat, and she could feel the heat of it behind her, though she wasn't close enough to be in the crook of it.

"I like your hair," he said, touching the ends of it with his fingertips.

"Thank you," Elizabeth said. "Some people think it's too short for a girl."

"I think it's great. It suits you. Something puckish."

"Puckish?" Elizabeth had to think about that. "I'm, like, an elf?"

"Well, yeah. You've got a bit of mystery about you. In a good way. A great way."

Elizabeth smiled at that.

"To be honest, it's a bit scary." He had a pleasant look on his face as he said it, but he didn't smile.

Elizabeth laughed. Her being scary. She couldn't imagine. But it did make her feel powerful, which she liked. A lot.

He turned so his body was facing her and she looked at him. What was he thinking? Was he going to kiss her? Could it really be? Elizabeth felt her stomach ball up with excitement. He's going to! I think he's going to!

Sure enough. He leaned forward and whispered, "If it's all right, I'd like to kiss you now."

She couldn't help herself, she was so nervous she snorted a laugh. "Sorry!" she said. "Sorry. Yes. I would love to kiss you."

He leaned forward so that his face was right next to hers, and she tilted her head so that her lips met his and a beautiful electric shock ran through her as their lips touched. His were soft and warm and gentle, and she moved her head to square her face a little better and to avoid his nose and it seemed like all of her was right there in their lips and it was wonderful. He finished the kiss slowly and pulled back and then looked into her eyes and smiled. "That was nice," he said.

"It was," Elizabeth said and meant it with all her heart. And all her body, which seemed to be tingling all over.

"Once more?" he said, raising his eyebrows.

She smiled and nodded. The second kiss was just as good as the first.

After that kiss was done, he said, "That was even nicer, but I wouldn't want to be greedy."

She laughed again and sat back against the seat and his arm fell across her shoulders. He gave her one good squeeze and then pulled his arm back, and said, "Food. You think?"

"Yes." She almost squealed it, she was so excited. He had kissed her! He was sitting right next to her! Oh, it was all so wonderful and unbelievable. This perfect specimen was right here.

As they were driving off the hill, Elizabeth thought of poor Jenna. She had felt this way with Charlie, and then Charlie had just up and left. Didn't even kiss her. Just left her hanging.

Elizabeth looked over at Teo. He didn't seem like them. He was from Jackson—he would stay.

Chapter 17

The next day, Geri and Patty were invited over for supper.
Jenna had decided she wanted to cook the main dish, and so
she spent all afternoon in the kitchen making homemade
lasagna. Elizabeth sat at the table and talked about what had
happened, but she changed the subject when Mom popped in to
answer questions and tend to her garlic bread dough. It was hot
in the kitchen, so they had the windows and door open and a
rotating fan going. Few of the houses in Jackson had air
conditioning, as there was only a day or two a year that reached
the 90s.

Geri and Patty arrived with a bottle of wine and their black,
white, and brown Corgi named Beckett. Beckett was a laid-
back small dog who acted like a big dog. He would lie at their
feet and pant companionably.

Dinner turned out well. The lasagna was sloppy but
delicious, and Jenna blushed at the compliments everyone gave
her. She was subdued throughout the meal, though. Mom had
put chunks of garlic in her loaf, and so it was mild and almost
sweet in the crusty bread. There was a salad of greens and fresh
tomatoes from the garden, and Livie had made orange-ade.

Colin was only mentioned once when Geri looked at Dad and said, "I saw your boy, Will, at the hardware store." Dad nodded and changed the subject with a glance at Mom. Patty told the story of a music festival she had been to recently, and Mom talked about how the city council was trying to make housing more affordable. After supper, Geri asked Elizabeth if she wanted to step out to take Beckett on a quick walk, and she said yes immediately. She really liked Aunt Geri.

"What's up with Jenna?" Geri said once they were out on the road. "She's not her perky self."

Elizabeth explained about Charlie and D'Arcy and Tiff and how Charlie seemed to really like Jenna but then they left and she thought it was probably Tiff and D'Arcy behind it. "I think if it was up to Charlie they'd still be here. I mean, if Charlie wasn't such a gadfly."

"Summer people," Geri said and shook her head. "I'm sorry Jenna's been hurt. Charlie sounds like a good guy, if not a little flighty. But that's the way it goes with summer people. They fall in love with Jackson and with summertime and with a pretty girl. There was this one rich chick who came in when I was in my early twenties and running the rafts. I thought she was something. But, well, you know. They're more in love with love than anything else."

"But this wasn't like that," Elizabeth said. "I've never seen anything like it. Charlie really liked Jenna, you could tell. He's been here before and so it wasn't just that. You should have seen the way he looked at her. And how he was so kind and did things for her. It wasn't just Jackson. He was head over heels. She was too. *Is* too."

"Poor Jenna. Love stinks."

They were at the highway by now and turned around to head back, Beckett sniffing among the weeds at the edge of the road and lifting his leg every so often.

Geri added, looking sideways at Elizabeth, "It'd been easier if it was you. You'd laugh at yourself sooner or later and bring yourself out of it. Poor Jenna, she's so earnest."

"Yeah, I've been trying to cheer her up."

Geri pulled up as an idea occurred to her. "Tell you what. I'll invite her to come stay with us. I'll use the excuse we need the help at the Deckle over the Fourth. It'll take her mind off it."

"Yeah! That's a great idea," Elizabeth said. It was always a good time staying with Geri and Patty. Their house was always full of interesting people, and they treated you like an adult. You could stay up with everyone, and their friends included you as part of the crowd. "I'm sure Mom and Dad will go for it."

They walked companionably for a while and then Geri said, "Speaking of your turn. What's up with you and Teo?" When Elizabeth made a fake-surprise face, Geri said, "Hey, I got eyes in my head."

"He's nice, that's all."

"Yeah, *nice*." Geri snorted. "I knew him as a kid, you know. When his dad was working for Pemberly."

"So you knew D'Arcy too, when he was a kid?"

"Not so much, I just heard he was a bit stand-offish."

"Sounds about right," Elizabeth said.

"I don't really *know* Teo, but I'll say this. You're too smart to fall in love just because someone tells you not to. But I'm not afraid to say: be careful. I don't have anything to say against him, but he'll be moving on one way or another. I know how it works."

"You said yourself, you don't really know him." Elizabeth hated that she sounded defensive and she was confirming what her aunt was saying.

"Yeah, but I know guys. Given the chance, they're after more than just a peck on the cheek. And Teo strikes me as a little—well, let's just say, he's looking out for number one. Just watch yourself."

"I'm not in love with Teo," Elizabeth said. "We're just hanging out, you know. It's not like I want to get serious with anyone."

"Right," Geri said with a twinkle in her eye.

"I'm *not*," Elizabeth side.

"Right. I said *right*," Geri said and chuckled. She put her arm around Elizabeth's shoulders. Elizabeth just shook her head.

They got back to the house. Patty had broken out her dulcimer, and the adults all sat on the porch and drank wine and sang old songs. The kids sat around for a while, and when Geri invited Jenna to stay with she and Patty, she agreed immediately.

"Can I, Dad?" she said.

Dad nodded. "Course."

Jenna looked as happy as she had in days.

Elizabeth, Jenna, and Livie then went inside to take turns playing cribbage and have some ice cream.

Chapter 18

Jenna went to stay with Aunt Geri and Patty. Her mood was better, but she still wasn't her upbeat energetic self. More than once, Elizabeth had found her slouched in a chair staring out the window. Jenna wasn't a sloucher, and that more than anything worried Elizabeth.

Jenna was only gone a day when Elizabeth's phone rang with Jenna's song. It was a little soon for Jenna to just be catching up, so Elizabeth answered as manic-happy as she could.

"What's the story, morning glory?" she said.

"Oh, Elizabeth," Jenna said, "you'll never guess."

"What?"

"Well, maybe you'd guess."

"What? What?!"

Jenna was quiet for a second. "I got an email from Tiff."

Of course you got an email from Tiff, Elizabeth thought. It couldn't be anything but bad news. That witch with a capital B! She tried not to let it out in her voice, though: "Yeah?"

"You were right," Jenna said, a scratch in her voice. "I hate to say it." She paused then continued. "You have to admit, though, you always think the worst in people, even though they

123

don't do anything to deserve it, just like I always think about how good people are."

"That's true," Elizabeth said. Some would say I'm just being realistic, she added to herself.

"Anyway, doesn't matter. Tiff showed her true colors. I don't think she ever liked me, even though she faked it pretty well. I don't understand why, though? Why was she nice to me when she hates me so much?"

Elizabeth could think of a dozen reasons off the top of her head, but it wouldn't do any good to say them. "So, what *did* she say?"

"Well, I have to admit that I sent her an email. Well, maybe a couple." Of course she had. Elizabeth couldn't blame her. "And so that's why she wrote me—so I wouldn't write another. She spent the whole time talking about herself. Didn't once ask about me or you and didn't once mention Charlie. It was like she was deliberately not saying anything that I wanted to hear."

Sounds about right, Elizabeth thought.

Jenna continued, "So, you were right. I don't want anything to do with that …" Jenna didn't finish, and she choked a little at the end. "Not only that, but Charlie hasn't emailed or called once. Not once." She was a little angry about that, Elizabeth was glad to see. That would help her get over him. "When I realized that, I realized it really was over." There was silence again for a second, and Elizabeth let her have the space. Then she continued, "I was still hoping, you know? Maybe just a little." Her voice was almost a whisper at the end.

"I know, my sweet Jenna," Elizabeth said. "Oh my gosh, I know. I'm so sorry." If she'd been standing next to Jenna, she would have given her the biggest hug. But she had to settle for trying to find the right words. She did the best she could. At least Jenna wasn't fooled any more. At least she knew, now, that Tiff was a phony and that Charlie really wasn't coming back.

Elizabeth tried to cheer her up by talking about what was going on around the house. Livie had tried to sneak out, but she'd made the mistake of stopping in the kitchen to grab a snack before she left, and Dad had caught her. "She and Dennis again, I'm sure," Elizabeth said. "That kid's nice enough, but he's bad news." Jenna told her about how busy it was at the Deckled Edge. She was making lattés and waiting on tables, and she came home exhausted. It was good, though, she said. They both knew what that meant—too tired to think.

Elizabeth started spending a lot of time with Teo. He even came over to the house once or twice and stayed for supper. Dad never once lightened up. His face looked like he'd swallowed a lemon. Thinking about it, Elizabeth suspected that since he'd been a teenage guy who'd apparently, uh, gotten girls pregnant, that he suspected all guys of being that way. It made Elizabeth see him in a new light, and she didn't like it at all. She'd always thought her dad was the coolest, and she was his favorite too—he wasn't supposed to have made mistakes. It made her mad. So when he stood there with his arms crossed giving Teo the eye, she glared right back at him. He had no room to be all judgy about it. Teo was nice guy. He was nothing like Dad had shown himself to be. Just the thought made her fume.

They kissed on their second date too. This time it was just a quick kiss as he dropped her off. On their third date, they kissed even longer. He tickled her lips with tongue, and so she stuck her tongue into his mouth. It was her first French kiss, and it made her tingle all over. Oh, it was all so romantic! So unlike her to be this way—all aflutter with romance—but she thought about him all the time. She thought about what a yummy body he had and even his smell was great. She wanted to just snuggle in the crook of his arm and stay there forever. She resisted the urge to write *Elizabeth Wick* all over her spare notebook.

They had been on a handful of dates when he invited her on a picnic. "It'll be cool," he said. "I know this spot. It's even got a little waterfall," he'd said on the phone. "Maybe we could go skinny dipping." His voice was all flirty when he said it.

She laughed. The thought thrilled her, but she knew better. The thought was enough. "Sounds fun," she said.

She got ready for the date. She borrowed Jenna's hair straightener to make her hair sleek behind her ears. She put in her fake diamond studs, opalized eye shadow, and sheer pink lip gloss. She decided on a fun flippy skirt, a soft turquoise top with a v neck, and sandals. *Girly*, she thought. *I feel girly.* She liked the feeling, which was unusual for her.

As she walked by stairs that went to the basement den, her dad yelled up, "Elizabeth, that you?"

"Yeah," she yelled down the stairs.

"Come here for a minute, will ya?" he yelled up.

This couldn't be good, Elizabeth thought. She pattered halfway down the stairs and stood, hands on the railing.

He glanced at her and laughed. "I'm not going to chew you out or give you a lecture or anything," he said.

She made a face at him and shook her head. How did he know that's what she was expecting?

"I wanted to say I'm sorry," he said. "You're getting to be such a grown up. You have feelings and instincts, and you know better than this old guy what you want."

Elizabeth tried to keep the shocked look off her face.

"I guess what I'm saying is to trust yourself. And don't let people push you around. Even me." He smiled wryly. "Well, do what I say, but you know."

"I do, Dad," Elizabeth said.

"I know. I just want what's best for you. To protect you."

"I know that." Elizabeth did, even though she was still mad at him.

"So I'm going to trust you with *this guy*"—he still wouldn't say Teo's name—"but be careful."

"I will, Dad," Elizabeth said. "I will."

Dad took a step forward like he wanted to say more, but then he shook his head.

Elizabeth pattered the rest of the way down the steps and gave him a quick hug. She still hadn't forgiven him, but it was all right. She smiled at him and skipped back up the stairs.

She glanced out the window. The sky was overcast. That would be a bummer if it rained. Then they couldn't picnic. "Please don't let it rain," she whispered to no one in particular.

Teo drove up in an old car—a big brown Buick LeSabre with a dented fender. It was his real car, as it turned out. He'd borrowed the red truck.

Elizabeth yelled bye to her mom and skipped out the door. She felt lighter than air. But then a couple of raindrops wet her arm as she crossed the yard. Dang! *Clear up*, she thought. *Clear up, dang it!* Teo didn't get out of the car to open the door for her, but they'd known each other long enough that

Elizabeth didn't mind. It was a sign that they were comfortable. She slid onto the front bench seat, slammed the door, and let out a big sigh. It smelled a bit inside, but Teo had tried to cover it up with a new car smell thing, which was considerate.

"Hello," she said, smiling broadly at him.

"Hey," he said. He was switching the radio station and hardly looked up. He flipped past a couple of stations and finally settled on thrash metal. Wasn't really Elizabeth's gig, but it was fine. It had a good beat.

He looked so nice. And smelled so nice. He'd put on a strong cologne. Maybe a little too strong, but it was nice anyway. That he cared enough to do that for her.

There was a box in the back seat that had some food in it. A few sodas, some store-bought sandwiches, and some chips. The picnic.

The rain went from a few drops splashing on the windshield to a steady stream, and as they drove out of Jackson it turned into a deluge. The windshield wipers couldn't keep up, and the road was blurry. They even hydroplaned a bit around the highway curves. Elizabeth wanted to tell Teo to slow down, but she didn't want to seem like a scaredy cat, so she didn't say anything.

Teo wasn't in a very talkative mood, so Elizabeth filled the silence with a story about Jenna helping out at the Deckled Edge. The lead up to the Fourth of July holiday was always busy, and Jenna had dropped a stack of plates. Elizabeth put in lots of exaggerations and emphasis. Teo was only half listening, though.

They turned off the highway onto a humpy bumpy two-track that had turned into a slick muddy mess with the rain. They slid from one rut to another.

"Maybe we should go somewhere else?" Elizabeth said.

"No," Teo said. "I want this to be perfect."

How sweet, Elizabeth thought.

Luckily it wasn't far to where he meant to go. The two-track went through some pines and then into an open meadow that was cut through by a fast stream. On the far side was a hill and a small waterfall where the stream splashed over rocks. The lump of Mount Moran loomed up behind it.

"This is great," Elizabeth said. "It's raining, though." She was not looking forward to getting out of the car.

Teo just sat and shook his head, his jaw clenching.

"Maybe we could eat in the car?" Elizabeth said.

"I really wanted to …" Teo said. "I have a blanket in the trunk. I was going to spread it out so we could eat on it."

"That sounds great," Elizabeth said, glancing from him to the rain on the windshield. "Well, that *would've* been great." She exaggerated her words, trying to make it funny to get a reaction from him. Something was up with him, and she wasn't sure what. "I guess we could sit here for a while and see if it clears up."

"Yeah," he said, his face brooding.

She slid halfway across the seat. "There are worse places to be," she said, smiling broadly. She reached up and took his cheek in her hand and turned his head toward her and leaned in and kissed him. It was weird, though, because he wouldn't let whatever he was brooding about go.

He kissed her back, gently but then more enthusiastically. She kissed him for a bit and then gave him a couple of pecks like you do when you're signaling you want to come up for air, but instead of letting her go he put his arms around her. All right, she thought and kept kissing. It went on, and then Elizabeth really did need to come up for air so she pulled back. He responded by pulling her tightly to him. He squoze her tightly for what seemed like a long time and then began kissing her again. She felt a little crowded, especially when he pushed his tongue into her mouth. She put her hands against his chest and tried to push him away, but he shifted his weight forward, with the end result she on her back on the bench seat and against the door with him on top of her. *Well*, she thought. *This is rapidly becoming a lot less romantic.*

It all happened so fast. She tried to say something, to tell him maybe they should take a break, but he put his mouth on hers so she couldn't say anything. She tried to turn her head but it was back against the door and propped to where she couldn't move it. He lay fully on top of her and started grinding his pelvis into her. She could feel his hot crotch through his shorts as it ground against her thigh. Elizabeth struggled to move, to let him know to stop, but he wouldn't move. He wouldn't get off her and wouldn't pull his mouth away. There's no way he couldn't have known she was trying to get him off her.

What the hell? Elizabeth lay there stunned as he put all his weight on her, pushing the breath out of her. She tried to shift, to push him away, but her arms were pinned and her head was pinned and her legs were pinned and she could hardly breathe. Then he reached down and put his hand up her skirt next to her crotch. He actually did it.

For a split second, she was paralyzed, and a bolt of sheer terror went through her. She couldn't move. There was nothing she could do. He'd brought her to a remote place, and now he was going to do whatever he wanted to her. What else was he capable of?

The thought sent rage shooting through her. *No fucking way*, Elizabeth thought. *Who does this asshat think he is?* And so she did the only thing she could. She jerked her head to the side and then bit his chin—with enough force to break the skin but not so much that she pulled a Jeffrey Dalmer.

Teo jerked back, falling sideways into the dash board. "Shit!" he said. "Why did you do that?!" He pushed backwards, bracing against the floor and the seat back.

Elizabeth was pissed. She felt the anger run through her and she let herself feel it. "What do you mean?" she said. "The part where you get all rapey?"

At the word, Teo's face looked shocked. "What do you mean? I thought we were having fun." He pushed himself back to the driver's side.

She just looked at him.

"You didn't say no," he said.

"I couldn't with your tongue jammed down my throat."

He just looked at her for half a minute, and a look of hatred came over his face. "So you're one of those," he said. "A cocktease. You get off on making guys suffer?"

Elizabeth thought she'd been mad before, but now she was so pissed she wanted to punch him. "Look, asshole," she said. "It's MY BODY, and I get to say what happens to it. I could be naked here, and I still get to say no."

"But I brought a picnic. I paid for your dinner the other day. I've put up with your dad. You owe me." His eyes were narrowed.

She just looked at him incredulously. The balls on this guy! What did he think she was? Her face got hot and she was sure she was red as a beet. Without a word, she turned and pushed the door open and jumped into the pouring rain. She began stomping back down the road, mud caking her sandals and flipping up her legs. She did not care. How dare he? That may work on some girls, but if he thought she was such an idiot, he was dead wrong!

She'd made it a quarter mile when the car slid up next to her. Teo rolled down the window and stopped, but she just kept walking. "Come one," Teo said. "It's fifteen miles to your house. Are you going to walk that whole way?"

She was. She really was.

"Don't be an idiot," he said. "I got the message."

She stopped and turned to him. "You ENTITLED asshole! How could you …"

"Just get in the car."

"No fucking way," she said. She kept walking, him in the car creeping along behind her. Finally, after a few minutes, he punched the engine and roared around her, spattering mud all the way up and down her body. "Fuck you," she said under her breath, and then she shouted it as loud as she could after him, almost slipping and falling on her butt in the process.

Rain dripping through her hair and down into her collar, mud soaking her dress and her legs, she pulled out her phone and dialed Jenna's number.

"Hey," Jenna said, her voice relaxed.

"Come get me," Elizabeth said. As she said it, tears of anger welled up inside her and she choked.

"What?! What's the matter?" Jenna said.

"Just come get me, please." Elizabeth told her where she was.

"I'll be right there," Jenna said.

Elizabeth fumed as she walked. I was such an idiot, she thought. I actually made small talk. To make *him* feel better. How stupid is that? And all that time, he'd been planning to, well, to make sure I went to bed with him. He didn't even try to sweet talk me. In fact, he tried to blackmail me. A lot of girls even would fall for that. Which really sucked and made her feel icky.

Within fifteen minutes Jenna was there. Elizabeth had reached the highway by that time. She flopped into the passenger seat and sat there shivering.

"What happened?" Jenna asked, but Elizabeth couldn't keep it together enough to tell her. It made her feel dirty and awful, and she just sat there, silent but hiccupping, shaking her head, tears streaming down her face.

"Well," Jenna said, "tell me when you're ready."

Elizabeth didn't know when she'd be ready. She felt weak, like she'd run a marathon. And maybe she had, metaphorically. It took days before she stopped obsessing about it, and she even had nightmares where there was a heavy weight on her chest and she knew that someone was going to stab her. She would wake up with a yell. She tried to rationalize it, tell herself it was all silly. Nothing really happened. But her body wasn't listening and had reactions of its own.

He didn't even text or apologize or anything. Of course. She bet he didn't think he'd done anything wrong, that it was her fault.

Chapter 19

Aunt Geri called Elizabeth a few days later. She made small talk and then said, "So, you still got the hots for Teo?"

"Don't even!" Elizabeth said. "What I mean is, he's a bastard, so don't even mention his name."

Aunt Geri laughed and then said, "That's good to hear. For a couple of reasons, but most of all because he's been in the café with some girl named Brittany. And they seem to be pretty close. Well, *close* doesn't half cover it. Velcro, more like."

Elizabeth snorted, but on the inside, she felt her stomach twist. That asshole! On to his next victim. She would have felt bad for Brittany—Brittany King, she was sure from the way she had seen them exchange looks—but from what she heard, Brittany might be on board. More power to her, Elizabeth thought, if that's what she's going for.

"May they live happily ever after," Elizabeth said, letting the nastiness come through in her voice.

It was Geri's turn to snort. "So you did like him," she said.

"No!" Elizabeth said. "Well, not that much. I was pissed, sure. But not *in* in love. And I'll tell you why. If I'd been really in love with him, I'd hate his guts right now. I did hate his guts, but not now. I feel sorry for him now. "

Elizabeth had thought about all this. She'd go all the way with someone one day. She wasn't saving herself for marriage or anything. It was her body—she could do what she wanted with it, as long as she took precautions. But the difference was that Teo had believed he owned her, that she didn't get any say in it. It was his right. If he didn't give her any more respect that that, he could jump off a very tall mountain. She hoped he'd gone home with blue balls, whatever that was—something she wasn't quite sure was a real thing but hoped he had it and that it was painful.

She needed to let it out, to tell someone, and so she hesitated and then told to Geri what had happened. That they had dated for a while and seemed to be doing great, but then he wanted to go further than she did. That had been scary. It wasn't something she would ever have told her parents, but Geri was someone you could tell anything.

"Good for you," Geri said, "for listening to your own gorgeous self. Listening to your gut. Only you can say what's best for you. You go, girl."

This made Elizabeth feel better. She thought a lot of Geri and her saying that meant a lot.

"You think Brittany can handle him?" Geri said.

"Well, from what I hear, they may be two peas in a pod."

"What makes you think that?"

"Well, rumors, you know."

There was silence on the line. "About that," Geri said. "I'd be careful before I jumped too far ahead of myself. I've had my share of rumors spread about me, as you can imagine. People like to take these things and chew them up and spit them out.

And then what they say—well, it makes you wonder about *them*."

This piqued Elizabeth's curiosity. "Like what? You can't just say that and then not tell me what they were saying."

"Well, that I was a pedophile, for one. Because, you know, if you're a lesbian you must be a pedophile too."

"*No. Way,*" Elizabeth said.

"Anyway, bottom line, I wouldn't jump to conclusions about Brittany just because."

"Fine," Elizabeth said, "she's pure as the driven snow. And he's a he-whore."

"I didn't say that at all," Geri said. "All I'm saying is that someone who knows her own mind and doesn't make a secret of it gets called out in public. Even if she doesn't deserve it. Especially if you're a woman. More power to her if she wants to sleep with him. And more power to him. To them. But if not, hopefully she's like you." There was a smile in her voice.

"Well, I'm sick of them both. Them all. Men in particular," Elizabeth said. "They're a pain in the ass." As an afterthought, she added, smile in her voice, "I think I'll switch teams."

"Oh, honey," Geri said, laughing. "Welcome to the dark side!"

Elizabeth laughed too. She liked guys, and Geri knew that. Still, it was funny.

"That's why you're my favorite niece," Geri said. They both knew that she said this to all of her nieces all the time, so it was a joke.

She went on, "Another thing, as long as I have you on the phone. Patty's playing in a music festival on a dude ranch over near the Idaho border in a couple of weeks. We thought it would be cool to invite you to come. You and I can hang while Patty does her thing."

"Oh, really, Geri? That would be fun!" It was a great idea, Elizabeth thought. Get her out of town for a few days. And Geri and Patty were just cool in a not-trying-too-hard kind of way.

Elizabeth's summer was looking up just a little. And then, later that day, Miley called to invite Elizabeth over to stay again, this time for a week. Two invites in one day, though Elizabeth really didn't want to go to Miley's. She loved Miley, but ever since Colin came into the picture and Miley had totally caved to some weird impulse, it wasn't the same. It made Elizabeth sad, and she hadn't called Miley much—not exactly avoiding her but avoiding her, if you know what I mean.

But because she had been avoiding Miley, she felt double guilty and so when Miley asked her over, she said yes. Besides, she really needed a change of scenery. Jenna was pretty much back to her old self, and Livie was fidgeting around the house like a caged panther. A good time to get the heck out of Dodge.

When Mom dropped Elizabeth off, though, Miley and Colin came out holding hands. *Icky*, Elizabeth thought. *That just nails it. Guys are just the worst.* First they make her sister fall in love and then ditch her, then they take her best friend away, then one tries to … well, she didn't like to think about it. Guys were just the worst.

Elizabeth smiled as wide she could manage and gave Miley a one-armed hug.

"Hey, girl!" Miley said. Colin nodded.

As they walked up the path to the house, Colin waved to some people who were walking down the sidewalk nearby. There was an older lady with dark sculpted hair and a stiff stance who was checking her phone, a teenage girl who looked elven with a shag cut, and a young plump Asian woman with straight hair pulled back in pony tail who was pushing an expensive-looking stroller. In the stroller was a well-wrapped baby. The woman and girl were obviously related. The girl smiled shyly. The older lady nodded in response but did not smile, but then she focused on them and gestured at Colin. He trotted over and spoke to her. They both smiled and nodded, and then Colin turned and caught up with Elizabeth and Miley as they went into the house.

"You know who that is?" Miley said as Colin shut the door behind them.

"Summer people?" Elizabeth said.

"Yeah. Well, kind of," Miley said, flopping down into a kitchen chair.

"No, they're not," Colin put in. "They moved here."

"Kind of," Miley insisted. "They still have a house back East."

"*And* the big house down the road," Colin said. "And some other places too, I guess."

Miley turned to Elizabeth. "That's D'Arcy's mom and sister. Sisters. The baby is his sister too."

"What?" *What?* Nobody said anything about a baby sister. And wasn't the woman a little old to be having kids? That was weird. And the parents were getting divorced. Half to herself, she said, "That was Gabby and … What's the mom's name?"

From what she'd seen, Gabby was pretty, in a sweet and misty kind of way, which made you want to protect her. No wonder Charlie liked her. Poor Jenna.

"Katherine," Colin put in. "I have to say they're really rich. And really nice. And, well, Mrs. Pemberly's been having me help her with things. She's got a bunch of things going, and I'm helping her with some financial software and getting things organized." He nodded and smiled like he'd been given an award or something.

Word had gotten out about Colin being good at computers, apparently. And he must be, if everyone was asking him for help.

"She is nice," Miley said. "She's, well, she certainly has a mind of her own." Elizabeth wasn't sure Miley meant that as a compliment. "The baby is Agnes," Miley continued. "And the woman with them is their nanny Meg."

What? Elizabeth was speechless. How weird to see D'Arcy's family. She could see the resemblance. They were all tall angular people with dark hair who oozed good taste. She imagined they were all snotty and stuck up, too, though Gabby's smile seemed genuine.

"Hmmm," was all Elizabeth could manage, nodding slightly.

"What was that about?" Miley asked Colin.

"We're invited over for a barbeque," Colin said. "They're just such generous people. Mrs. Pemberly, well, she's just ..." Colin couldn't seem to find the word.

"Yeah, she's pretty great," Miley said in a voice that seemed to be more about agreeing with Colin than meaning what she said.

"So, you ready to cook your heart out?" Miley asked Elizabeth. Turns out, Miley was trying out a couple of Southern recipes for her mom, and she planned on enlisting Elizabeth in the effort. A sweet corn pudding called spoonbread and a combination of ham hocks and greens called potlikker. "You know it's got to be good with a name like potlikker," Miley said, grinning.

Elizabeth had expected Colin to go off and do his own thing, but he didn't—he stayed and helped. Well, *helped* in loosest sense. He wasn't very handy. He had a lot of opinions about things, but when it came to chopping vegetables or stirring frying ham hocks, he most likely would chop off a finger or end up with third degree burns.

"Don't even think about it," Miley said to him when he picked up a carrot. "This can opener has safety handles—try that." She took the carrot from him and handed it to Elizabeth, who was chopping collard greens.

Colin was clueless for sure, but he was also sweet in a weird way. He followed Miley like a puppy, and she bossed him around. It was the arrangement they had, but it worked for them. "Stop!" Miley would say sternly, as Colin froze, his finger poised to dip in and taste something. "Yes, you may," she would say when he moved to kiss her cheek.

And Miley. Elizabeth had never seen her like this. Miley always spoke her mind, but this was over the top. She bossed him, and he just smiled. In fact, he seemed to enjoy it. Tough as nails Miley even giggled. And, once or twice when they thought Elizabeth wasn't looking, they did that weird things couples do when they just look at each other with drooly looks on their faces. It would've been sweet if it wasn't just weird.

"Get a room," Elizabeth said finally, which made both of them blush—Elizabeth could tell Miley was blushing by the way she squinted her eyes. Which made Elizabeth think that's exactly what both of them wanted.

"Hmmph," Elizabeth breathed.

The sweet corn pudding turned out to be a cross between creamed corn and custard. Even though it didn't have any sugar, the corn itself was pretty sweet, and the browned top was really yummy. The potlikker was a rich soup with big pieces of ham, collards, and cornbread croutons, with a gooey melting of cheddar and Monterey Jack on top.

"Damn, you are a good cook," Elizabeth said to Miley after they'd stuffed themselves.

"The one thing I don't mind inheriting from my mom," Miley said with a lopsided smile.

Chapter 20

The next afternoon, Elizabeth, Miley, and Colin went over to the Pemberlys' for the barbeque, which turned out to be more like a formal dinner.

Elizabeth wanted to wear her jeans, but she figured dressy might be better so she put on her flippy green skirt, a brown tank, and a long-sleeved off-white lacey cover-up. When she came downstairs, Miley had not yet come down. Colin looked at her raised an eyebrow. He shook his head slightly and said, "Don't worry about what you're wearing. The Pemberlys usually dress down for these sorts of things. Mrs. Pemberly won't think bad about somebody just because of how they're dressed."

Elizabeth flushed to the roots of her hair. Colin showing his true colors again. What he said made Elizabeth think two things. First, that that's exactly what Mrs. Pemberly would think—she'd think bad about someone not all dressy—and second, Colin was trying to make her feel better in his bumbling way but what he was really doing was letting Elizabeth know how wrong she was. And he was totally clueless about it.

143

Colin was wearing khakis and a short-sleeved collared plaid shirt. She was surprised he wasn't wearing a tie.

She was trying to think of a smart comeback when Miley came downstairs in a beautiful long skirt and an embroidered tank. She caught the look on Elizabeth's face and raised her eyebrows, but Elizabeth just shook her head.

The house was just down the street, but it was tucked way back on a huge lot surrounded by trees and had a spectacular view of the mountains. The whole place oozed good taste, and even the intricately cast door knobs looked expensive. From the front, it didn't look too big on the outside, but that must have been a trick because the inside was huge. It sprawled down a small hill. There were lots of deep brown leather couches and chairs and oriental carpets on shiny wood floors and big windows with views to the blue toothy mountains. The kitchen, which flowed into the living room, had two ovens and flagstone floors and granite countertops. Colin explained that there was a second kitchen in the basement that was just for entertaining. The two-story grate room with a two-story lichen-stone fireplace and a wall of windows. A balcony on the second floor overlooked the grate room, and the chandeliers felt western without being kitschy. The big-screen TV was huge, and there was a hot tub out on the deck.

Mrs. Pemberly met them at the door. She looked like she was from a stylish European country or was married to the president of the United States. She was thin and seemed taller than she really was, which was tall, and she held herself very stiffly, like a ballerina. She wore a perfume that was musky and nice at first but then became overpowering pretty quick. Her dark hair was soft and loose around her face but very controlled. Her makeup was perfect, and her black slacks and ivory sleeveless silk top were perfect, and her jewelry was perfect. Her face, not so much—she was one of those women who suffered from resting bitch face.

D'Arcy *was* related to her.

"Welcome, thank you for coming," she said in a surprising deep voice. A smoker, Elizabeth thought.

Colin took a step forward like he was going to say something, but then was totally tongue-tied, and so Miley said, "We're so glad you invited us." Miley introduced Elizabeth. Mrs. Pemberly looked her up and down. All it took was a second, and she nodded her head, like she had Elizabeth pegged, and invited them into the living room.

Definitely related to D'Arcy. Two seconds, and she'd made up her mind about somebody.

Gabby was sitting on the edge of a loveseat, but she jumped up when they came in. She came over, and Mrs. Pemberly introduced her and then told her to quit slumping, to pull her shoulders back. Gabby was skinny and gawky but stylish at the same time. She curled in on herself like people do when they're really shy, and she bowed her head and looked at them under her eyebrows. She looked like she'd been sick—she was pale and had a thick sweater that she kept pulling around herself like she was cold. Elizabeth wondered whether she was just getting over something or she was always like this.

"And where's that sweet Agnes?" Miley asked, looking around. She turned to Elizabeth, "When I have a kid, I want her to be just like Agnes. So sweet." Tough girl Miley had a thing for babies.

145

Mrs. Pemberly glanced at Gabby as she said, "Meg just put her down for a nap. She'll be out later." Gabby nodded.

Colin finally managed to find his voice. "Your house. Ummm. It's … it's so *affluent*." His eyes widened when he said this, and then he tried to recover, "Er, comfortable. Yes, comfortable. In a nice way. A really nice way." He blushed.

Miley looked uncomfortable on his behalf. "What he means is it's a dream house," she said as an apology. "He really likes your house," she added. Then she seemed embarrassed too.

"Thank you," Mrs. Pemberly said and held up her hand for them to walk to the windows. They walked over to them. "We have a great view," she said, as if she could take credit for it. "But it's even nicer when there's more snow on the peaks." Elizabeth wondered if she was always this critical. She couldn't even take a compliment without being all judgy.

Mrs. Pemberly then invited them to sit down on the couches and Gabby brought in hors d'oeuvres from the kitchen. There was fresh fruit, chicken livers wrapped in bacon, crab stuffed mushrooms, and sparkling apple cider. They each took a little plate and made small talk until dinner was delivered to the kitchen door. Meg had joined them by that time, coming in so quietly Elizabeth almost didn't notice. Meg answered the bell and had the delivery guy bring in the food.

As soon as they sat down for a dinner of beautiful lasagna, Mrs. Pemberly started talking. Everything she said, she said with absolute certainty, not up for negotiation or disagreement. She asked after Miley's mom and dad and Colin's mom—they must have been the subject of her close questioning before because she seemed to know a lot about them. "And you two are half-siblings?" she said, glancing back and forth the between Elizabeth and Colin. Colin looked like a deer in the headlights as he nodded, and Elizabeth was sure she blushed to the roots of her hair.

Then Mrs. Pemberly turned her questioning on Elizabeth. She asked about where Elizabeth lived and who her parents were and how many other siblings she had. She asked about high school and what subjects she was taking and her grades and where she was going to go to college and what major she was considering.

Every answer Elizabeth gave was met with specific and detailed advice. When Elizabeth said she had two sisters, one older and one younger, Mrs. Pemberly rolled her eyes and said, "Girls are just the worst." She didn't even glance at her own daughter, who looked embarrassed on her behalf. "Girls," she continued, "are weak-minded and easily duped by men. And there's three girls in your family, you say? Your poor parents. I hope your dad has a shotgun."

"We take care of ourselves just fine," Elizabeth said, holding her gaze when Mrs. Pemberly looked sharply at her.

When Elizabeth told her she was thinking of going into wildlife biology, Mrs. Pemberly snorted: "Wildlife biology? Why in the world would you want to do that?"

"Because I like being outdoors. Because I like science," Elizabeth said.

"Out in the wilds. Don't you think that's dangerous? Especially for a girl?"

"My dad is a wildlife biologist."

"Exactly," Mrs. Pemberly said, as if it proved her point. "Exactly."

"I don't think there's any reason that a *woman* can't be a wildlife biologist," Elizabeth said.

Mrs. Pemberly shook her head. Then she stopped and folded her arms. "Colin, didn't you say you just recently came to Jackson? Your first time here?"

"Yes?" Colin answered.

"Your family lives here—well, your dad and step-family—and you say you've never been to Jackson before?"

Colin gulped and nodded. Elizabeth was starting to feel sorry for him. He couldn't seem to get his footing.

"Interesting. Then what you're saying is that you haven't seen your family before. Why is that?"

Colin just shook his head. Well, Elizabeth thought, shock and awe must be Mrs. Pemberly's modus operandi. Seems like she went through life like a bull in a China shop. Well, Elizabeth could break a few plates herself, if she wanted to.

"Mrs. Pemberly," she started as sweetly as she could. "It's really nice of you to be so interested in our family. We're actually not very interesting."

"Odd, isn't it? He's your brother and you haven't seen him? Did you even know?"

Elizabeth refused to answer and just looked at her. When Colin tried to say something, Elizabeth waved her hand at him and he closed his mouth.

Mrs. Pemberly continued, "A shame. Keeping secrets like that. Everything out in the open is my motto. Secrets just fester and soon the whole family's fighting." Mrs. Pemberly nodded her head once sharply and took a bit of her salad.

Elizabeth couldn't help noticing Gabby's face at her mother's words. Her eyes got big, and then she bowed her head and looked at her plate and didn't even glance up for a full ten minutes. Elizabeth's Spidey sense went crazy. She thought of what D'Arcy's dad had done to Teo. No skeletons in your closet, eh? Elizabeth knew better. She tilted her head to the side but kept her eyes on Mrs. Pemberly's face. She said, "The thing about closets. Once you open them, you never know what you'll find." She kept her eyes on Mrs. Pemberly's face just long enough to see her arch her eyebrow, and then she gathered up a roll and started buttering it.

"Hmmph," Mrs. Pemberly breathed.

Miley then turned the conversation to the food. As they were having a dessert of rich chocolate cheesecake, the baby monitor on the wall crackled with Agnes's cooing and the wet sounds of raspberries. Meg smiled to herself and nodded as she left the table.

Mrs. Pemberly looked after her and said, shaking her head, "Three girls, huh. You seem to feel quite at home speaking your mind, Elizabeth. Are your sisters the same?"

"Well, Jenna's the oldest, and she's not much like me. She's very sweet. You would like her." Elizabeth felt pretty sure about that. "My younger sister Livie, though, is even more strong-willed than me, if anything."

Elizabeth smiled, remember Dad meeting Livie at the door in the middle of the night when she'd been drinking beer with Dennis. Dad had chewed her out, but the whole time she'd just looked at him. Then, when he was done, she'd said, slurring a bit, "Thanks for your concern, Dad. Are there any leftover pork chops?"

Elizabeth continued, "Yeah, she's only fourteen and she's already been grounded for drinking. A wild child, that one.

When she was eight, she tried to drive the pickup into town to get ice cream."

Mrs. Pemberly raised her eyebrows. "That would not happen in my house."

Elizabeth thought that that was probably true.

Meg brought in baby Agnes, who had passed the gawky stage of a newborn and had just started to fill out. She had on a sweet pink and white dress with lace and ruffles and brightly colored leather slippers. She was awake and curious and looked at everything. Something would catch her eye and she would stare, and then a broad smile would dawn on her face, and she would beam. She would shake her hand up and down in delight and let out an excited "Aaah!" Everything delighted her.

I wish I was like that, Elizabeth thought. Then immediately she thought, no, that is not me. So cute, though.

Miley was totally in love, though. Meg let her hold Agnes, and Miley did all the over-the-top things girls do. She cooed and tickled and jiggled and giggled. When Miley offered to pass the baby along, though, Elizabeth smiled but shook her head.

What was really curious, though, was that Mrs. Pemberly hardly seemed to notice the baby. She kept on talking. It was Gabby, along with Meg, who kept a close eye on Agnes, and when Meg offered the baby to Miley and then Miley to Elizabeth, Gabby flinched visibly and narrowed her eyes. The smile quickly returned to her face though.

Hmmm. Maybe Gabby was Agnes's main caretaker besides Meg. Elizabeth wouldn't put it past Mrs. Pemberly to make up her mind to pass along childcare duties.

They stayed just long enough to finish their desserts and compliment Mrs. Pemberly on her house and on the dinner and on sweet Agnes. "She is very accommodating," Mrs. Pemberly said. "I don't know where she gets it," she added—and she seemed completely unaware of the irony of what she said.

Glad that's done, Elizabeth thought when they got back to Miley's. Not something she wanted to do again.

Two days later, Elizabeth realized that they could see the Pemberlys' back deck from Miley's. Just as she realized that, she saw a tall thin figure with his dark head bent checking his phone. She recognized him immediately. It was D'Arcy. Elizabeth squinched her face. That sucked. Hopefully they wouldn't run into him. But just as her mind told her that, her body went a little liquid, a little zazzle. Her eyes widened. What's up with that?!

Chapter 21

That weekend, Elizabeth and Miley and Colin decided to go to the rodeo. Colin had never been to one. And so Elizabeth and Miley dressed in their cowboy best—jeans and westerny shirts. Miley pulled her beautiful long hair into two beaded braid wraps, and Elizabeth stopped home to get her cowboy boots. Colin wore his usual khakis.

It was a night rodeo, and they got there a little late. The lights were bright above the arena, and it smelled of horse manure and mud and dust. The saddle bronc had already started, but they knew the whole thing would go on for hours so they weren't in a hurry. They stopped by the concessions stand. Miley and Elizabeth each got their own nachos, Miley piling hers with jalapenos, and Colin got a corn dog, nachos, and a powdered sugar funnel cake. They also got huge drinks—Miley got a strawberry lemonade, Elizabeth a diet Pepsi, and Colin a chocolate milk. The stands were pretty full, so they found a place way up against the back rail.

"This is it?" Colin said through a mouthful of corndog as he looked around.

"What do you mean?" Miley said. "What did you expect?"

"I don't know. A big screen TV. And, well, a little better view."

"We could sign you up," Elizabeth said. "Put you on a bull. You'd have a great view then."

Miley snorted. "Or the kids' sheep ride. We could put you on a woolly." Her eyes were bright with amusement.

Colin looked startled. "Are you kidding me?"

Miley gave in. "Yes, we're kidding you. You're too big. It'll have to be a bull."

Elizabeth nodded, trying to keep a straight face.

"No way," Colin said. "That's crazy." He knew they were joking but looked a little worried nonetheless.

They settled in to watch. The bareback finished and then came the steer wrestling and team roping. There would also be saddle bronc, goat tying, barrel racing, then bull riding. Elizabeth liked rodeos. She had lots of great memories of hanging out at rodeos and eating sticky fatty food and playing behind the stands. Elizabeth's dad had tried to get her to be a barrel racer or maybe goat tier, but she'd taken a pretty bad spill coming around a barrel and her mom had put her foot down. "Will," she'd said, "our daughter is quite tough enough already." And that was the end of it.

Colin was starting to get a little bored, and so he and Miley held hands and did lovey dovey kinds of things. Elizabeth decided it was a good time to go pee. She ran down to the concrete bathrooms and had to wait in line—the woman in front of her was dancing, she had to go so bad.

Elizabeth came out of the bathroom wiping her wet hands on her jeans, and then she decided she'd grab a candy bar on her way back. She made her way along the wall and almost tripped over someone on the floor. "Oh! I'm so sorry," she said and then realized it was George, the Billingsleys' guy, the great cook. He was sitting on the floor, his back against the wall, arms at his sides, legs splayed out in front of him.

"Thass no problem," George said. His head swayed as he turned and looked up in Elizabeth's face. "No problem," he said, shaking his head slowly. He was obviously and spectacularly drunk.

"George! I didn't realize it was you." Elizabeth hesitated. "Are you okay?"

"No, I'm not okay," he said, then paused. "No, that's not right—yes, I am okay. Drunk as ten monkeys, but since that was what I was going for …" A smile spread slowly over his face.

"Is there anything I can do for you? Get you? Coffee?"

It took George a minute to register what she meant. "Coffee? Naw, that would wreck things." He focused back on her. "You're … You're Elizabeth, Will and Holly's daughter."

"Yes. Yes I am," Elizabeth said.

He smiled again, his head wobbling. "You know, I had a huge thing for your mom, back in the day. A huge thing." His face got serious again and it even looked like he was going to cry. "You look just like her. You're beautiful." He raised his hand toward her but then let it flop back to the floor.

"You? And my mom?" That was weird. And not something she thought she wanted to hear. She'd never thought about her mom having admirers before.

"Oh, don't worry. I don't think she even knew." His eyes widened. "Shshshsh! Don't tell her."

"I won't," Elizabeth said. "I promise." That was a promise she was pretty sure she could keep. Awkward. Then she got an idea. Maybe George could tell her something about Charlie and what happened before, since he was their guy. "Say, George, do you know if the Billingsleys are coming back this summer?" Maybe she could help Jenna after all.

"Billingsleys? No. It was just Charlie and Tiffany, and then they decided to leave." He got a secretive look on his face and tried to lean forward but then fell back. "They left because of a *geeerl*." He let the word roll around in his mouth for a while. "He got a huge crush on her, and so the Pemberly boy convinced him they needed to go back to the city. Best thing, really." He nodded.

Well, he must be drunk enough he didn't remember that *that girl* was Elizabeth's sister.

"Why?" Elizabeth realized her voice was pretty sharp, so she softened it. "I mean, was there something wrong with the girl?" It felt strange calling Jenna *the girl*.

"No," George said. "She was nice enough, but she was kind of cold. D'Arcy told Charlie that she didn't like him near as much as he liked her. That's when they left."

I knew it! Elizabeth thought. D'Arcy shows his true colors again. She gritted her teeth and narrowed her eyes. And Charlie *did* like Jenna! She knew that too. She didn't know what she would do with the information—it wouldn't be good to tell Jenna—but she stored it away. It would be useful sometime, she was sure of it.

She focused on George. "Are you sure there isn't anything I can do, George? Can I call somebody?"

"No. That's really nice of you, but no. My wife's up in the stands flirting with some *cowboy*, but she'll be coming for me soon."

TMI, TMI, Elizabeth thought. "Oh, okay. Bye," she said and went back up to where Miley and Colin sat leaning against each other watching the bullriding.

The next morning, Miley decided to make eggs Benedict with homemade Hollandaise for breakfast—English muffins topped with Canadian bacon, poached eggs, and a creamy buttery sauce.

"You've got to be kidding me," Elizabeth said, but she let her real reaction—YUM—come through on her face. It was bound to be scrumptious.

"We're out of butter, though, to make the sauce," Miley said. "Colin?"

Colin was sitting at the table with his laptop, tapping away at the keys. "Hmm?" he said.

"Store. Butter," she said.

Colin nodded up and down but then shook his head back and forth. "Sorry. Your mom. Got to be there in twenty minutes."

"Why are you just lollygagging, then?" Miley said, shaking her head. She turned to Elizabeth. "Please? Got to have me some Benedict. Please?"

Elizabeth was still in her yellow SpongeBob pajama bottoms and a black tank. She looked at Miley, down at her clothes, and back at Miley, raising her eyebrows.

Miley dramatically batted her eyelashes. "Please?" *Bat bat*.

"Oh all right," Elizabeth said. "But only because I know it's going to be mouthwateringly delicious." Sighing, she pushed herself up from the kitchen table where she had been sipping coffee and slipped on her tennis shoes, shrugged on her jacket, and grabbed some money. She hadn't yet combed her hair, but she had splashed her face with water earlier. The store was just on the next block, she thought. Who's going to know?

"Really?" Miley said, cocking her head and looking at her clothes. "You got no pride?"

"Do you want your buttah or not?" Elizabeth said, smiling.

Wouldn't you know it, she'd walked half a block and there, sitting on the grass in a small park with his back against a tree, was D'Arcy. He was reading on his phone. Seven-thirty in the morning on a Sunday. Personally, she couldn't really blame him—who'd want to hang out with that old battle axe—but did he really have to choose now to take a nature walk? Really?

My luck with guys, Elizabeth thought. Are there no good ones out there? And me looking like a rotten zombie. Why couldn't I have at least ran a comb through my hair? She touched her hair and then forced her hand to her side.

Another problem. When she saw him, she just happened to notice how scrumptious he was. How long and lean his legs were in those shorts and how broad his shoulders were and how his hands seemed so, well, dexterous. Which meant capable and … well, she didn't know. But the thought of his hands sent a sweet sensation through her. Really, she thought to herself. Really?!

She stopped. She was going to flip around and go back and around the block the other way, but then he looked up and saw her. He pushed himself up immediately and came toward her. Not knowing quite what to do, she just kept walking. For a minute, she tried to act like she hadn't seen him, but then it got kind of silly when he walked right up to her.

"Oh, hey," she said and kept walking.

He fell in beside her as he tucked his phone into the pocket of his shorts.

"Hey," he said.

They walked a couple of paces. What in the world was he doing? "I met your mom," she said finally.

"I heard," he said.

"I bet."

He didn't say anything to that.

She thought about what George had said, and her anger flared. Let's see what he's got to say for himself, she thought. "You all left pretty quickly. Before. You and Charlie and Tiff. Just like you said. Charlie must have just up and changed his mind, like he does. That how it happened?"

D'Arcy's face flushed. "Pretty much," he said.

"Charlie doing good, then? Oh, and Tiff? *How's Tiff?*" She let the sarcasm drip all over her words.

"They're good," he said.

Elizabeth was upset enough she kept walking faster and faster, and by this time they were striding down the walk. D'Arcy's legs were much longer than hers, though, so he kept up easily. Elizabeth realized what she was doing and then stopped in her tracks and turned toward him. He stopped with a jerk.

"Was there something you wanted?" she said, glaring into his face.

He looked startled. "No," he said. "Yes. … No. No. There was …" He stood there shaking his head.

"Well, then I've got some *buttah* to buy." She turned abruptly and strode off, leaving him standing there on the sidewalk. When she came back, she took another route and kept her eye out, but he was nowhere to be found. What had that been all about? What could he possibly have wanted?

When she told Miley, Miley snorted. "I bet he was stalking you. It'd be just like him."

"Well, of course," Elizabeth said. "Who wouldn't want to stalk a gorgeous babe like me?" She pulled on the side of her SpongeBob pajama bottoms and shook her hair and laughed. "Gawd! I'm such a mess."

"Yeah, how can I stand the sight of you?" Miley said, laughing too. "You could shower while I make the Benedict. There's time."

"It's a deal," Elizabeth said, grabbed Miley's shoulder in a quick hug, and went upstairs.

The day was a gorgeous one, started off right with a great breakfast. That afternoon they sat on the porch talking about college—where they might want to go and what they might major in. Miley had been thinking about fashion design or something art-related, but since she hooked up with Colin she was thinking more toward video game design. There was a university in Colorado that offered a degree in gaming and game design, and Miley's grades were good enough to get in. Elizabeth was still thinking wildlife biology, although she would have to admit secretly, because of everything with her dad, it wasn't as appealing as it had once been. She wasn't quite so sure she wanted to be just like her dad.

"Look at that," Miley said, looking past Elizabeth and down the street. "Here he comes."

"What?" Elizabeth said and turned. There was D'Arcy walking toward them. Twice in one day. He wasn't ambling like he was just taking a walk. No, he had his head set in determination, and it was obvious it was them he was coming to see.

"*Stalking*," Miley whispered.

"*As if*," Elizabeth whispered back. "We have a mutual agreement. He hates me and I hate him."

He walked up to the porch and fixed his eyes on Elizabeth. "Uh, can I talk to you?" he said. His face was so focused and intense, he looked almost angry. He totally ignored Miley.

Elizabeth glanced from him to Miley. Elizabeth opened her eyes wide. *Should I*, she said without saying. Miley shrugged, saying, *up to you*. Miley lifted her eyebrows, though, which meant, *I got your back, girlfriend*.

"Sure. Have a seat," Elizabeth said, holding her palm out to a chair.

"Alone," he said and glanced at Miley. Then he seemed to realize he was being rude and said, "If that's okay," glancing back and forth between them.

Miley shrugged and got up to go into the house. She gave Elizabeth a meaningful look as she left.

There was an awkward pause until Elizabeth said again, "Would you like to sit down?"

"Uh, sure," he said and perched on the edge of the chair Miley had just left.

Elizabeth felt no obligation to fill the silence. This was his thing. So she just sat looking expectantly at him and didn't say a word. Let him squirm.

After a minute, he kind of smiled and said, "Wow. You don't make this easy."

"Whatever *this* is," she said, "I don't intend to."

He snorted, swallowed, and then launched in. He didn't look at her as he spoke. "I tried really hard," he said. "But I can't help it. I like you." His words tumbled out quickly. He was shaking his head, like he couldn't believe it himself.

Elizabeth froze. What? What? She wasn't sure she'd heard it right. He liked her? It blindsided her, and for once in her life, she was totally speechless. But. But. He hated her. And she hated him. Well, maybe not hated. Intensely disliked. They agreed on that. They were both comfortable with that. How could he go and do this? She sat there, shaking her head.

They were both silent for what seemed like forever. He fidgeted in his chair, started to get up, but then settled back. "I can't help it," he said again. "I think about you all the time." His face turned red when he said it but he didn't pull it back. "I … I looked you up on the web. You're going to be a junior here in Jackson. You like horses and the outdoors and science. You broke your leg on a horse when you were twelve. You're smart and you have a wicked sense of humor. You have two sisters, and your mom and dad are from Jackson. You're …" He faltered. "You're beautiful."

Elizabeth listened in wonder. He *had* been stalking her. Just a little. Hopefully just a little. She wasn't sure how she felt about that. But she softened. It was flattering. He'd liked her enough to check her out.

But then he said fiercely, "I don't *want* to like you, though. It doesn't make any sense. I'm from, well, not here, and I'm supposed to have this life that's, well, big. You're from

161

Jackson, Wyoming, and you've probably never been out of the state. Your family is …" His voice trailed off, like he couldn't find the right word. "Well, anyway. We aren't very much alike." His expression was open, like he was asking her why he liked her, why he couldn't convince himself he didn't.

Well, just when she thought she might soften a little, he goes and says that. "Well, gee," she said. "What girl wouldn't be flattered to be stalked and then told that it was against his better judgement? That it was a mistake. You really know how to sweep a girl off her feet." She said this is a totally flat voice and stared into his face.

If anything, his face got more red. "I'm not … Well, I'm not good at this sort of thing. Can we …? I mean, you're smart. You know what I mean." He clenched his jaw. "What I mean is, would you go out with me?" In that moment, his face looked like a little boy's—so wide open and vulnerable.

She once again softened, felt a little sorry for him. She looked at him for a minute and was about to answer when he continued, defensively, "It's not like I'm a total loser." He said it with such confidence that it made her mad all over again. Just like him to point out how much better he was than other people.

"I suppose I'm supposed to be grateful," she said, "for *the favor*. How generous of you."

He half-smiled until he got her tone. Then his forehead wrinkled and he frowned. This wasn't going the way he'd imagined, however that was.

"I wouldn't go out with you if you were the last guy on earth," Elizabeth said.

His eyes widened with shock. "Why?" he breathed. "Why not?"

She snorted. "You've treated me like shit from the very first time we met." She made her voice low, "*Oh, the girls aren't very pretty 'round here.* You go out of your way to insult me. If that wasn't enough, you break my sister's heart by convincing Charlie to leave, all because in your opinion she doesn't do enough of those silly things girls do. And what about this? You made sure your dad didn't help Teo out, give him what he promised. There's that. What's up with you, sticking your nose where it doesn't belong and destroying other people's lives? And then you have the nerve to come here and say, *Oh, against my will.* And I'm supposed to feel flattered? How CLUELESS can you be?" Elizabeth was really really pissed, and by the end of it, she was shouting.

He stood up and clenched his fists and looked one way and then another, like he didn't know quite what to do. He was towering in his fury, and for just a second, Elizabeth was afraid of what he would do.

To cover, she said, more softly, "Isn't that right? Is that how it happened?"

He closed his eyes and took a deep breath, and in half a second he composed himself and became furiously cold. "Sure, guilty. I told Charlie that Jenna didn't seem to like him. I was doing him a favor—advice I should have given myself, apparently."

"What about Teo? You go out of your way to mess up other people's lives. You're hateful and proud and snide and mean."

"Yeah, *what about* Teo? If you only knew," he said, half to himself. "And you seem really interested in him. Just a friend,

163

I'm sure." There was a choke in his voice, like this got him more than anything. He stood there for a minute, and Elizabeth thought his eyes might be a bit shiny. But then he clenched his jaw. "Now I know what you think of me. Thank you for that. You know what I think? I think you're stuck on yourself. Your pride gets in the way. That's the reason you're being such a bitch."

"And damn proud of it," Elizabeth shot back, her voice low and loud.

He shook his head back and forth, looking one way and another, and then let out a frustrated "Aaaaaugh!" clenching his fists and shaking them. Then he took a deep breath, focused on her with a bottomless look, and said, "I'm sorry. I really am." Then he rushed down the stairs and stalked away.

Elizabeth's hands were shaking, and she took a shuddering breath. She realized her body was tense all over and she took a long deep breath and forced herself to relax. As soon as D'Arcy made it to the sidewalk, Miley scuttled out and sat in the chair.

Looking after D'Arcy, Elizabeth said to Miley, "Did you—"

"Yeah," Miley interrupted. "I heard it all." Then she added quickly. "I hope that's okay?"

"Course," Elizabeth said.

They talked for almost an hour about what it meant, dissecting every part of it. Elizabeth was left with a conflicted and unsettled feeling. She had to admit, it made her feel good that he'd wanted her, but why was he such an asshole?

Chapter 22

Elizabeth obsessed about D'Arcy. She couldn't help it. She went over everything he had said again and again. Even when she and Miley were out back shooting baskets, her mind kept going back to it.

What an asshole! she thought. How could he have been so clueless?

"Quit it," Miley said in a stern voice—she knew exactly what Elizabeth was thinking about. Then she easily sunk a shot over Elizabeth's head. "Teach you to obsess over *a boy*."

Tired and sweaty, they collapsed on the grass. Miley was laughing at Elizabeth's wilted hair when Elizabeth's phone buzzed. She'd gotten an email. She didn't check it till they went inside and she went up to change, and she got the shock of her life. It was D'Arcy. Again. What was up with him? Hadn't she told him exactly what she thought?

The email began: *I know I should just let it go, but don't worry. I won't try to ask you out again. I got that message loud and clear.*

She would hope so. She couldn't have been more direct if she'd cussed him out.

It went on:

I couldn't let it go, and you owe it to me to hear me out. Then I won't ever bother you again. You accused me of two things—of upsetting your sister by getting Charlie to go back to the city and of stopping Teo's getting what's coming to him.

As far as me getting Charlie to leave. I did do that. I saw that Charlie really liked Jenna, but she seemed like she was just playing with him. She didn't seem like she really liked him. It seemed like she was using him for his money or at the very least it was a summer fling. She was always nice enough, but kind of reserved, so I thought, well, I told you what I thought. But you know your sister better than me. If you say she really liked him, then I must have it wrong, and I'm sorry that I had a part in making her feel bad. Jenna's really nice and I wouldn't want to make her feel bad. Tiff agreed with me, BTW, that Jenna wasn't really that into Charlie. Even then, I'm sorry.

I can only imagine what Teo told you. He's told lots of stories. I imagine he told you that his dad worked for my dad. Did he say my dad fired his dad? That was one story he was spreading. You may not believe me, but that's not what happened. But don't take my word for it. Look it up. It was in the papers. I'm sure it's online. His dad's name is Sonny Wick. Sonny wasn't fired. He went to prison for embezzling from my dad. He got away with it for a while because we were home back east and Dad was busy with other things. When Dad found out, he wasn't even going to press charges because Sonny had worked for him for so long. We were friends, his family and ours. Which, if you knew my dad, you'd know was huge. My dad doesn't just let things go. He thinks people should do the right thing, and if they don't he goes after them like a shark. But then Sonny started talking smack about the

166

*company and spreading rumors, and so my dad didn't have
any choice but to let the police know so that his company
wouldn't be ruined. A lot of oil business is done on a
handshake, and my dad couldn't afford to have his reputation
ruined.*

*I suppose Teo told you that my dad promised him
something. A loan or a job or something. Well, Teo was right
there with his dad spreading rumors. He even implied to me,
but I didn't tell my dad, that we needed to pay him some money
or he would ruin us. He actually said that, "I will ruin you, D."
So of course my dad didn't give him a job or a loan or
whatever.*

*And there is one more thing. I shouldn't tell you about it
because it's a secret. Promise me you won't tell anyone? I'm
going to trust you on this. And I do because I know you're
pigheaded (like me) but you do the right thing (also like me),
even if what you see as the right thing is cockeyed. After I tell
you, you'll see why you. So please please. I'm trusting you.*

*My sister Agnes, the baby, is not my sister. She's Gabby's
baby. Last summer when the shit hit the fan, we spent a lot of
time in Jackson to get things straightened out. I didn't so much,
but Dad and Mom and Gabby did. We didn't know it but Teo
came to the house one day when no one was around but
Gabby. I don't know why. Maybe he had the idea before he
came, or maybe he got the idea when he found her alone. He
started talking to her. She'd been out back in the pool in her
bikini, she said. She tried to get him to leave but he got this
look in his eye. He wouldn't leave her alone. He kept talking
and pushing and talking. I can only imagine what it was like.
God. And then what happened happened. I could've killed the*

bastard. What a fuckface! To this day I could rip out his guts and feed it to him. Gabby is such a sweet kid. She said she couldn't remember whether she actually said no. She felt guilty. Can you imagine that? This bastard rapes her and then she's the one who feels guilty about it. It about wrecked her. She's just now getting back on her feet. And what could we do? We couldn't press charges because then everyone would know, plus there's the whole he-said-she-said thing. And my mom has really strong feelings about abortion, and so here we are. I have a new baby sister.

And so now you understand why I can't stand the sight of that bastard. He tried to ruin my dad. He ruined my sister. I hope he rots in hell.

And so now you can believe me or not. But this is the truth.

He didn't type his name at the bottom.

Elizabeth's first thought, when she started reading, was that he was going to ask her out again, but he quickly shut that down. Thank god, she had thought. And so she continued reading, ready to not believe a word he said. When he said he did turn Charlie against Jenna, she expected him to defend it and get all huffy and tell her she was wrong, but he actually apologized. That was a first. He was so proud and snotty, but he actually apologized. Huh. Then she read about Teo. She was skeptical at first. His word against Teo's, she thought, even though she herself didn't have that high opinion of Teo. She still wanted to believe D'Arcy's guilt more than she knew Teo was a bastard. But then when she read the part about Gabby, it all clicked into place. She knew about this part of Teo—she had experienced it firsthand. She found herself nodding and then feeling tears spring to her eyes when she read what he did and then when D'Arcy explained how angry he was, she got angry too. Gabby seemed like such a sweet kid, and Teo was older. He'd pushed and pushed, like he does. He'd raped her! Rape—the word was so ugly, but there wasn't any other word for it. It didn't matter if she said no or not. Any self-respecting person would have seen that she wasn't into it and stopped. But Teo had ignored that, the asshole!

Why hadn't they charged him? Certainly they could have done a DNA test to tell if the baby was his. That would be proof of his guilt. But then she thought about it a little more. Last year, he wouldn't have been over 18, so they both would have been minors. And, like D'Arcy said, would everyone have believed Gabby? She wouldn't have made a very strong witness, Elizabeth suspected, because she was sweet and could be bullied so easily. Heck, her mom had made sure of that. She could see what would happen, if it went to court. She'd seen enough courtroom dramas. Poor Gabby would be skewered. And for what? What could they get from him? They wanted nothing more to do with him, and he and his family had caused enough scandal. There was nothing they could do. This made her even madder. By this time, she was pacing the room, and she wanted to break something, to rip something to shreds. So she did the only thing she could do—when she had been mad as a kid, her teacher had taught her to take a tissue and rip it up or to punch a pillow, to take her frustrations out on that, and so that's what she did. She grabbed a tissue and ripped it into a thousand pieces and, not wanting to cause a mess, threw them in the garbage. Then she did another and another. Soon she took a stack and grunted as she tried to pull it apart but only ended up bending it—the stack was too big. She threw them away in disgust and flopped on her back on the bed.

She didn't want to admit that one of the things that really got her was that she believed D'Arcy. She was wrong. She had totally misjudged Teo. As she thought about it, though, she realized some other things. The first time they met and went to the coffee shop with everyone, he'd been a little too willing to dish dirt on the Pemberlys. She hadn't even asked at that point, she suddenly remembered. She'd been wondering about it, but then he'd just started talking smack about them. She'd wanted to hear it, so it didn't strike her as funny. And the day he tried to go too far. He had treated her like dirt, really. It was like he was sure of her, sure of what he was going to get, so he didn't have to pretend anymore. He could just take what he wanted and it didn't matter what she thought. He had her right where he wanted her.

The more she thought about it, the more she began to turn her mind to D'Arcy. If he was anything, he was straightforward. He prided himself on it. He wasn't the type to make things up and sneak around and lie about it—that was Teo. And so, while he might believe something that was wrong and say it as the god's honest truth, he would never intentionally lie. It just was the way he was. He said things, even if they hurt people. He had *principles*. And he was a good friend—at least to Charlie. When he'd thought his friend was going to get hurt, he'd not been afraid to say something and to try to help him, just as she was with Jenna and Miley. She also realized that maybe she'd been pretty mean to him as well. She hadn't made it easy for him. She'd went out of her way to return it all, tit for tat. She'd gone into the whole thing with her mind made up.

Now she felt ashamed of herself. It was all such a train wreck, and she'd been right there waving the train on. She wouldn't really admit it to herself, but one of the things that really got her was that she prided herself on being such a good judge of character, and she'd been wrong about D'Arcy and she'd been wrong about Teo. Here she was, a smart girl with a healthy skepticism about everyone, and she'd misjudged both of them. Jenna was right—looking for the worst in people wasn't always good either.

And yet after all that D'Arcy'd wanted to go out with her. After she'd been a bitch and told him off in one way or another every time she'd seen him, he'd still liked her. It took her aback and made her think about it all. She remembered how her body against her will had reacted when he was around. How scrumptious he always looked. Even when he was frowning at her, she had been attracted to him—yes, that was it. Her brain was busy saying *no flipping way* but her body had had other ideas. Teo, she'd kind of decided to be attracted to. Her mind and body had agreed. But with D'Arcy she'd been attracted even when she hadn't wanted to. She was so conflicted and confused, she felt like crying. Why wasn't this stuff easier! But she didn't cry. She just took a deep shuddering breath.

In that frame of mind, she went downstairs. Miley and Colin were playing cards on the dining room table. Miley caught the look on Elizabeth's face and raised her eyebrows, but Elizabeth just shook her head.

"Hey," Colin said. "We think Mrs. Pemberly's son was here for you."

"Shshsh!" Miley said. "What'd I say? Let it go."

"But he stood outside for ten minutes," Colin said. "Shouldn't we tell her?"

"No! I told you not to mention it," Miley said sharply. She looked at Elizabeth with apology on her face. "He stood out on the sidewalk for a while just staring at the house. But he never came up and then he went away."

Elizabeth took a deep breath and said, "No problem. He was probably just doing a bit of light stalking." She said it jokingly and Miley smiled and Colin shrugged, but on the inside her stomach knotted in a ball. Even after all that, D'Arcy had come over. Maybe he'd hoped she'd read his email and come out and talk to him. She was glad she hadn't known.

The days passed, and Elizabeth didn't see any signs of D'Arcy for the rest of her stay at Miley's. But in her spare moments she read and reread his email till she knew it by heart.

Chapter 23

The morning Elizabeth was leaving, she came down for breakfast and there was Colin eating a bagel and cream cheese and sewing a button on a shirt. He glanced up with a lively expression, like he was expecting Miley, but when he saw it was Elizabeth, his face blanked and he looked back down at the shirt in his lap.

"Hey, Colin," Elizabeth said as she poured herself some coffee.

"Hey," he said.

After standing for a minute, Elizabeth decided to go back upstairs, but then when she turned to go, Colin said, "Wait. I wanted to say something."

She turned back around and stood with her coffee clutched in her hands.

"It's been hard for me," he said.

Elizabeth didn't say anything.

He continued, "It's probably been hard for you too."

Understatement, but at least he was trying to see things from her point of view.

"I'm not going to say this right—because I never say things right—but I need to say it," he said. "I hope now that you've got to know me, you'll see I'm not a bad person. You'll probably never call me your brother, and I understand that." Which made Elizabeth think that that's exactly what he'd been hoping for, which made her sad for him. "But I didn't mean to wreck anything. I really didn't."

"I know that," Elizabeth said in a soft voice.

"And I wanted to tell you that I'm not going to bother your dad any more. He's got his reasons, and even though it isn't right"—his voice took on a hard edge—"I tried and he couldn't give any more and that's that." Colin stared down at his hands.

Elizabeth realized all of a sudden that she was actually more on Colin's side than on her dad's, really. Her dad was in the wrong, and all Colin wanted was to be acknowledged. Who wouldn't want that? Still, she wasn't ready to welcome him into the bosom of the family, so to speak, but she said, "What Dad did wasn't right. It wasn't fair." She cocked her head to one side and thought for a minute. Then she said, "I know it's a little late, but maybe there's something I can do."

Colin looked at her wide-eyed, and an honest-to-god tear rolled down his cheek. He didn't reach to brush it away though.

"I can't promise anything," she continued, "but you need to at least come over for dinner sometimes." Maybe she was ready, at least a little bit.

Colin's jaw clenched, and then he pushed up from the table and turned his back to her. He cleared his throat a couple of times and then after a minute he said over his shoulder, "I'm not sure he'll, well …"

"Don't worry about Dad," Elizabeth said. "I'll work on him."

"You'll work on who?" Miley said as she came downstairs.

"Nobody," Colin answered for her. "You want I make some tea?"

Miley could tell something was up but she didn't say anything. "Sure, whatever," she said. "Thank you."

They ate breakfast and Elizabeth packed her bag to go back home. Miley was going to drive her. As they were headed out the door, Colin told Elizabeth, "Thank you for everything," with a meaningful look.

"Least I could do," Elizabeth said.

It felt good to be back home, and Jenna had come back from Aunt Geri's. She seemed to be back to her old self, smiling all the time and relaxed. That night as they sat next to each other on the couch watching a movie, Jenna whispered, "Sorry about Teo. I know you liked him."

"All guys are scum," Elizabeth whispered back. Then she told Jenna what had happened with him.

Jenna was horrified. She just kept shaking her head but didn't even try to justify anything. "Did you hear that he and Brittany broke up too?" she said.

He probably tried to go too far with Brittany too and she booted him. Some guys should just have huge warning signs pasted on their foreheads. Maybe with blast horns. He was just bad news.

Just then Livie came in. She plopped down next to Jenna and said, "What you watching?"

"You know," Jenna said. "Flirt flirt, smooch smooch." It was a fun but forgettable romcom.

"Cutaway right when they get to the good parts," Livie said.

"You'd want to watch that?" Jenna said.

"Next best thing to doing it," Livie said.

Elizabeth snorted and Jenna rolled her eyes.

They watched for a bit, and then Livie said, "I was thinking. Can you guys help me with something?"

It was said nonchalantly—too nonchalantly. Elizabeth was pretty sure her answer was going to be no.

"Wendy invited me to help them out with their river guide service. You know, cleaning rafts and some light entertaining."

"Isn't rafting kind of dangerous?" Jenna said. "Seems like somebody drowns every year or two."

"That's not true," Livie said. "Besides, I wouldn't actually be going on the rafts. Wendy said I'd have to have a permit and take safety training and stuff to do that."

"Who's Wendy?" Elizabeth asked.

"You know," Livie said. "Wendy Hernandez. She's married to George?"

"George. The Billingsleys' George?"

"I don't know. I just know her from swim practice."

"Anyway," Jenna said. "Why do you need our help?"

Livie glanced down at her hands. "Because, you know, Dad and Mom will freak out. They think the only reason I'd be doing it was to sneak out to be with Dennis."

"Well, isn't it?" Elizabeth said.

"No. I broke up with Dennis. He's, well, he's more interested in hanging out than anything else."

"Good to hear," Elizabeth said.

"You promise that's true?" Jenna said. "You and Dennis broke up?"

"Stick a needle in my eye," Livie said. She looked at them steadily as she said it—too steadily.

Jenna glanced at Elizabeth. Elizabeth still didn't totally trust Livie, but there didn't seem to be anything particular that raised alarm bells. She shrugged but shook her head.

"She's going crazy around here and dragging the rest of us after her," Jenna said, a question in her voice.

Elizabeth considered for a minute. Her gut told her that Livie was up to something, and when her gut told her something, she paid attention. "That's true, but I …. I'm not sure," Elizabeth said.

"Well, I don't really need your help anyway," Livie said with a sniff, pushing herself up off the couch. "Aunt Geri's on my side. She thinks everyone should be a river guide. Good for the character. And so Dad will go along with it."

"Whatever," Elizabeth said as Livie left the room. It was true that she'd been driving everyone crazy.

Geri and Patty came for supper the next day, and Elizabeth had a sneaking suspicion it had all been arranged by Livie. Sure enough, shortly after dinner started, the subject came around to river guiding, when Livie asked Geri what it had been like. Geri told a story about the time a famous movie star, an action hero type of actor, came on a trip and how scared he'd been. He was white around the gills and visibly shaking when they started. They went through the rapid Big Kahuna and he had such a fit they had to pull out before the next one, Lunchcounter.

"You should've seen him," Geri said. "He was screaming and bawling like a baby. I bet he wet his pants. Not that you could tell, since we got pretty doused at Big Kahuna."

Everybody was laughing. Soon as it died down, Livie piped up, "So, Aunt Geri, would you say being a river guide was a learning experience? Was it good for you, being a guide?"

Dad snorted loudly and looked over at Mom. Mom shook her head, not in a you-can't-do-it kind of way, but in a what's-she-up-to-now kind of way. Dad said to Livie, "You want to guide, huh?"

"No!" Livie said. Then after a minute, she said, "Well, yeah." She glanced between Dad and Mom and Aunt Geri. "I mean, it'd be good for me. Take out some of my *excess energy*." She said it in the way Mom did: *Go outside with all that excess energy.*

Mom immediately said, "I don't think so. First of all, it's dangerous. Second, even though you're not still grounded, we need to keep our eye on you. Third …" She kept rattling off reasons. But the whole time, Dad just sat there, neither nodding or shaking his head. Elizabeth knew that this meant he could and would be persuaded. He was for it, really. Mom must have sensed that because she turned to Aunt Geri and said, "Geri, what do you think? Is it a good idea for a *fifteen-year-old girl* to go and live in dorms where she's around *a lot of boys* and she's proven in the past that she's *unreliable*?"

Geri raised her eyebrows and said, "I am *so* staying out of this one." But she couldn't resist because she added, "Though I was fifteen when I started."

Mom rolled her eyes. "It was different with you, I think. You hadn't just gotten in trouble for drinking with boys."

"Maybe I had. Maybe I hadn't," Aunt Geri said and glanced at Dad. "But that's neither here nor there. I'm not saying another word." She got up and started clearing the dishes.

"Please?" Livie said. "Pleasepleasepleasepleaseplease?"

There was silence at the table until Dad said, "She's been cooped up in the house all summer, Holly."

"Yes!" Livie said.

Mom was shaking her head. "Whatever, Will, but mark my words, there'll be trouble." She looked over at Livie. "Huh, Livie."

"No, Mom. Never. I realized my mistake. I was immature before. Now I'm not." Livie was very pleased with herself, bouncing up and down.

And so it was settled. Livie was going to live in the dorms for two weeks and help Wendy with the rafting business.

But Elizabeth still didn't like it. On one hand, she should keep her nose out, but she knew Livie would get in trouble, just like Mom said, and so she had to say something. The next day, she found Dad on the porch reading the newspaper.

"I don't think you should let her go, Dad," Elizabeth said. "You know what she's like."

Her dad smiled to himself as he said, "Not everyone can be as forthright and outspoken as yourself, Elizabeth."

"This isn't about me," she said. "She's going to get in trouble. She can't handle that much freedom without causing a ruckus."

Dad sighed and said, "That may be true, but, you know, Livie isn't going to rest until she self-destructs in one way or another. How can we expect to her to really put her heart into it with us holding her back?" Amusement came through in his voice.

"She'll take us all with her," Elizabeth said, frowning. "Next time, it's going to be much more serious."

Dad scrunched his face in a mock frown. "Did Livie embarrass you? Poor you. What's being a teenage about if not being mortified by your siblings?"

"I'm not embarrassed by her. What she does is her own fault, and it isn't about me. This is about her. And you." Elizabeth let her anger come through in those last words. Didn't he remember how he got in trouble when he was about their age? Couldn't he see that Livie was headed the same direction? How blind could he be? "If you don't tell her no, nobody will, and she'll—well, it won't be good."

Her dad didn't take the bait. He just smiled. "Everybody gets wild when they're teenagers, and Livie will probably be wilder than most. Sure, I'm not going to let her do anything dangerous, but this will let her stretch her wings a bit while still being near. George and Wendy will be there, but she'll have a little bit of freedom."

Elizabeth just looked at him.

"We can't lock her up, Elizabeth," Dad said. "Nor would we want to."

There was nothing else Elizabeth could say, but at least she'd tried. And so just a two days later, Livie sang as she left with Mom, "Later, alligator, after while, crocodile." She seemed to say it with more force than necessary.

Chapter 24

Aunt Geri and Aunt Patty picked Elizabeth up for the music festival on a bright Monday afternoon. Summer was winding down and it was less than a month before school started. Elizabeth had really been looking forward to the trip. Staying with Geri and Patty was invariably a blast but relaxing too. They were the best combination of family and friend—they let you do pretty much whatever you wanted but they also called you on your shit. Anticipation of trip took on a comforting glow. No guys, no sisters, no parents, no pressure. One last real break before school started.

Another reason Elizabeth loved being with Geri and Patty was that they were such a sweet couple. They were always doing nice things for each other, and they were very respectful and caring. For example, Patty had packed a bag with things they might need just on the drive. There was a first aid kit, sunscreen, sunglasses, and jackets, but there was also Geri's favorite munchies—sunflower seeds, jerky, and ripe pears. Patty would put her hand on Geri's thigh, and when Geri wasn't shifting she'd lay hers on top of Patty's. When they'd had the car before with a bench seat in front, Patty had always ridden slid over in the middle right next to Geri.

Geri also took care of things for Patty. On winter mornings, Geri started Patty's car, which was a highly impractical Chevy stingray convertible, and when Patty was low on gas, Geri would drive to the gas station and fill up for her. When Patty started getting a little stir crazy, like she did in late winter, Geri would call up all their friends and have a big party with lots of food and lots of music.

If Elizabeth ever imagined herself married, it was Geri and Patty's relationship she hoped for, even though she knew she'd marry a guy.

Their little Subaru was stuffed to the gills with music equipment and camping gear and food and Geri's photography equipment. They'd created a little nest complete with pillow and blanket in the back seat for Elizabeth, though it would take an hour or two to get there.

"That way you can sleep or read or just look out the window," Patty said. Her curly hair was pulled back with a peacock-colored scarf, which trailed down her back, and she smelled of patchouli oil.

"Thank you," Elizabeth said. And she really was grateful.

Aunt Geri took her time driving. They all sang songs to the radio, which was hooked up to Patty's iPod. The sun was setting gloriously red and purple behind the high mountains when they pulled off the highway and down the gravel road to the dude ranch. The Double X was tucked up against the mountain in a valley that opened out into a broad meadow surrounded by pine trees. There was a long lake where beaver had dammed the creek, and a large herd of horses grazed in a pasture and up into the trees. There were a lot of buildings—a main lodge, small guest cabins, a huge barn where there were dances and where the music festival would take place, barns for the horses, corrals, and so on. There was even a boat house where you could take out paddle boats or borrow fishing equipment. During the winter, the place was a hunting and snowmobile lodge.

Waved in by an attendant, they parked their car in the meadow that apparently doubled as a parking lot when the lodge was busy. They walked to the main lodge and checked in. On the inside, the lodge was everything you'd expect it to be—elk antler chandeliers and manly print couches with lots of natural wood and big rugs on polished wood floors. A huge fireplace crackled away, and servers and hostesses wore white tux shirts and black pants. Elizabeth couldn't help wondering if they were just local kids from Wilson or Victor who picked up spending money whenever this place was busy.

They had a suite in one of the larger buildings close to the main lodge. Geri and Patty had a large room with a huge plate-glass window overlooking the lake, while Elizabeth's room was smaller and off to one side. Its window overlooked the inner courtyard between the building and the lodge. It did have one of those huge tubs with jets and sprayers. It looked so relaxing. She made a mental note to spend as much time in there as possible.

The week was everything Elizabeth had hoped for. Every night there was music in the main barn and dancing and good food and good drink. Then there was an after party where just the musicians and their families got together and played their instruments and talked and drank and ate. Elizabeth stayed up till two or three in the morning every night, and so she slept until noon most days. While Patty was hanging with all the musicians she had known for decades, Geri and Elizabeth would hike up the mountain or use the lodge's fishing gear to try their hand at fly-fishing. Geri was an avid flyfisherman. When they went out, Elizabeth had to practically drag Geri back to the lodge.

Early in the week, they went on a guided trail ride with a group of others, but it drove both of them crazy because they rode nose to tail the whole way and the guy who was their guide talked and talked and talked. He was always drawing their attention to something or another. Two girls about Elizabeth's age obviously had the hots for his cowboy act, but Elizabeth was pretty sure by the newness of his clothes and his accent that he was all hat and no cattle—someone just in to work for the summer. His swagger took on the aspect of overcompensation.

The ride had been so disappointing that the next day Elizabeth asked if she could take a horse out by herself, while Geri went fishing again. She explained that she'd ridden a lot, and she liked the looks of a bay mare she'd seen under another experienced rider. The wrangler said sure, that she had a good eye, and she gave her directions how to make it to the top of the ridge and up toward the peak of the mountain if she wanted. When Elizabeth asked Geri, Geri said, "Go! Have fun. You have to be sick of our cuddlebugs by now."

It was a great day. She made a point of getting up early, even though the bed was so warm and cozy. She was the first one in the barn, and the wrangler, who was in her thirties and was named Val, caught the horse for her and led it over to the tack. Elizabeth started saddling the mare, and Val tried to help her, but Elizabeth waved her off. "Been around horses," she said. Val watched her for a bit and then nodded when she was satisfied that Elizabeth did in fact know what she was doing.

The beautiful bay horse, who Val said was named Josephine, was everything Elizabeth had hoped for—which actually surprised the heck out of her. Horses who are rode a lot by non-riders tend to have iron mouths—out of necessity from all the frustrated yanking and pulling by dudes. But Josephine was a dream. Her trot was like a boat on a stream, and when Elizabeth reined, she responded. Elizabeth crested the first rise just as the sun was breaking over the ridge, and it was beautiful. She rode up the ridge, down the swale, and on to the next ridge and the next and the next. She rode to the top of the highest ridge near the dude ranch, and she had a view of beautiful Tetons all around her and toward Idaho and Gros Ventres to the east around Jackson Hole. She could see the earth curve in the misty distance. The air was fresh and cool with pockets of warmth from the sun. It was heaven.

She rode back. When she was almost back at the lodge, she was riding down a steep switchback trail on a pine forest slope when she saw a horse and rider off in the distance. As the person came into view, he or she stopped and dismounted, and so out of courtesy, Elizabeth took a cutoff that avoided passing right by the rider. She was enjoying her solitude, and she was sure this other rider was too.

But something in the way the rider stood reminded Elizabeth of someone. She couldn't think just who, but she was sure she'd seen that tall slouched figure before. It was a man—she was sure. He wore boots but that only his only concession to riding, as the rest of his clothes were not cowboy at all. He wore a ball cap and athletic pants and shirt.

The horse Josephine, though, wanted to go over to the other horse—horses are such social creatures—but Elizabeth reined her firmly away. She nickered, though, and raised her head, and the other horse, black with a white blaze, raised its head and nickered back. The guy then glanced her direction, and Elizabeth immediately knew who it was.

For heaven's sake, it was D'Arcy!

By this time, Elizabeth and Josephine were down the slope beyond them, but she was certain the shock on D'Arcy's face was mirrored on her own. Neither of them waved or acknowledged or anything. They just stared at one another for the split second before Josephine turned a corner on the next switchback and a tree blocked the view.

Elizabeth obsessed about it for the final fifteen minutes of her ride. Had he been there the whole time and she just hadn't run into him? Would she run into him again? They had a few more days of the music festival, and she couldn't very well ask Patty and Geri to leave early. She was tempted to though. *I'll act like I'm sick*, she thought. *Yeah, that's it*. But even then she knew she wouldn't.

When she got back to the corral, Val took the reins from her, saying, "Good ride?" Even though Val was probably in her 30s, she looked older. She had a tanned wrinkled face and thin smiling eyes like she was part Native American or Asian. They crinkled in a great way.

"I can curry her," Elizabeth offered.

"Nah," Val said. "Management would frown on it." She led Josephine over to the trough, where the horse noisily sucked in water.

It occurred to Elizabeth that Val might know something about D'Arcy, since he'd probably gotten the horse from her. Here was someone she could pump for information. "Say," Elizabeth said. "I have a question."

"Yeah?" Val said as they walked into the shade of the barn.

"There's a guy staying here. I'm pretty sure he's staying here. I saw him out on the trail. A long tall drink of water. Dark hair, grouchy—"

Val interrupted her, "D'Arcy Pemberly. Yeah? What about him?"

"You know him?"

"Of course. Remember that *management* I mentioned?"

"He manages the place?" Elizabeth couldn't picture it.

"Not manages, owns. Well, his father does. They've owned this place for fifteen years. One of their first acquisitions when they were starting their oil business. Because Mrs. Pemberly really likes the West."

So that explains it. She'd put it down to her tremendously bad luck when it came to guys. "So, they come and visit a lot?"

"Sure. At least a couple of times every summer," Val said and paused. "Got a thing for the son, then?" There was a sparkle in Val's crinkly eyes.

"No! No," Elizabeth said, with maybe too much emphasis. "What I mean is, I know him from around."

"Right." Then Val added, "Tell you what, if'n I was twenty years younger, I'd try to snag him."

Elizabeth just shook her head.

"Seriously," Val continued, "he's never said a cross word. Always willing to pitch in and help out. Got his favorite horse that, while he's here, he takes care of. Never demands special treatment. All of our staff adores him."

Now that was weird. So different from what she knew of him, and Miley and Jenna would agree with her. They all knew him as stuck up and entitled. But here was someone—someone who worked for him, no less—saying what a good person he was.

Val saw the look on Elizabeth's face and continued, "I've known him since he was a boy. He's always been the sweetest kindest person. Even when he was a kid, which tells you something. You know how little boys can be." She flipped Josephine's rein over a stall rail and said, "Here, let me show you."

Val led Elizabeth to the end of the row of stalls to a tack room. On the wall was a large framed picture of a family. Elizabeth recognized Mrs. Pemberly right away. She hadn't changed much. Standing next to her was a man not quite as tall as she but with the same level gaze. He was broad in the way older guys are when they're powerful—plenty of muscle, plenty of fat. Standing in front of the two were D'Arcy and Gabby, but they were just kids. Gabby looked like she was eight or nine, slender and not looking at the camera like she didn't want her picture taken. That would make D'Arcy in his early teens, eleven or twelve. He was already tall, and he had an amused look on his face like he'd just been telling a joke a minute before.

The picture made Elizabeth feel weird. On one hand, seeing him so young made her feel empathy for him. She liked his expression—what happened since then? she wondered—and it made her want to know him better. But then the memory of his snottiness made it all uncomfortable. And then the fact that he had wanted to go out with her. She realized in that moment that she actually really wanted to go out with him. She wanted get to know that boy in the picture, the one that Val spoke so highly of. You know a lot about a person by how they treat waiters and their employees, Elizabeth's mom had said, and it really seemed true.

"The daughter and some of the Pemberlys' friends will be here tomorrow," Val said as she stepped out of the tack room ahead of Elizabeth. "We always get notice so we can get everything ready for them." Then Val stopped and said, "Speak of the devil."

A jolt went through Elizabeth. That could only mean one thing. Sure enough, when she stepped out of the tack room, there, riding into the barn, was D'Arcy. He rode to the middle and then dismounted in one smooth motion. It crossed Elizabeth's mind to wonder where he'd learned to ride, but then he had his own guest ranch.

"Looking to get your head knocked in?" Val said to D'Arcy.

"Huh," he said, turning around.

"He spooks in here, and that's your head bashed in by the rafters," Val said. "As I've mentioned before."

He was about to say something, and then he saw Elizabeth. He blushed to the roots of his hair, and Elizabeth was sure she had too. He immediately walked over to them, leading the horse.

"Elizabeth," he said. "I hope Val is treating you well?"

At a loss for words, Elizabeth nodded. She expected him to ignore them, drop the reins, and walk off.

"And the Double X? Is it good? You've had a good stay, I hope?" His voice was strained but extremely polite.

She continued nodding.

"Are you here for the music festival?"

"Yeah. Uh, yeah," Elizabeth said. "My aunts—well, one of them—plays the dulcimer."

"And your sister? How's she doing? And your mom?"

"Uh. Good."

He was nodding, a blank but bright look on his face.

Well, he'd asked about her family. Then she started—it was only polite to return the favor. "And your mom and sisters and … the babysitter?" All names had gone out of her head.

"Well, Mom's mom—you know. And everyone else is good." He half-smiled and looked at her expectantly.

But then neither of them could find anything else to say. Val saw their awkwardness and stepped in and said, "I'll put Inigo away for you."

"Nah," he said to her, "I got him." He glanced at Elizabeth. "Well, I hope you have a good stay. If you need anything, don't hesitate to let them know—let me know." He blushed again. He led the black horse away.

Elizabeth's mind raced for the next hour. Would he think she'd come on purpose, that she knew this was his family's and that he'd be here and she'd come to run into him? And then he'd talked to her! Like a human being. He'd been nice, for heaven's sake. Like he was regular human in a regular social situation. What's up with that? It was like he was a completely different person.

That night, supper was a barbecue on the patio. Elizabeth, Geri, and Patty gathered their plates and found a table tucked in a corner in the shade. They'd just began eating when Patty glanced past Elizabeth and then nodded her head to her. D'Arcy had walked up behind Elizabeth's chair.

"Oh," Elizabeth said when she looked over her shoulder. "Oh." She pushed her chair back and stood, almost knocking the chair over. She swallowed her bite and said, "D'Arcy. Hello."

"Hello," he said. "Is everything good? They really do things well here, but you never know."

"Yeah. Oh, yeah. The food's been fabulous."

They both stood in silence for a second, until Geri said, "Introduce us, Lizard Breath." She had a smile in her voice.

Elizabeth shuddered at the sound of her nickname. Patty patted Geri's arm and shook her head slightly, telling her now was a not a good time to razz Elizabeth.

"Uh," Elizabeth said. "D'Arcy, I'd like you to meet my aunts, Geri and Patty." She held her hand out to each one as she named them. "This is D'Arcy." She said to Geri and Patty. "He's, well, his last name is Pemberly. His family—"

"Is in the oil business. I know," Geri interrupted. "It's nice to meet you." She rose from the chair and shook his hand.

Patty shook his hand as well. "We run the Deckled Edge, there in Jackson," Patty said.

"Oh," D'Arcy said. "That's a great place. You carry Jamaica Blue. I love that stuff."

"When we can get it, yeah," Geri said. "And thank you. We try."

"Well, then," D'Arcy said, like he was ready to leave, but then he just stood there. There was a silence, and Elizabeth wasn't sure if she should sit down to show the conversation was over or if that would be rude.

"How about you join us?" Geri said after a minute. "That is, unless you're busy? I'm sure Elizabeth's tired of the company of old folks." She'd been glancing between the two of them.

Before Elizabeth could blurt out that she was sure he had better things to do, D'Arcy said, "Sure. I'd love to." He sat down next to Elizabeth, pulling his chair close enough to Elizabeth's to make her uncomfortable in both a bad and a good way.

After a few fits and starts, they began talking about music. D'Arcy asked how they liked the music festival and asked about Patty's music. She talked about all the great music festivals she'd been to back in the day and that this one was shaping up to be pretty great too. D'Arcy talked about his sister Gabby and that she played the violin. "She's pretty good," he said. "She's taken lessons from Anthony Aibel and is considering Juilliard."

This sent Patty over the moon. "Oh, I always always wanted to go to Julliard! From when I was a little girl. I got in for bass, but then I couldn't go. Tell her she has to—if it's her dream, she can't let it go. She'll regret it, always." Patty was clutching her hands in front of herself.

"I will do that," D'Arcy said. "She'll be happy to hear that there's others in Jackson who love music as much as she does."

"Patty has connections to the music scene here and all the way to Canada and down through Colorado and New Mexico. Sedona. Marin County, California. Places like that." Geri said.

"She's been playing so long, I think she's got an ancient lute around here somewhere."

Patty snorted. "Listen heeeeeere, sonny," she said in a high creaky voice. They all laughed.

"Say," Patty added, "bring your sister by the Deckle on Fridays. We sit around and play. It's a great time. Anyone who wants to can grab an instrument. Or bring their own. If she loves music, she'll love it."

"We try to make it like the pubs in Ireland, where whole families come and bring their instruments on a Friday night and sing and everything," Geri added.

"That would be great," D'Arcy said, and Elizabeth could tell he really meant it. What he said took on deep meaning since Elizabeth knew what had happened. He glanced at her but didn't show anything.

They talked about Jackson and about the guest ranch. D'Arcy told a story about the first time their family came to the ranch and how he expected Indians to storm over the hills. He'd been watching a bunch of westerns. There was a funny bit where as a kid he'd imagined one of those wooden carved cigar store Indians on a horse. He tried to figure out how the guy would be able to mount and ride with all those cigars in his hand. "You'd think I'd never been around a Native person before," he said, blushing.

They talked about fishing, and Geri's eyes glowed as she told the story of going fishing with her dad when she was five and how she was in charge of the creel. It got really heavy by the end of the day, she said, and her hands and arms were covered with dried and peeling fish slime because she'd insisted on petting them all day. D'Arcy noticed the gleam in her eye and invited her to come fishing on the property any time. "Dad brings out clients he wants to impress, mostly, and we don't give permission to anyone other than guests, so it'd be pretty quiet. I'll make sure to tell them." Elizabeth was sure he would by the way he said it. It was so generous. He didn't have to do anything like that.

As they all talked, Elizabeth marveled at this different person. He was kind and considerate and seemed so changed that she had to remind herself of what he'd been like before. He told funny stories and seemed very aware of his social obligations and entertaining them. Which in turn made her think again about the picture in the barn, and going on a date with him crossed her mind again. She kicked herself now—she really really wanted to go on a date with him, but then he had offered and she had thrown it in his face and he'd taken it back. It wasn't totally her fault, but she regretted it.

And as they sat there, his leg bumped up against hers once or twice, and she sucked in a quick breath. Had he done it on purpose? Whenever she talked, he watched her face with an intense look, and whenever he talked, Elizabeth felt her body drawn to his. Just like she'd seen Tiff do, hanging over the chair armrest, she reminded herself, and pulled away a little. Still, she was drawn back toward him.

Finally, it was time for Patty to go play her music. She and Geri exchanged a quick smooch, and Geri said in a low voice, "Knock 'em dead, tiger." Patty smiled and left. D'Arcy took it as a cue to leave as well, even when Geri insisted he stay. "We don't have anything to do for the next hour. You should stay," she said.

Elizabeth agreed wholeheartedly. She wanted this new improved D'Arcy to stay.

But he wouldn't. "I would love to," he said, "but I've got to get some things ready for tomorrow. My sister Gabby's coming." He glanced at Elizabeth and then added, "And a friend of mine, Charlie Billingsley, and his sister."

Charlie and Tiff too. This was the group Val had mentioned.

"But I look forward to seeing you all tomorrow," he continued. "I'd love to have you join us for lunch. We have our own dining room." He seemed a little embarrassed by that.

"That'd be great," Geri said, just as Elizabeth said, "Yes. We'd love to."

"It's settled then," he said and, nodding, left.

He was barely out of earshot when Geri leaned over to Elizabeth and whispered, "Maybe not as smooth and yummy as Teo, but he's got a good heart."

Elizabeth shook her head back and forth but then nodded. She totally agreed about his good heart—now—but she thought he was a lot more attractive than Teo. Teo's good looks had turned all slimy and gross, while D'Arcy's shone like a star. The thought made Elizabeth clench and tingle all over.

Chapter 25

The next day, Geri and Patty made the excuse that Patty had promised to go to lunch with some old musician friends, which they couldn't get out of it. Elizabeth suspected Geri had talked to Patty and they'd decided to make themselves scarce. On one hand, she would have loved to have them around as a buffer and to take the pressure off conversation, but on the other, she kind of liked the idea of being able to hang out with D'Arcy. Even though he'd been a pain before with Charlie and Tiff, she had kind of enjoyed hanging out with them all, something she had a hard time admitting to herself. She'd liked Gabby a lot, and so she looked forward to seeing her. She was kind of a split mind on seeing Charlie. On one hand, it wasn't really his fault he'd ditched her sister, really, but then it really was. Let the blame lie where it should. But then again he was a great guy who made everything a lot of fun. Mixed feelings. She was flat-out dreading seeing Tiff.

She thought about playing sick to get out of it, but then she told herself, *What am I, a chickenshit? Let's see this through.* And, of course, there was the carrot of D'Arcy.

She dressed carefully. She didn't want to seem like she was trying too hard, so she kept her makeup light and natural. She used product to get her natural curl to hold. She wore jeans but then put on a deep blue sleeveless shirt that showed off her arms and dangly earrings. Feeling armored up, she headed out to the private dining room. There was a lounge area outside of it, and that's where D'Arcy met her. He was by himself.

"Hi," he said when she walked up.

"Hi," she said back.

"Where's your aunts?"

"They had this thing. They said to say they were sorry they couldn't make it."

"Ah, that's a shame," D'Arcy said. "I like them."

Elizabeth nodded. There was lots to like.

"Gabby will be disappointed," D'Arcy added. "I told her about the music."

"Oh," Elizabeth said. "Make sure she comes to the jam session tonight. Patty said to tell her to come."

D'Arcy nodded. Then he walked over to her, a little too close for comfort, and stared down into her face, searching. She looked back into his eyes and then let her face soften and open up. A smile flicked on his lips. He held for another second and then turned away, saying, "They're in here."

Elizabeth took a deep shuddering breath—recovering from his look but also anticipating meeting the others—and followed him.

There was a lot she wanted to do. She wanted to see how D'Arcy was with Tiff, and she wanted to deflect all Tiff's nastiness. She wanted to see if she could figure out Charlie's feelings. She wanted to make friends with Gabby, if she could. Most of all, she wanted to spend time with D'Arcy. Also she wanted to try to figure out how she felt about everything—that was maybe the hardest. It was all so complicated.

They walked into the dining room. It turned out to be a lot less formal than she'd expected. It was more like a dining room in a house than a place where executives ate with clients. It was right next to the Pemberlys' suite with a view of the mountains to the north. Paintings of landscapes and western scenes covered the walls, and there was a regular rectangular table of dark polished wood and beautifully carved chairs in the middle of the room.

Gabby was standing over by a window, Tiff was sitting in a chair off to the side, and Charlie was sitting at the table. Charlie immediately got up and came over, trailed by Gabby. Tiff didn't move.

"How are you guys?" Elizabeth said, glancing between them.

"Good," Charlie said. "Taking it on the down low." He smiled his charming smile, and Elizabeth felt the warmth of his personality surround her. She had been half-ready to ignore him because of what he'd done to Jenna, but he was so genuine and uncomplicated that she melted right away.

Gabby looked at Elizabeth under her eyebrows, chin tucked in, but smiled. "I like your beautiful shirt," she said quietly.

"Thank you," Elizabeth said. That was sweet.

"And you remember Sniffy Tiff, don't you?" Charlie said, glancing over to his sister.

Elizabeth nodded.

Tiff looked up at them grudgingly and said, "Hey."

D'Arcy stepped forward. "We can eat any time. You all want to sit down?"

And so they did. D'Arcy sat on the end, and he invited Elizabeth to sit next to him on his right. She was happy to do it. With a resolute look in her eye, Tiff sat down on the opposite side of the table on D'Arcy's other side but avoided Elizabeth's eyes. Gabby sat next to Elizabeth, and Charlie sat at the other side.

A waiter brought menus, and they all decided what they'd have. Elizabeth had a half BLT and a cup of chicken noodle soup, D'Arcy and Charlie got hamburgers, Gabby had a club sandwich, and Tiff ordered a salad.

While they waited for their food, they talked about the dude ranch and about horses and other neutral things. Elizabeth watched them all closely. Charlie and Gabby were sitting across from each other, but they acted more like brother and sister than like they liked each other. So much for Tiff implying that Charlie liked Gabby. Elizabeth couldn't wait to tell Jenna. D'Arcy basically ignored Tiff, who seemed unhappy with everything, and he kept his attention focused on Elizabeth. Tiff and Gabby didn't seem particularly close. They hardly looked at each other. One thing Elizabeth could tell for sure— D'Arcy and Gabby and Charlie all went out of their way to include her and make her feel like part of the group. They were determined to like her. That made her feel good—and a little sorry for Tiff.

Elizabeth thought of Jenna. Charlie was his old self. She didn't know what to think about that. Did he still like Jenna? Or not? She glanced at D'Arcy, who was taking a big bite of his burger. What did he think about Charlie and Jenna now? She had no idea. Charlie asked in a general way how her family was doing, and he made a reference to the last time he had seen her, which made her think that maybe, just maybe, he hadn't totally forgotten Jenna.

The whole feel of the group had changed from before. Before, D'Arcy and Tiff had held back and given snide remarks or glowering looks, but now D'Arcy said positive things and smiled. Tiff was the only one who had a shitty look on her face.

Throughout lunch, they talked about everything and nothing at all. Elizabeth told Gabby about Patty's music, and Gabby talked about her violin. Elizabeth invited her to Patty's jam session that night, and Gabby's face shone. "All right. All right," she said shyly. Elizabeth couldn't help noticing that whenever Elizabeth said anything, Tiff looked at her through cold narrowed eyes. D'Arcy told a story about a year or two back stepping over a log on Inigo, the black horse, and Inigo spooking at something and D'Arcy ended up half in and half out of the pond, Inigo calmly munching grass on the bank. "What? I didn't do anything," D'Arcy said in a goofy voice, imitating Inigo's look.

Charlie put in that it was because D'Arcy was such a walking stiff—a stiff rider, a stiff conversationalist—and D'Arcy didn't object. He just laughed and nodded in agreement. Tiff started to object and defend D'Arcy, but Charlie cut in, "We talked about this, Tiff. When it's the truth, it's the truth."

D'Arcy looked at Tiff, really looked at her, for maybe the first time during lunch, and said, "It's nice of you." His face was kind but distant, his eyebrow arched. Tiff got a wide-eyed hopeful look on her face, but then D'Arcy added, "But there's no need. We're all friends here." As he said it, he looked over at Elizabeth and held her eyes. It was as if he'd reached out and took her hand. Elizabeth couldn't believe what she was hearing. Her whole body flushed with warmth and she held her breath, her eyes on his face. After what seemed a long time, he glanced back over to Tiff, whose face turned white, a look of horror sliding over it.

"But," Tiff said. "But …" She shook her head back and forth in disbelief. Then her eyes narrowed again. Her voice smooth and low, she said, "By the way, Elizabeth, I meant to ask you. How's *Teo*? You seemed so concerned about him last time we talked." A mean smile spread across her face.

Elizabeth was sure her own face showed her shock. Tiff must not know about Gabby and what happened, or she never would have brought it up. Not even Tiff was that mean. Elizabeth, D'Arcy, and Charlie all glanced quickly over at Gabby, whose eyes widened and face drained of color, but she didn't say anything. So Charlie must know about it too. The set of Gabby's jaw made Elizabeth think that anger was helping her through it all. *Good for you*, Elizabeth thought. *Hold onto it.* That might mean she was blaming the person who deserved to be blamed—Teo—instead of herself. That was good.

"Tiff," Charlie said in a low voice. "You are so out of line. You have no idea."

A shocked and confused look on her face, Tiff stood up so fast, her chair fell over with a clatter. She froze for a half second, looking at their faces, before bending down, yanking the chair back upright, and rushing out of the room.

There was silence around the table. D'Arcy was looking at Gabby with raised eyebrows, asking if she was okay.

Just then, Elizabeth's phone went off. It was Jenna's ring. Everyone glanced at her. What was she going to say to Jenna with Charlie and D'Arcy right there? Not a good time, so she pulled it out of her pocket, silenced the ring, and set it beside her plate. In the silence, everyone reached for their drink glasses at the same time. But then Elizabeth's phone rang again. Exactly what Elizabeth would have done—if Jenna hadn't answered, she would have called right back. She silenced it again and made a face like, *what can you do?* More fumbling with silverware. "So," D'Arcy said, but then Jenna called a third time, and so Elizabeth glanced at D'Arcy and said, "I guess I better get it." He nodded.

Elizabeth poked the button as she pushed up from the table. "Hey," she said, deliberately not saying Jenna's name. "What up?"

"Elizabeth. Finally," Jenna said. "Answer your phone when I call." There was a strain in her voice.

"I did," Elizabeth said.

"The third time!" But then Jenna added, "Sorry. Not your fault."

"What's not my fault?"

"Livie's run off with Teo Wick."

"LIVIE RAN OFF WITH TEO WICK?!" Elizabeth repeated in a loud voice and then realized where she was and who was listening. Her back had been to them, and she spun around and all three of them were staring at her with shock on their faces.

"What?! When?"

"Well, she was only at the rafting dorms for a couple of days before off she went. Makes us think that's what she planned all along."

"You think?" Elizabeth said. That conniving little rat. Just like Livie to do something like this. *I told Dad. I told him.* But then Livie didn't know what she was getting herself into. Teo's past record was not at all good. "But Teo ..." she said but then trailed off, glancing at Gabby, who returned her look.

"I know," Jenna said. "You told me. I just keep thinking that Livie would put up a fight, you know?"

"She would. That's true." Other thoughts came to Elizabeth—much darker thoughts. "I wonder if he would ..."

What immediately came to mind were the infamous cases of Amy Wroe Bechtel and Lisa Marie Kimmel. Amy Wroe Bechtel was a woman who disappeared around Lander in 1997 when she went out running. The case had never been solved and her body was never found. Lisa Marie Kimmel was a college student in 1988 traveling from Billings, Montana, to Denver, Colorado. She disappeared in Casper and was found a week later in the river. She'd been raped and tortured for six days and then bludgeoned and stabbed and thrown off a bridge. It was made a cold case and featured on *Unsolved Mysteries* and *Cold Case Files*, and then DNA linked it to this really creepy guy in prison named Dale Wayne Eaton. It was called the Lil' Miss Murder because that was what was on her license plate. Ironically, Dale Wayne Eaton was also suspected of Amy Wroe Bechtel's murder, but it remained unsolved.

Elizabeth didn't like Teo, but he wasn't a Dale Wayne Eaton, she was pretty sure.

D'Arcy stood up and took hold of the back of his chair and watched her, not even pretending not to listen.

"I know what you're saying, and I don't think so," Jenna said, "and here's why. He's an opportunist. He pushes himself on girls, but he's never been violent. Even when people push back, like you did. A little too gutless wonder. He wouldn't hurt her. He's basically a lily-livered bastard."

"You got that right," Elizabeth said.

"Not only that, but Livie left a note for Mrs. Hernandez. Sounds like it was her idea too."

Yep. "Sounds about right."

Well, that was a comfort, kind of. And it made sense. Livie was always ready to do the wrong thing. Elizabeth wasn't sure, though, if she knew just how wrong it was and what the consequences could be. Livie was all heart, all Livie, and very little brain.

"I bet Dad is ready to kill her," Elizabeth added.

"Yeah, but he was all for it, remember?" Jenna said. "You and I didn't think it was a good idea."

"Turns out, we were right," Elizabeth said. Her mind jumped ahead to what needed to be done. The music festival was on for one more day, but they obviously wouldn't stay for it. Patty would be the first to say they needed to go home. Then it would be all hands on deck trying to find those two. "I'll get Aunt Geri and Patty. We'll be home in a couple of hours."

"I'll tell Mom and Dad," Jenna said. Elizabeth was about to hang up when Jenna said, "Oh! I meant to ask. How was your week?"

"It's been, aah, interesting," Elizabeth said.

"What's that supposed to mean?" Jenna said. "What?! You can't just say that and not tell me."

"Uh. Well. I've got to round up Geri and Patty and get on the road. Tell you what. I'll call you from the road." She glanced up at the three in front of her and then turned away from them.

"There's something you're not telling me. Did you do something wild and crazy too? Did you hook up with a musician? Did you join the circus? What is it?" Jenna's voice was intense with curiosity.

"You have *no idea*. I can't talk now, though. Love you. Call you later." Then, despite Jenna's loud protests, she pushed the end button.

Elizabeth looked back over her shoulder, and D'Arcy, Charlie, and Gabby were all watching her.

D'Arcy was the first one to speak. His voice was deep as he said, "Livie's your sister?"

"Yeah," Elizabeth said.

"This isn't good," Gabby said with an edge in her voice. "How old is she?"

"She's fifteen," Elizabeth said. "But she's a little different than you in that she went with him on purpose." She realized her mistake the second the words were out of her mouth.

D'Arcy winced, just as Gabby stood up and said, a quaver in her voice, "You TOLD her?"

"I—" he began, but then Elizabeth stepped forward with her hand out and said, "It wasn't his fault. Don't blame him."

Gabby's face was bottomless with pain and anger. "You *told her*. Why would you do that?"

"Gabby, please don't be mad at him. Please?" Elizabeth said as she went forward and stood right in front of Gabby, not too close but close enough, and held her hand out, not to ask for anything but to hold her in place. "First of all, I would never tell a soul, never ever. Swear to god." Gabby stared at her face, and Elizabeth tried to keep her face as open as possible. "Second, the reason your brother told me was because Teo tried to do to me what he did to you." That wasn't strictly the truth. D'Arcy'd told her about it because she'd defended Teo to him, but nonetheless it was to set the record straight. It came from a good place—wanting to warn her. Maybe a little jealousy too, but that was totally understandable, considering.

D'Arcy's face opened in shock and then clenched in anger when he heard what Elizabeth said. He mouthed the word *What?* but didn't say it out loud. Charlie looked back and forth between Gabby, D'Arcy, and Elizabeth, his face firm with concern. Gabby was still angry but her eyes were on Elizabeth's face. She was listening.

Elizabeth lowered her voice and started to go on, "Gabby, he—" but she didn't get the chance to finish. D'Arcy came over and slumped into the chair next to her and took her hand. He bent over but looked up into Gabby's face. "I'm so sorry, Gabs. I, I, I would never hurt you on purpose. You know that."

Charlie came in closer too, hovering on the edges.

Elizabeth tried again to say something, "I totally—"

"STOP," Gabby almost shouted. She stepped out from the middle of them, around the table, and next to the windows. She started pacing back and forth. "I am *so sick* of all of this." Her voice dripped with anger. "All these secrets. The Pemberlys don't have secrets, remember?!" She glared in their direction but not at any one of them. "Why does he get to be the one who has all the power? Why do we not talk about it? I did nothing wrong. It is not my fault." Her voice became quieter. "It is not my fault," she almost whispered, but then she spun around. "People treat me like glass and try to make me feel better. I DON'T WANT TO FEEL BETTER. I want to get mad. I want to get even. I want him to feel just a little bit of what I'm feeling. Is that too much to ask?" She looked to the ceiling like she was trying to ask the gods or something.

Gabby stopped and stood thinking for a minute. Then she focused intensely on D'Arcy, "I don't know if I'm ready to forgive you, but I do know one thing. I'm not a fucking little girl. Don't treat me like one." D'Arcy nodded slowly. She continued, "We're not going to be quiet about this any more, I don't care what Mom says. That's how he does it. Everybody's afraid and ashamed, so he gets to go his merry way and keep doing it. That's not right. I'm important too, and what happened to me is important. Too important to let it go." Tears were streaming down her face by this time.

There was silence. They all stood just looking at each other.

Chapter 26

"You've got to go," Gabby said, sniffing, to Elizabeth.

"I'm so sorry," Elizabeth said, not wanting to leave things the way they were.

Gabby shook her head. Then she walked over to Elizabeth and took Elizabeth's hand in both of hers. "Don't worry about it," she said. She didn't smile, but she had an open look on her face. She nodded. "If we had said something, maybe he wouldn't have done what he did to you. Maybe your sister wouldn't be where she is."

"But that's no excuse … I mean …" Elizabeth said.

"I know, but there's much more serious things right now. Go."

"Uh, okay," Elizabeth said. "And I hope …" She didn't know exactly what she hoped for. That maybe she and Gabby could be friends some day. Gabby was an amazing person.

"I know," Gabby said. "Me too."

"You okay?" D'Arcy said to Gabby.

"Stop it," she said but with soft look on her face.

"Right," D'Arcy said. Then he turned to Elizabeth and said, "I'll walk you out."

Charlie and Gabby said goodbye. Charlie said, "I hope you find them," and Gabby nodded.

As Elizabeth and D'Arcy walked down the hall, D'Arcy shook his head. He asked about what happened with Livie. She told him what little she knew. She jumped when he slapped the wall with the flat of his hand, making a loud thump. "Gaaah!" he said, shaking his head back and forth. "If only I'd … It's my fault. I should have said something." His fists clenched at his sides as he strode on.

"That's true," Elizabeth said. "But what would I have said then, if you'd told me? Considering you then and me then." She glanced over at his face.

"Good point," he said, his face softening.

"And, really, it's my fault," Elizabeth said. "I tried to get Dad to not let her go but not enough. And I also should have said something. I told Jenna about him, Geri too, but I didn't tell anyone else. It's like Gabby said. Being quiet only helps him." She shook her head. "What a horrible mistake."

D'Arcy didn't answer. He just shook his head.

What he must think of us, Elizabeth thought. We're such white trash. She wished things hadn't happened the way they did. She wished Jenna hadn't called while she was at lunch with them. She wished she hadn't blurted out about Livie. She wished she hadn't let on that she knew about Gabby. It was all such a mess. And now D'Arcy had every reason to think they were one of *those families*. Now that she knew what he was really like, she knew he'd be nice about it, but all the more reason why he would never speak to her again.

He walked her to the door of her suite. "Here I am," she said, gesturing toward the door.

He nodded and said, "I'm so sorry about all this."

"I'm the one who's sorry," Elizabeth said and looked meaningfully into his face, "for everything."

He nodded, looking into her face for a long second, and then said, "Well, bye."

"Bye," she said.

He turned and walked back down the corridor.

Elizabeth watched his back and felt an unaccountable urge to cry. She really liked him. Contrary to what she'd thought, he was a kind and caring person, and this had been probably the last time they'd be in the same room together, hanging out, everything so great. The last time she'd be able to see his beautiful chest and shoulders, his long neck muscles, his supple hands, his muscled calves. The last time his knee would bump up against hers, with the memory of its heat warming her leg. The last time his dark eyes would focus intensely on her face as she spoke, and his voice would make her shiver.

And he was also just like her. He was strong willed and opinionated—just like her. He defended those he cared about and didn't care if other people were upset about it. He was smart and fun and great to talk to. He was a good person, and Elizabeth considered herself a good person. He was actually perfect for her. She felt very sad. What she wouldn't give for him to ask her out now, like he had before.

She went into her room and called Geri and told her about Livie. There was silence on the line for a half a second and then Geri said, "Well, she just grabs life by the balls, don't she?"

Elizabeth snorted.

"Let me get Patty and we'll be right there. Get packed," Geri said.

"Will do."

As she threw things into her suitcase, she thought about Livie and Teo. She hadn't seen anything between them. Not so much as a flirt. And Dennis was Teo's best friend. Livie had said she and Dennis had broken up, but was that before or after Teo? And what about the fact that Livie was fifteen and Teo was eighteen? That would be statutory rape. And what about the fact that Teo had a history? Come to think of it, Livie had a history too. She wasn't an innocent in all this. But … It was hard to reconcile things. Livie was underage yet she was also someone who knew her own mind, even if what she wanted what she wasn't supposed to have. They'd all joked that she was someone who would burn brightly. What they didn't say was that they hoped she wouldn't go down in flaming wreckage, even though Elizabeth was sure that was what they all were thinking.

She just wanted to be home. It felt so helpless being this far away. Just then there was a tap on her door. Patty poked her head in to ask if Elizabeth was about ready. Elizabeth said she was and then added that she was sorry Patty would miss the last day of the music festival. Patty winked at her and said, "Not a problem. That's something you learn as a performer. You want to take your bow before everyone's sick of hearing your songs."

They made it back to Jackson in record time—Geri turned the wheel over to Patty, who drove like a maniac, even in the Subaru. Elizabeth got a little sick in the back seat because of the curvy road.

211

When they got to the house, no one was home, and the cars were all gone. Mom had left a note: *Dad's out looking for Livie, and Jenna and I are going to the Police Department for the third time. If you could get supper, that would be great. Don't know anything more. Mom*

Geri glanced at the note, nodded her head, rubbed her palms together, and said, "Geri's world famous veggie frittata. If there's any eggs." She looked at Elizabeth. "Looks like you're in charge of biscuits." They got to work.

Dad arrived home shortly before five and then Mom and Jenna got back. They sat and ate, and Mom, Dad, and Jenna filled them in on what little they knew. Mom had dropped Livie off at the rafting dorms. She had worked for two days, but at the end of the second day she'd said she was catching a cold, so when she didn't show up the next day, everybody just assumed she was sick. It was a whole nother day before anyone thought to check. All her stuff was gone except for a note that was addressed to Mrs. Hernandez. Livie must have snuck out in the evening, or possibly when everyone was at work the next day, though no one had seen them. Someone must have picked her up, and everyone knew who that someone was.

Mrs. Hernandez had given the note to the police, but they'd also given Dad a copy.

Livie wrote:

Wendy –

You'll never guess where I'm going. Remember we talked about yummy guys and about how you and George eloped? Well, that's what I'm doing! Can you believe it? It's fifteen in Idaho with parents permission, and I can fake their handwriting. My family's going to be really pissed, but they're pissed at pretty much everything I do. I'm sure you know who, too, if you're not dumb. My family is. They have no clue!!

It's Teo Wick. I love him with all of my heart. I will love him from today to the ends of time. He is my own personal angel. He is my knight in shining armor. And he's the yummiest guy I've ever met. And he treats me like a princess! Like a queen! He's just as stoked about it as I am. We're so compatible, just like you and George. We're going to be happy forever. And we're going to go on huge adventures. Teo is going to get his degree and then we're going to travel the world. I told him he had to take me to Africa and Japan—and there's no way he's getting out of it.

And you don't need to tell my dad if you don't want to. He's going to be mad, so you don't have to be the one. Ha! I wish I could see his face when he finds out! That would be a laugh and a half!

Anyway, thank you so much for helping out. I wouldn't have been able to pull it off without you! You and George are such an inspiration to me! You keep the fun in your lives.

Livie

TMI about George and Wendy Hernandez's relationship, Elizabeth thought, but she did wonder whether Mrs. Hernandez had really known what was going on or Livie had just used her. It was unclear from the letter.

Everyone had been looking all over for them. Livie wasn't answering her cell or texts. She hadn't posted on her Facebook page or tweeted. The police were on the job, and the authorities over in Idaho were also on the case, as Livie had said they were going to hop the border to get married. The police had come to the house and searched Livie's room, taking her diaries and laptop with them. They'd issued an amber alert and put out fliers for tips. Mom had contacted all of Livie's friends, and Jenna had even got ahold of Dennis. The police had talked to Dennis too, as well as Livie's other friends. Dennis had been pretty laid back about the whole thing to Jenna, though he had said, "I don't like to share my ladies," which led Jenna to believe that Livie hadn't broken up with him before she'd at least flirted with Teo. That meant it was before Elizabeth and the aunts went to the music festival. Maybe even before Teo had broken up with Brittany King. Why had those two broken up, anyway? Elizabeth had assumed that it was because Teo tried to go too far, but maybe there had been another woman. Thinking of Livie as a woman, much less the other woman, made Elizabeth's head ache.

Even with everyone looking, they hadn't turned up anything. Teo's credit card hadn't been used, according to the police, and no one had spotted them. No real tips on the tip line—just some crazies reporting she'd been abducted by UFOs. Teo had quit his part time job as a janitor at an office building, so they hadn't seen him. There'd even been talk of a press conference, and Dad and Mom would speak to the press. Geri and Patty said they'd put out the word and put flyers up at the café and anything else they could think of. It was all such a mess.

They had to stop Livie and Teo before they got married, everyone agreed. Elizabeth was as vocal about it as she dared to be. She hadn't told Mom and Dad about Teo, and she was of a mixed mind about it. Secrecy was Teo's game, but Elizabeth didn't want to alarm them any more than necessary. But if it came down to it, she definitely would tell them. Geri did, though, give Elizabeth a significant look when they were talking about Teo.

The next day, Elizabeth told Jenna everything that had happened at the music festival. About D'Arcy being at the dude ranch. How nice he had been and about Gabby and Tiff showing up. And Charlie. She added this last bit offhandedly and then watched Jenna's face fall. She told her about what D'Arcy had done to influence Charlie and why Charlie had left.

Jenna just sat there, her head shaking back and forth. "Is nobody what they seem?" she said. "Has the whole world gone crazy?"

"That's the difference between you and me," Elizabeth said. "This surprises you."

"And I hope it always does," was all that Jenna would say to that. After a minute, she said, "Was Charlie ... Did he say anything about me?"

"No," Elizabeth said. She had to be honest. "But he did ask after *my family* and mentioned a few things about before. I think he was hinting."

"Fat lot of good that does," Jenna said, shaking her head, which surprised Elizabeth. Pretty negative for Jenna. She usually kept those kinds of things to herself, if she even thought them.

Days passed. No one heard a thing from Livie or Teo. Dad went over into Idaho and checked all the places they might be. He checked at hotels and motels, justices of the peace and marriage license places. He stopped in at police departments. Nothing. They'd vanished off the face of the earth. The police weren't turning up anything on where they were either. It was like they'd just disappeared. In this day and age of video cameras and the internet, how do you just disappear? One thing that did turn up, though, was that running off with underage girls wasn't the only thing Teo was up to. He'd written a few checks at businesses around town that he apparently didn't have quite enough in his account to cover. In fact, it'd started long enough ago that they'd gone to collection, and there was even a warrant out for his arrest in Idaho.

Miley called to commiserate. She'd heard through the grape vine what happened. They talked about Livie and how she was headed for a life a crime if she didn't watch it. "And it's not that she's not smart," Miley said. "She's totally smart. The Dark Side just pulls on her a little too much. She's the Anakin Skywalker of Jackson, Wyoming."

"Know the power of the Dark Side," Elizabeth said in a low voice.

Miley laughed but then there was silence on her end. "What …" she said to someone on her side of the phone. There was mumbling. Elizabeth couldn't hear what she was saying. "Oh, all right," Miley finally said to the person and then to Elizabeth she said, "Colin wants to say something." Her voice did not sound happy.

"Elizabeth?" Colin said when he got on the phone.

"Yeah?" What could Colin want to say that was so important?

"Your sister is acting like slut," he said.

"What?!" Elizabeth said.

"Yeah, she's going to ruin everything, not just for herself but for her family too. For you. I thought I should warn you."

"You what?!"

"She'll ruin her reputation and take you with her. I say, you should disown her. Actually. Is your dad there? Our dad? I should talk to him."

"Colin," Elizabeth said, trying to keep the intense rage out of her voice. Just when she was thinking he might be okay, he shows his clueless true colors once again. She made her voice as low and calm as she could, "Colin, I'm only going to say this once. Take some sensitivity lessons before you hurt yourself. I beg you."

"What?" He seemed genuinely shocked.

"Put Miley on the phone."

"For the record, I'm saying this for your own good."

"For the record, you're an asshole. Put Miley on the phone."

There was arguing on the other end. "Just give it to me," Elizabeth heard Miley say before she came back on the phone. "Sorry about that," Miley said. "He is officially in the doghouse. Forever." Miley was obviously saying that for his benefit.

"I'd hope so," Elizabeth said.

"And maybe some dog training. I think we might have a long discussion about just why that was so wrong."

In spite of the rage boiling inside her, Elizabeth laughed. "You go girl," she said. "I'm counting on you."

"Never underestimate the power of the Dark Side," Miley said in a low voice. They both cracked up.

Chapter 27

One evening, Elizabeth saw Dad sitting out on the porch swing, staring off into space with his brow furrowed. He'd taken weeks off work and he'd been out every day searching for Livie. Elizabeth felt bad for him.

She went out and sat next to him on the swing. He glanced over at her and gave her a half smile. He shook his head and said, "People do the most screwed up things. They're nothing but a messed up bundle of wants and hormones."

"Yeah," Elizabeth said. "You've been having some long hard days."

She knew that she'd been right about not letting Livie go for this job, and her dad knew that she'd been right, and she knew that he knew that she knew. Neither one of them had said anything about it, though. But then Dad did say, "My own fault."

"Not really," Elizabeth said. "Livie's, mostly."

"Livie's, sure, but it's my job to keep her safe against her will."

Elizabeth just nodded, not sure what to say.

"Being a parent isn't all it's cracked up to be," he added and put his arm around her shoulders and gave her a squeeze.

"Being a daughter's no picnic either," Elizabeth said.

"Especially when your old man screws up royally. You warned me."

Elizabeth nodded but then shook her head back and forth.

He couldn't let it stand though. He said, "And I don't hold it against you that you were right. See how great I am?" There was a smile in his voice.

"So generous," Elizabeth said.

"That's it," he said. "None of you girls are ever going anywhere. I'm locking you in your rooms and you won't get out till you're thirty."

"Hey!" Elizabeth said. "I was the responsible one, remember?"

"And if you're good for fifteen years, I'll let you have some ice cream." One of his eyebrows raised as he looked over at Elizabeth.

Elizabeth shook her head and laughed.

Just then, Dad's cell rang, and he glanced at it.

"Who is it?" Elizabeth asked.

"It's Geri," he said with surprise in his voice. He answered it.

Elizabeth could only hear Dad's side of the conversation, which went something like this.

"Hey, Ger. ... What?! When?"—his voice became urgent—"How did you find them? ... Liv's okay? Is she, well, is she okay? ... Okay, okay. Yeah, we'll see you in a half hour. Thanks for calling. Thank you. ... Yeah, I will. See you later." He hung up and stood.

"What? They found Livie?" Elizabeth said.

"Yeah. Where your mom?" Dad said.

"She's up in your room."

He pushed through the screen door and into the kitchen. "Holly?"

"Dad, is she okay? What happened?" Elizabeth said.

"Hang on. I'll tell you both as the same time." He shouted up the stairs again, "Holly?"

Mom trotted halfway down the stairs. "What?! Did you hear something?"

"Yeah. She's fine. They found her. Geri found her. How she did it, I don't know. She said she'd fill us in when they got here. The police are bringing her home, and they should be here in a half hour or so. Geri and Patty are following in their car."

"Oh my god," Mom said as tears started rolling down her face. "Oh my god, Will."

Dad went over and put his arms around Mom and they stood there hugging, Mom sobbing with relief.

Jenna came up from downstairs and said, "What?!"

"They found Livie," Elizabeth said. "She's fine. Aunt Geri found her."

"Geri?" Jenna said, and then, "Thank god."

Elizabeth and Jenna stood with their hands at their sides as Dad comforted Mom.

It was forty-five minutes before over the hill came a police car, followed by Geri's Subaru. They stopped out front and out popped Livie. Mom and Dad had gone out to meet her, and Elizabeth and Jenna stayed on the porch. Livie had a huge smile on her face as she ran over to Mom and gave her a big hug. Mom held her for a long time. Dad went over and talked to the police officers, a man and a woman, who had brought her home, and then talked to Geri and Patty. He ignored Livie.

Dad and Mom thanked the police and shook their hands. Livie stepped up and shook their hands too and said, "Thank you, officers. You're not at all what I expected." The officers smiled pleasantly but glanced at each other with a significant look.

"Well, thank you," the woman said in a deep voice, "and good luck."

They all came into the house, and Mom, Jenna, and Patty put out the stuff for sandwiches. They sat at the table. Geri told them that Livie and Teo had been staying at a Forest Service cabin up in the national forest. That's why no one could find them. Livie said that Teo had stayed there a couple times as a kid. His family always tried to get that cabin when they went camping for the summer. "It was really nice," Livie bubbled. "It even had water and plumbing, and Teo brought munchies." Livie couldn't stop talking as they fixed their plates, and everything she said made Elizabeth wince. It was Teo this and Teo that and when anyone said anything she'd answer with, "Well, Teo thinks such and such." Dad did not say another word and had a stony look on his face.

At one point, as they ate, Livie licked the mustard off her fingers and said, "Isn't it funny how I'm the one with a boyfriend, and Jenna and Elizabeth tried to land boyfriends all summer."

Livie has no shame, Elizabeth thought. She swallowed her potato salad and said, "First of all, we weren't *trying to land* boyfriends. Second, when I want advice from *my baby sister*, I'll ask."

"I'm just saying," Livie said.

"*I'm just saying*," Elizabeth said, "that I don't like your particular way of getting boyfriends."

There was silence around the table.

"He's not your boyfriend," Dad said.

"He is," Livie said.

"You are grounded," Dad said.

"Teo and I are getting married, and so you don't get to say what I do," Livie said breezily.

"You are not getting married because you need our permission," Mom said.

"I am getting married," Livie said.

"I've had enough," Dad said. "Go to your room and stay there."

Livie pushed up from the table and said, "I'm pregnant."

"What!?" Mom and Dad and Geri and Elizabeth said at the same time. Jenna and Patty had shocked looks on their faces.

"I'm pregnant. We checked. Just yesterday."

"How did you—" Dad said but then interrupted himself. "Never mind! How could you …"

"Well, you see, the guy has a penis, and the girl—" Livie was really enjoying this.

"You little shit," Dad said. "How dare you?"

There was silence around the table as Livie and Dad locked eyes.

Geri put in, "Livie, you don't have a clue what you're getting yourself into."

"What does that mean?" Livie said, her voice heated for the first time. "Dad got another girl pregnant while he was married to Mom. The whole town hates your guts because you're gay. And I'm the one that doesn't know anything?"

Geri's expression didn't change. "You can get an abortion. That's what I'm saying." Always the practical one. She glanced at Dad and then at Mom.

"Absolutely not," Dad said at the same time that Mom nodded slightly.

"If I wanted an abortion, I'd get one, *Dad*, and you couldn't stop me," Livie said. "There's ways. Teo and I talked about it. He knows people."

I bet he does, Elizabeth thought.

Livie glanced at Mom and then back at Dad. She continued, "But I don't want to. I want to marry Teo and I want to keep it. And if you don't give me permission, I can talk to the court and ask if they'll let me anyway. A judge can order it."

"Not without our permission," Dad said, but he didn't seem really sure about it.

"Yes, without your permission. That's what the law is for," Livie said.

"She's right," Geri said quietly.

Dad got a furious and terrifying look on his face, stood from his chair, and stomped from the room.

Shaking her head, Mom looked at Livie and said, "Livie, you may be right, but you're really really wrong. And you just broke your father's heart." She stood. "We'll work it out," she said over her shoulder as she followed Dad out of the room.

"Don't be such a bitch, Livie," Elizabeth said. "Think about someone other than yourself. For once."

Looking like she didn't have a care in the world, Livie took another bite of her sandwich. She shrugged.

Geri sighed and said, "If you do this, life's going to be really tough for a bit. You know that, right?"

Livie shrugged again. "It's what I want."

"Well, you make your choices and you live with them, but you need to realize you're going at it the hard way. If you go into it knowing that, that you only have yourself to kick, then you're farther along than some people."

"But that doesn't mean you don't ask for help," Patty put in, "when you need it."

Geri sighed and nodded.

Elizabeth wasn't going to let it go. Livie really didn't know what she was getting herself into. "Livie," she said. "Teo's a predator. He's sweet as pie at first, but then he's all, well, he wants what he wants. He goes too far." She hesitated and then decided it wasn't a good idea to tell Livie about Gabby. Besides, she'd promised she wouldn't. So she said, "Teo tried to go too far with me." She didn't want to use the word *rape*. Was it really rape? It certainly was with Gabby, but maybe not with her. One thing she did know—he'd tried to go further than she'd wanted to, and he'd kept trying even after she'd pushed him away.

"Oh, he told me about that," Livie said.

Elizabeth tried to keep the shock off her face. "He what?"

"Yeah, he told me. You're as cold as a dead fish. All he wanted was to snuggle, and you acted like he'd tied you up and stuff."

"That is not what happened," Elizabeth said. This was all making her feel like a prude. She wasn't a prude, and that's not what happened at all. This was how he got away with things, twisting the story like this.

"Whatever," Livie said. "That's not the way it is with us. In fact, I jumped his bones first. He went along with it, though." There was pride in Livie's voice.

Geri had an unsurprised look on her face. Patty was just watching and looking sad around the eyes.

Even though Elizabeth was really mad, she thought she'd try one more time. It was her little sister, after all. Then she'd let it go. Livie was bound and determined. "Look, Livie. You're in love so you don't see what Teo's like. I was the same way." She could admit that, that she had been in love with Teo. "But he's not what he seems. He comes across as one thing, but then when he has you where he wants you, he treats you like dirt. He uses people."

"And how do you know all this? He didn't treat you like a princess, and so now you're mad and you're going to blame him." Live was picking at the chips on her plate, eating them slowly.

"Whatever," Elizabeth said, shaking her head. Let her go to the devil, as Grandma always said.

"People do that to Teo," Livie said. "He was born under an unlucky star, he says. But that's changing. I'm his lucky star." She smiled a satisfied smile. "D'Arcy, when he stopped by the cabin, said—"

Both Geri and Elizabeth interrupted her at the same time. Geri said, "You weren't supposed to say anything about that." Elizabeth said, "D'Arcy was at the cabin?!"

Then Elizabeth turned to Geri and said, "You knew?"

"We promised we wouldn't say anything," Geri said, glancing over at Patty. "All of us promised we wouldn't say anything," Geri added, looking at Livie.

"Whoops," Livie said without conviction.

"D'Arcy was at the cabin?" Elizabeth said. It didn't make any sense at all. It was unfathomable. Was he in cahoots? What?

"Well, since you know," Geri said. "You'd told him about Livie. He started looking too. He knew about Teo and about the cabin from when they were younger so he went with a hunch. He drove out and caught them. They were going to take off, but he took their keys so they couldn't leave. Then he didn't quite know what to do. He didn't want to call you, so he called the Deckle looking for me. I came out and then we called the police."

"He punched Teo," Livie said. "He's lucky Teo doesn't press charges." She paused and then continued. "It's all okay, though. Teo forgave him. He gave Teo some money. A whole handful. And he said that if he was ever in a tight spot in the future, Teo could call him." Livie said it breezily, like it was just another thing, but it hit Elizabeth what this meant. She glanced at Geri and Geri raised her eyebrows. D'Arcy had basically given Teo permission to take advantage of him whenever he wanted to. Whenever Teo got in a mess, which knowing Teo it could be often, he could call D'Arcy. Talk about inviting the devil into your house.

Elizabeth looked at her sister. She wondered for the hundredth time whether Livie was really as clueless as she acted, or if it was a clever act. It didn't seem like an act.

"You're lucky *Dad* doesn't press charges," Elizabeth said.

"What?" Livie said.

"Against Teo. For statutory rape," Elizabeth said. She wasn't quite sure the rules and the ages, but she'd heard about a guy who got in trouble for it with his girlfriend because he was older and she was younger.

"He wouldn't do that, would he?" Livie said.

"I wouldn't be so sure," Geri said.

For the first time, Livie looked worried.

Chapter 28

The house was quiet for two days. Dad gave Livie the silent treatment, Mom walked around looking worried, and Livie acted like nothing was wrong. Mom took away Livie's phone and, though they'd gotten her computer back from the police, Mom wouldn't give it to her.

Elizabeth went down to the kitchen in the middle of the night for some leftover pumpkin pie. She flipped on the light and caught Livie sitting on the floor talking on the landline with Teo. She was so fed up with Livie that she just flipped the light back off, skipping the pie, as Livie smirked up at her. She loved her sister, but Livie was screwing up royally and treating everyone like shit, and there was nothing she could do about it. Her parents didn't seem to know what to do about it either.

On the third day, Elizabeth was in her room when Jenna poked her head in and said, "Better come down. It's going to hit the fan."

Elizabeth hopped off the bed and followed her down the stairs. Finally, she thought. The tension had really sucked. When they entered the living room, Dad was sitting slumped forward on a chair, his elbows on his knees, and Livie was sitting on the couch with her arms folded across her chest.

Mom was standing next to Dad. She glanced at them when they came in and gave them a worried smile.

"We could make it so you never see him again," Dad was saying. "We could turn him in to the authorities over in Idaho and he would go to jail."

"It doesn't matter what you do," Livie said. "The minute you aren't looking, I'm going to run away to be with him. If I have to wait a few years to do that, I will, but I'm not going to hang around here while you treat me like I've done something wrong."

"You just don't know," Mom said, turning around, "how much you've done wrong. You're the baby and you've never taken care of a baby before."

"I have too," Livie said. "I babysat that neighbor baby."

"Actually, I did most of the sitting, if you remember right," Jenna put in.

"You were only ten and you forgot about the poor kid," Mom said.

To everyone's surprise, Livie burst into tears. "You always do that. You all do. You treat me like I'm incompetent. You point out all the things I do wrong. Of course I do things wrong—I'm always younger than everybody." She was shaking her head, tears running down her face. "Well this time, I'm not going to let you. This is my thing. This is what I want to do with my life. I don't care if I'm young. I may not know about babies, but I'll learn. I want my own life. I want to get married and have this baby."

The sight of Livie crying really bothered Dad. He stood up and went over to the window and looked out, his back rigid.

Mom went over and sat next to Livie. She didn't try to reach out or anything, and she didn't even look at her, but she said, shaking her head, "Livie, if you do this, this is your decision. What I mean is, your dad and I don't want another child of our own. We would love to help out, but you would be the one getting up three or four times a night to care for him or her. We'd babysit, but you, and the baby's father"—she glanced at Dad—"would be the ones buying diapers and changing them and being there twenty-four seven. You're the ones who would need to take responsibility."

"I know that," Livie said.

"I don't think you do," Mom said. Then, to no one in particular, she said in a low voice, "I don't think any of us do. We just go in blind."

Dad turned back around and looked at Livie, his mind working.

Livie took a deep shuddering breath, looked back at Dad, and said, "Dad, you don't think I'm responsible enough. I don't know if I am either, but I think I'm strong enough. I get things done if I put my mind to it."

He looked at her for a long time and then took a deep breath and let it out. Livie's face relaxed a bit at his reaction. The decision had been made. They all knew it. Livie would keep the baby. Mom glanced between them. She looked at Dad. "Okay," she said, "and what about her marrying him?"

Dad shook his head and turned back around to the window.

Elizabeth stepped forward. She was going to say something about Teo, tell them about what he'd done to her, maybe even about Gabby—this was her sister, after all, and that took precedence over Gabby's feelings—but then Livie gave her the

dirtiest meanest look. *Shut up*, she was saying. *Don't say it.*
Elizabeth stopped. A battle raged inside her. Mom looked
expectantly at her. She looked once more at Livie and then
glanced over at Jenna. Jenna was shaking her head—not saying
no but more like she didn't know what to do. She shrugged her
shoulders.

"Never mind," Elizabeth said, her stomach in knots.

Livie smiled then—with relief and, Elizabeth liked to think,
maybe a little gratitude. Elizabeth just hoped she was wrong
about Teo, but she didn't think she was. *You can lead a horse
to water*, she thought.

Dad turned back around. Elizabeth could tell by his
expression that he'd made up his mind. He didn't like it, but he
was going to let Livie do what she wanted. He would sign the
permission for them to get married.

That was that. For the next couple of weeks, there was a
flurry of activity as they got ready for a quick and quiet
wedding. Not even a wedding, really—just two people getting
married. Mom took Livie to a doctor, and sure enough she was
pregnant. She got prenatal counseling while they were there.
Livie was given back her phone and computer, and Teo finally
was allowed into the house. He was invited over for supper,
which was awkward all the way around. Afterwards, Dad
invited him out to the porch for a talk, and it went on for a long
time. Dad paced while Teo sat on the porch swing with a
whipped look. When they came back in, it had been decided
that Teo was going to enlist in the National Guard. He admitted
that he didn't have the money to go to college and he didn't
have any support from his family—his dad was in prison and
his mom had been drinking a lot—and so if he could get a

guard scholarship, that would put him through. If he couldn't, he would go full-time military. He would either go to a community college in Idaho Falls or go to the University of Wyoming. Depending on what Teo decided, Livie could stay in Jackson and finish high school there or she could get her GED or her online high school diploma. There was no mention of Livie going to college—she had never expressed an interest. Livie said she wanted to try for her online diploma. She wanted to get it out of the way before the baby came, if she could. "Good idea," Mom said dryly.

Mom brought up the idea of Livie living at home for a while and maybe Teo moving in too, but Dad nixed that idea. "If she's going to make this decision, it's going to be all up to her. She's a big girl now—she better put on her big girl pants."

Every time Teo visited, Livie stuck to him like glue. "PDAs," Mom would say when she came across Livie wrapped around Teo on the couch. Dad just glowered. Livie called Teo all kinds of cute names and she bragged about him to everyone. Teo spent most of his time with a hang-dog look. He was pleasant enough, but he just wasn't present.

During one of Teo's visits, Elizabeth came across him sitting near the window by himself playing with his phone. She'd been avoiding him as much as she could, not even looking at him. It made her angry just to be in the same room with him. He didn't seek her out either. Elizabeth glanced around—nobody was in the room—and then went over and took the chair right next to him. He looked startled and glanced around too, and when he didn't see anyone, he got a bit of a deer-in-the-headlights look.

Elizabeth leaned forward and looked into his face. He pulled back. She said, "You're going through with it?"

"Uh, yeah. I think so," he said.

Well, that didn't inspire confidence, but at least he said yes. Elizabeth continued, "Well, you treat her well. Treat her well or else." She said it low and with force.

"What?"

"You know what I mean," Elizabeth said. "You may have Livie hornswoggled but I know what you really are and you know that I know. If you treat her bad, I'll tell her about Gabby and about your dad and all the other stuff." She really didn't know other stuff, but he didn't know that. And she was sure there was other stuff.

"What? You ..."

"I'm just saying—" Elizabeth said loudly and then Livie walked into the room and interrupted her.

Livie stared at both of them and then loudly—if you can do an action loudly—came over and sat on Teo's lap and put her arm around his shoulders. "Everything all right, Tay-Tay?" she said to him but looked at Elizabeth.

"Everything's fine," Elizabeth said before Teo could answer. She got up and left the room.

Since Livie wasn't 16 yet, she and Teo would have to go over to Idaho to get married. It was 15 there with parental permission. Livie cornered Mom to remind her that they couldn't go into Idaho because Teo had a warrant out for his arrest for bad checks. Mom spent a week talking on the phone with a lawyer. The lawyer got the judge to schedule an arraignment, so Teo wouldn't be arrested the minute he crossed the border. Then Mom and Livie figured out where they would get married. Mom, Dad, Livie, and Teo would drive over for the ceremony, and then there would be a dinner at their house with just family.

"Does your Mom want to help or go to the wedding?" Mom asked Teo.

"You can ask her if you want," he said, looking embarrassed, "but I think she'll probably be too, aah, busy." Mom called her, but she was didn't say much. "Getting married, is he?" she said. She said she'd come to the dinner and bring Teo's two brothers who were younger. She didn't offer to bring anything. "She didn't seem well," Mom said, which Elizabeth and Jenna understood to mean she was drunk.

And so the day of the wedding came. Mom, Livie, Jenna, and Elizabeth spent the day before getting things arranged at the house for the dinner. Then Dad, Mom, and Livie got up early to go over to Idaho. Dad and Mom took a car, and Teo and Livie took his old beater car—Livie insisted. While they were gone, Elizabeth and Jenna cooked and got all the final things ready. The group returned mid-afternoon, and Livie was through the roof with happiness. She showed them her ring, which looked old and a bit tarnished, and talked a blue streak. It wasn't long before others started showing up. Aunt Geri and Patty came, of course. Teo's mom and two younger brothers came, but Teo's mom was already half in the bag and spent most of the time sitting in a chair with a pleasant but vacant look on her face. Teo's younger brothers were rambunctious but sweet. They spent most of their time outside, and at one point Dad took them to the barn to see the horses. Elizabeth had invited Miley, and Dad had invited Colin, but Colin refused to come and so Miley didn't either. Colin had said he wanted no part of it. "Tight-assed young man, ain't he?" Dad said. They asked Teo if there was anyone else he wanted to invite and he just shrugged. Now that's just sad, Elizabeth thought and actually did feel a little sad for him.

They had a dinner of prime rib, which was really good. Dad gave a half-hearted toast wishing them well. He refrained from making any smart-alec jokes, at least, which surprised Elizabeth. She saw the steely-eyed look in Mom's eyes, though, and figured she probably had something to do with that. Mom was all business and never seemed upset all day. And then it was over. There were hugs all around, and Teo and Livie left in his car as everyone waved. Teo's mom was passed out in a chair, and so Dad drove her and her two boys home. And that was that. Teo would start basic training within the week, and Livie would live at his apartment.

It was going to be really hard for Livie, Elizabeth thought. From everything everyone told her, having a baby was really hard, and how were they going to make a living? But Livie was tough. That was one thing Elizabeth knew. Hopefully she'd really made up her mind. Hopefully she'd grow up a lot.

D'Arcy also crossed Elizabeth's mind. He'd been so decent through this whole thing. And he didn't even want any credit. He'd just done it because it was the right thing to do. It made Elizabeth miss him, when there wasn't really anything to miss. They hadn't really spent much time together. Maybe I miss the idea of him, she thought.

Chapter 29

Elizabeth's phone rang with Miley's ring. Elizabeth answered, "What up, girlfriend?"

"Price of hogs," Miley said with a smile in her voice. It was something her dad said. Then Elizabeth and Miley talked about things. Elizabeth told Miley about the wedding, and Miley told Elizabeth that Colin's mom had come to visit.

"How was that?" Elizabeth asked.

"Aaawk-ward," Miley said. "She doesn't let him alone. She's always mothering him."

"Well, she's his mother." Elizabeth wondered what would happen if Dad ran into her. "Is she still here?" she asked.

"Naw," Miley said. "She was just here for a couple of days."

Good, Elizabeth thought. She'd had enough drama to last her for a while. She was ready for things to settle down and people to get along.

She'd heard Dad on the kitchen phone just the day before. She was sitting reading the paper when it rang, and he'd picked it up. It was obvious that he was talking to Colin. What had surprised Elizabeth was that Dad's voice had been relaxed. He'd even made a joke or two. When the conversation came to an end, Dad had said, "That'd be fine, Colin. We'll work on it." Whatever it was that Colin had asked, Dad had agreed—or at least agreed to think about it. She'd tried to hint to Dad a couple of times that maybe it wouldn't be the worst thing if Colin stopped by. He'd just raised his eyebrows. *Well,* Elizabeth thought, *I guess I'll have that brother after all.*

"Oh," Miley continued, "I meant to tell you. Charlie? That kid that Jenna liked? He's back in town."

"In town?" She'd seen him out at the dude ranch, but she didn't figure he'd stick around.

"Yeah. He came into the restaurant with his family."

He was here with his whole family? Hopefully Jenna wouldn't find out.

They talked about school, which would start in a couple of weeks. They were excited to start their junior year. They gossiped about their other friends and what had happened over the summer. It had flown by.

The next day, Elizabeth and Jenna changed into cutoffs and tank tops and put on goofy gardening hats to pick vegetables in the garden. It had been a good year for the garden, and they were under orders to pick a little of everything, so the wheelbarrow was piled full of potatoes, beets, carrots, lettuce, cucumbers, kohlrabi, and loads and loads of zucchini. Mom was going to make some casseroles and freeze them. Next week they'd start doing some serious canning. Elizabeth thought of the pickled mixed vegetables that she loved. Crispy carrots and cauliflower and cucumbers and whatever else they felt like in a butter pickle. When they had them in January, it reminded her of summer. One year, she had insisted that Mom put food coloring in the jars, and so they'd had blue pickles and green pickles and red pickles. Dad had made a face and said, "Remind me not to put you in charge of food."

"She's an artist," Mom had insisted.

It was a nice day. It would be hot later, but for now it was just right, the sun shining down on them, the cool dirt between their toes.

"Veggie delight," Jenna said, the juice of a tomato running down her chin.

"Veggie paradise," Elizabeth said, laughing.

"Veg-edible."

"Vegelicious."

"Vege-mighty."

"Here, let me get that," Elizabeth said, indicating she would wipe the tomato off Jenna's face, but instead she smeared mud on Jenna's cheek.

Jenna gave Elizabeth a mock-mad look and tried to rub it off.

There was a low rumble on the road. It was so low, at first Elizabeth couldn't figure out what it was, and then she realized it was vehicles coming down the drive.

"Jenna," she said, just as two motorcycles popped up over the rise down the drive. Elizabeth and Jenna looked at each other in surprise as they both realized that it was D'Arcy and Charlie on their motorcycles. Elizabeth's heart jumped into her throat, and adrenalin coursed through her. D'Arcy! It was D'Arcy! What in the world? She glanced over at Jenna. Jenna's face was pale, and her eyes were wide.

"What the ..." Jenna said.

Elizabeth just shook her head.

Then they saw a figure going out to meet the motorcycles. It was Dad. The bikes pulled up and turned off, and the two sat straddling their bikes and talked to Dad for what seemed like a long time. Finally, Dad looked over toward Elizabeth and Jenna and pointed. The motorcycles started up, and Charlie and D'Arcy putted over.

"Do I look okay?!" Jenna asked. "Do I still have mud on my cheek?"

"Just a little. Here," Elizabeth said and helped her rub it off. "We must look like bumpkins," she added.

"I look a mess," Jenna said, "but you look amazing."

It made Elizabeth feel better, her saying that. "Hardly, but you *look* amazing. You always do."

They turned and went over to meet the boys.

Charlie and D'Arcy turned off their bikes and put out the kickstands and parked them. They dismounted and walked over to meet them halfway.

"Hey," Charlie said, looking at Jenna.

"Hi, Charlie," Jenna said. Charlie probably couldn't tell it, but Elizabeth could—Jenna was vibrating like a plucked wire, but she came across as cool as a cucumber. That gal just has grace, Elizabeth thought. "Hi, D'Arcy," Jenna added and glanced from him to Elizabeth and back.

"Hello, Jenna," D'Arcy said. And then he added in what seemed like an afterthought, "Hello, Elizabeth." He didn't meet her eyes.

So that was how it was going to be. He was so nice at the dude ranch, so outgoing and everything, and now we have prickly D'Arcy back. Elizabeth felt her insides wilt.

"We were out riding, and we thought we'd stop by," Charlie said. "You said you had property. This is beautiful." He glanced around and smiled.

"It's not, well, grand or anything, but we like it," Jenna said.

"No," Charlie said, "it's really cool." And when he said it, it made everything all right. Charlie did not put on airs.

"You think so?" Jenna said.

"I really do," Charlie said.

Charlie and Jenna moved closer together. It was like they couldn't help it.

Elizabeth wasn't watching them, though. She was watching D'Arcy. She wanted to see if he'd be all disapproving about Charlie and Jenna. He didn't look disapproving at all. He looked distant, like his mind was elsewhere. That little voice in Elizabeth's head, though, said *he looks amazing and yummy*. She told that little voice to shut up.

They began talking about the garden. Charlie remarked how beautiful the tomatoes were, and Jenna said it was a good year for them. Charlie listed all the things he loved to make with tomatoes—turns out, he really did like to cook. D'Arcy put in that he'd predicted a long time ago that Charlie would become a chef. Or a food writer, Charlie added. Charlie and Jenna started talking recipes, and they were off. The rest of the world went away, as far as they were concerned, and Elizabeth and D'Arcy stood awkwardly next to them. It was as if the whole music festival thing hadn't happened. At one point, Elizabeth smiled at D'Arcy, and after a delay he smiled back. It looked genuine, but it had taken a minute. Elizabeth's insides wilted a little more.

They decided to go inside for a snack.

"It won't be anything special," Jenna insisted.

"We could do some caprese," Elizabeth suggested quietly

"Do you have some nice bread?" Charlie asked.

"Sure," Jenna said.

"Let's make caprese crostini," he said.

Then he and Jenna set out toasting bread and chopping tomatoes and basil, while Elizabeth made some lemonade and D'Arcy sat off to the side looking uncomfortable. When it was done, they took it out to the porch and ate, looking out over the horses grazing in the pasture and the mountains beyond.

As they were finishing up, Jenna said to Charlie, not quite meeting his eyes, "Would you like to go for a walk?"

"That'd be great," Charlie said. He glanced at D'Arcy, asking if it was okay, and D'Arcy shrugged. "We have a bit before we need to be back," D'Arcy said.

Jenna and Charlie strolled off toward the barn, talking, their shoulders almost touching.

And so it was just Elizabeth and D'Arcy on the porch. It was very awkward. D'Arcy didn't say much, and it was as if Elizabeth's brain had went on strike. She literally couldn't think of a single thing to say. Finally, the whole thing with Livie came to mind, and so she said, "I wanted to thank you, by the way."

"For what?" D'Arcy said, his hands tightly folded in his lap.

"For Livie. For finding them. For helping out."

"What?" D'Arcy said, focusing on her.

"For tracking them down and going to the cabin and finding them. I don't know where we'd be if you hadn't."

D'Arcy didn't say anything for a minute and then said, "You weren't supposed to know about that."

"I know. But Livie has a big mouth," Elizabeth said.

D'Arcy nodded like he agreed but then glanced at her.

Elizabeth continued, "I'm really glad she did. Because you didn't have to do anything, and you did. That was really nice."

D'Arcy shrugged.

"Really. The family doesn't know about it, just Jenna and I. Oh, and Geri and Patty, of course. But I personally am really really grateful."

"Well, you're welcome," D'Arcy said. "Least I could do."

After that, they struggled to find things to say, and so they finally lapsed into silence and looked out over the view. It was still really awkward, but Elizabeth wouldn't have had it any other way. D'Arcy was right there. Even without looking at him, she could feel his presence as he breathed and shifted. She felt like he could have been all the way across a room, and she would have known exactly where he was. Her body and her brain were like locating devices. And so she sat there, and it became a lot less uncomfortable. She relaxed. All that mattered was he was there. The past didn't matter. The future didn't matter. He was there now, and it was enough.

After a long time, Charlie and Jenna came back. They were holding hands, and Jenna had this look of pure joy on her face. A flush crept up her cheeks, and she was smiling wide and genuine. Charlie, too, looked relaxed and happy and he was smiling broadly.

"What happened to you two?" D'Arcy said.

"It's a beautiful view," Charlie said.

To that, D'Arcy snorted.

Charlie turned to Jenna and said with apology in his voice, "We've got to go."

Jenna said, "I know," but she didn't look at all sad. There was irrepressible high emotion as she looked in Charlie's face.

"Thank you for …" D'Arcy started to say to Elizabeth but then he stopped and they both watched as Charlie took both of Jenna's hands in his and leaned down and kissed her gently. She kissed him back.

Elizabeth took a quick involuntary breath. Now that was uncomfortable, and so she turned away to look at D'Arcy. D'Arcy had a pained look on his face, and Elizabeth didn't know if it was because he disapproved or what. She couldn't tell.

"Thank you for everything," D'Arcy said as they ignored the couple. "I mean that." His voice was forceful and sincere.

"I don't know what for," Elizabeth said, "but *thank you*. I'm the one who should thank you."

Charlie and Jenna finally finished kissing, and then Charlie leaned over and whispered in Jenna's ear. Jenna smiled up at him and nodded. He squeezed her hands and then turned to D'Arcy. "Ready?" he said.

"Yeah," D'Arcy said.

"Tomorrow?" Jenna said to Charlie.

"I won't forget," Charlie said but didn't seem aware of the irony of what he said.

Jenna nodded.

D'Arcy nodded to them both.

Charlie and D'Arcy went back out to their motorcycles and started them up. Elizabeth and Jenna watched them go. "Tomorrow?" Elizabeth asked.

"We're going on a date," Jenna said, her face shining.

"Oh Jenna, that's great! Do you think Dad will let you, after all … you know."

"He'd better," Jenna said darkly.

Charlie and Jenna. Elizabeth was so happy for her. Her sister had finally gotten what she wanted—and what she deserved.

"Oh, I'm so happy," Jenna said to the air. She glanced at Elizabeth. "I wish you could be this happy."

"Aah," Elizabeth said. "You are so sweet." She put her arm around Jenna's shoulders and squeezed. "If I had forty Charlies I couldn't be as happy as you. You are just such a good person. Such an *optimist*." It was the old joke between them, and Jenna smiled. Elizabeth continued, "Give me time. Maybe I'll find my very own Tay-Tay."

Elizabeth chuckled darkly and Jenna snorted.

Chapter 30

It wasn't even eight the next morning when Mom came into Elizabeth's room without knocking. Elizabeth had been laying there thinking about D'Arcy, about how he seemed like one thing and then like another. He was complicated. Then the thought came to her—she was complicated too. Did she give mixed messages like he did?

"There's someone here to see you," Mom said. "Better get up."

"Who?" Elizabeth said.

Mom just shook her head and left.

D'Arcy? Elizabeth's heart leapt in her chest. She jumped up, changed quickly, ran a comb through her hair, and splashed her face with water. It still looked a little puffy from sleep. Ah well. She went down to the living room.

But it wasn't D'Arcy. It was D'Arcy's mom Katherine. She was sitting talking with Mom.

"Mrs. Pemberly?" Elizabeth said.

Mrs. Pemberly gave her a dark look, which shocked Elizabeth. "Can I talk to Elizabeth alone?" Mrs. Pemberly said to Mom.

Mom glanced from her to Elizabeth and back. "I … guess," she said.

Elizabeth shrugged at Mom, and so Mom hesitated and then left the room.

"I won't beat around the bush," Mrs. Pemberly said.

Elizabeth hadn't expected her too. She nodded.

"You probably know why I'm here," Mrs. Pemberly continued.

"I don't have a clue," Elizabeth said. "Really."

Mrs. Pemberly fixed her with a look. "Don't mess with me. You know very well. Word has it that you're dating my son."

Elizabeth couldn't keep the look of pure shock off her face.

"Are you dating my son?" Mrs. Pemberly asked forcefully.

"You came out here to ask me? Why don't you ask your son?"

"He's not speaking to me," she said.

Elizabeth nodded with surprise. Small wonder, though.

"You can't be," Mrs. Pemberly continued. "It's just not right. He's, well, he's got a bright future ahead of him. He doesn't need *entanglements*."

Elizabeth did not like this, not one bit. The way Mrs. Pemberly just invaded Elizabeth's house to accuse her of things that weren't even wrong in the first place. It got her hackles up, so she said, "Well, there you are. You said it can't be, so it must not be."

Mrs. Pemberly relaxed for a half a second but then shook her head. "What? Are you saying you aren't dating?"

"If we are, shouldn't it be D'Arcy who says something? Why are you asking me?" Mrs. Pemberly was so in-your-face, it brought out the mule in Elizabeth.

Mrs. Pemberly just looked at her with a narrow look.

"He's your son," Elizabeth said, "but you're not my mom."

At that, Mrs. Pemberly looked really mad. "You can't date my son."

"Whatever," Elizabeth said.

Mrs. Pemberly stood up in a huff. "Answer me," she almost yelled.

Just then, Mom came back in and glanced questioningly between them.

"Your daughter is a brat," Mrs. Pemberly said.

"What?" Mom said. "What happened?"

Elizabeth shook her head at her mom. "She came here to chew me out, I think."

Mom raised her eyebrows. "You came here to yell at my daughter, to tell me she's a brat?" Mom looked shocked. "How dare you?"

"I came here," Mrs. Pemberly said, "to get answers. And all she does is play games."

Mom's jaw clenched. "I don't know what's going on, but you're not coming into my house and shouting at my kid. Whoever you think you are."

"Well, I never," Mrs. Pemberly said.

"I think you should leave," Mom said.

"I guess I should," Mrs. Pemberly said and with a pointed glance at Elizabeth swept out of the room.

Mom walked over to the window and watched as Mrs. Pemberly got in her car and drive away. She turned back around and said, "What was that about?"

Elizabeth didn't know quite what to say so she told the truth. "She doesn't want me to date her son."

"And she came all the way out here to tell you that?"

"Yeah."

Mom shook her head. "A bit of a dragon lady, I'd say."

"Yeah, definitely."

"Well," Mom said, coming over and putting hand on Elizabeth's shoulder. "Well," Mom repeated.

"Exactly," Elizabeth said.

Later that day, Elizabeth's cell rang as she lay on her bed reading a book. It was a number she didn't recognize.

"Hello?" she said as she picked it up.

"Elizabeth?" It was D'Arcy. What in heaven's name?

"Uh, yeah?" Elizabeth said. "This is she."

"Can I talk to you?"

"Sure," Elizabeth said. First his mom and now him. It was turning out to be a really weird day in a long line of weird days.

"Can I come pick you up on the bike?"

"Sure." She hoped that Dad would say okay.

"I'll be there in about twenty minutes."

They hung up. Elizabeth felt like screaming, she was so excited and unnerved. And what did his calling have to do with his mom coming by? Was he going to apologize for her? Was he coming to yell at her for getting his mom all riled up? She had no idea. It could be bad. But then another part of her whispered, *I get to be with him.* That was so amazing she wanted to shout it to the world. Even as she told herself it might be bad, she jumped up and danced around the room. Then she flopped back on her bed and stared at the ceiling and smiled.

She got up and threw on jeans and put on a little makeup. She grabbed her jacket. She cleared it with Mom, which was easy, and then with a deep breath she called her dad at work.

"Hey, Dad," she said. She was nervous all of a sudden. She wouldn't put it past him to make good on his promise of not letting her go anywhere. "Uh, could I go out for a motorcycle ride?"

"Who with?" he asked.

"D'Arcy Pemberly," she said. "That guy who was here the other day with Charlie Billingsley."

To her surprise, he said, "Sure. He seems like an upstanding young man."

Elizabeth scrunched her forehead. "Oh, okay," she said. "Thanks."

"You don't want to go?" he said.

"No! I do, I do."

"Well then," he said. "Have a good time. Don't do anything I wouldn't do." He said it with a smirk in his voice, then added, "Really."

"Got it," she said with a snort.

She waited for D'Arcy on the porch, and it wasn't long before he pulled up, his bike alternately roaring and putting. She went out to meet him. Letting it run, he put out the kickstand, stepped off the bike and propped it, and removed his helmet, tucking it under his arm.

"Hello," he said. Elizabeth had worried that he'd be like last time—distant and with drawn—but he wasn't. He walked up to her and looked intently down into her face. "Hello," he said again.

"Hello," she said back.

He nodded and turned. He set his helmet on the seat and removed a second helmet that was strapped to the back. "You better put this on."

She nodded and took it from him and pulled it onto her head. It was a little big. She pulled the strap over to the loops and tried to thread them through, but because it was under her chin she couldn't see to work it. He came over and stood right in front of her and threaded it through and pulled it tight. His hand brushed her chin as he did it. It was the first time he had touched her on purpose, and it tingled. She could also feel the heat of his body next to hers. She leaned ever so slightly toward him, drinking it in.

He finished and then gently tapped the top of her helmet with his palm, making her wobble. "That good?" he said.

She laughed in surprise. "I think so," she said.

He put his helmet back on, swung his leg over the bike, pulled it up, and then kicked up the kickstand. He nodded to her, and so she got on behind him. It was awkward swinging her leg over. She ended up way on the back of the seat, almost falling onto the rack.

"You're going to have to hang on," he said over his shoulder.

She looked at the black leather of his jacket and thought, this is exactly what I want at this moment. I am in heaven. She scooted forward so that her body was right next to his, and then she wrapped her arms around his waist and hugged him tight, her face buried in the back of his jacket. It smelled of leather and of him—warm and pleasant. She found the pegs with her feet.

He revved the engine and then eased down the drive, going slowly over humps and bumps. Elizabeth felt his body lean and tense as he steered around potholes and balanced the bike. She tried to lean with him and not hold so tight he couldn't move but enough she knew which way he was leaning.

They made it to the highway, and he took off, the engine loud and the wind whipping at them. It scared her but thrilled her, and she squeezed him hard around the waist. She closed her eyes and felt the air moving around her, smelled the pockets of marsh and dry hot grass as they blew past them. She was aware of the highway whizzing by just inches from her feet and how dangerous that was. If her foot slipped off the peg, or if D'Arcy made one wrong move, they really could die. But it didn't bother Elizabeth in that moment. She trusted D'Arcy. She realized that now. It was as if she'd fallen back into his arms without even looking. She trusted him that much.

They drove for a few miles toward town but then the biked jerked and slowed as D'Arcy downshifted. He turned off onto a gravel road that wound down through some hills to a creek that was lined with tall cottonwoods. He pulled up onto the short metal bridge, across it, and then on the other side he pulled off onto a gravel pullout. He parked the bike, and reluctantly Elizabeth unwrapped her arms and pushed herself away from him. Once it was stopped, she flipped her leg over and stood, swaying. It felt like getting off a carnival ride—she was off balance.

He took off his helmet, and so she fumbled with hers and finally managed to pull it off, smashing her ear in the process. They hung them on the bike's handlebars. Without saying anything, they both walked back onto the bridge and out to the middle over the stream. The trees were brilliant green and rustled in the slight breeze. The water in the creek tinkled over mossy rocks and the gravelly bottom and sparkled in the bright sunlight. It smelled of mud and moss and green things.

D'Arcy was ahead, and when they reached the center, he stopped and turned. She stopped and put her hand on the railing to steady herself, waiting expectantly.

"Sorry about my mom," was the first thing he said.

"I bet she isn't easy to live with," Elizabeth said.

"You could say that."

Not sure where he was going with it, she waited.

"She came and talked to you," he said.

"Yeah."

"That's why ... That's what made me think ... What you said to her." He glanced at her face and then looked out over the water. Then he focused back on her face. "It made me think ... It gave me hope that you, you ..."

She nodded, encouraging him.

He took a deep breath. "I know you well enough that you'd have told her to go to hell, that you wouldn't go out with me in a million years, if that's what you wanted."

"Yes," she said and laughed under her breath. "Yeah. If I can be bitchy to you, I certainly could be bitchy to your family." She hoped he'd catch her irony.

"You weren't a bitch," he said. "What you said was right. Telling the truth isn't being a bitch. If anything, I was the bitch." He shook his head.

"You were not," Elizabeth said. "Anyway, we shouldn't argue about who was the bitchiest. I mean, since then, we've both improved." She smiled.

"But I was really an asshole," D'Arcy said.

"You certainly took me by surprise at the dude ranch, being that nice."

"That was what I was hoping," he said. "You taught me a lesson."

"I—" she started to protest, but he broke in, "No, I needed it. Thank you."

"I thought you hated me," Elizabeth said.

"Hate you? I was mad, but I couldn't hate you. I …"

He hesitated and then slowly closed his mouth. He blinked, and Elizabeth could see thoughts moving behind his eyes. Then he seemed to make a decision. He stepped forward, his eyebrows up, questioning. He leaned forward and tilted his head and stopped, looking into her face.

He was going to kiss her! Oh my god oh my god! Elizabeth felt joy bubble up inside her and threaten to burst out of her mouth. She smiled at him and then on instinct reached up and cupped both his cheeks with her hands and pulled his face to hers, tilted her head, and kissed him. He kissed her back. At first it was just a light touch, but then he put his hands on her waist and she leaned into him and they pressed against each other. Elizabeth had never felt this way before. Her body melted and exploded at the same time. She wanted this moment to go on forever.

They kissed, and then he pulled away and looked into her eyes and took a deep shuddering breath. He leaned in and kissed her again and she kissed him back. He wrapped his arms around her and buried his face in her hair, and she wrapped her arms around him and hugged him as tightly as she had when they were speeding down the highway. She felt dizzy with it all. Emotion rose in her chest and threatened to overwhelm her.

They hugged, and then they pulled apart. D'Arcy reached out and took her hand and placed his other hand on top of it. He patted her hand, holding it up and looking at it before looking into her face, like he couldn't quite believe that it was all real. She squeezed his hand and then burst out laughing.

All around her, the world rushed on and she was there at the center of it, with him.

The End

Acknowledgements

I want to thank the sneak-readers, those who don't fit, the other-world mittys, and the geeks dreaming of online glory. I want to thank those whose families suck, those who are struggling to make it through the day, those who are sure their friends are way cooler than they are, those who hate gym class, and those who are hiding in their hoodies or under their hair.

I want to thank you. You. The one reading this right now. You matter, and I love you.

May the worlds in books save your life like it did mine.

– Tamara Linse, 2020

About the Author

Tamara Linse grew up on a ranch in the 1880s. Thank goodness for time travel! They don't tell you about outdoor plumbing, do they? Spiders and cold seats and splinters exactly where you don't want splinters. Ahem. … Tamara's favorite things are happy accidents, internet rabbit holes, fangirling, the world she's currently creating, writing code that works, and veggie sandwiches. Hey, don't knock them till you try them! Didn't you read *Harriet the Spy*? Tomato sandwiches? Eh? … Anyway, Tamara's also pretty keen on her twins—a gamer and an artist. The Wyoming Chronicles is an attempt to write something they'd like to read. So far so good. They only occasionally give her the evil eye when she comes down the hall with a book. … Oh, and the Wyoming Chronicles brings together two things Tamara loves, her home state and British classics. Usually loves. I mean, have you tried to read *Tristram Shandy*? That's like trying to walk backwards to Vermont! Anyway, you can find her online at wyomingchronicles.com or tamaralinse.com.

.

Made in the USA
Columbia, SC
17 January 2021